PHARAOH
FANTASTIC

Edited by
Martin H. Greenberg
and Brittiany A. Koren

DAW BOOKS, INC.
DONALD A. WOLLHEIM, FOUNDER
375 Hudson Street, New York, NY 10014
ELIZABETH R. WOLLHEIM
SHEILA E. GILBERT
PUBLISHERS
www.dawbooks.com

First Printing, December 2002
1 2 3 4 5 6 7 8 9

THE MAGIC OF ANCIENT EGYPT AWAITS YOU

in thirteen original tales of the Pharaohs, god-kings and -queens of one of the most powerful and fascinating civilizations of our past. Let the master scribes of the fantastic chart a course through the shifting sands of time to reveal such wondrous discoveries as:

"Beneath the Eye of the Hawk"—Their quest to find a legendary lost pyramid, holding unimaginable wealth, would lead them into peril great enough to rouse the dead. . . .

"Whatever Was Forgotten"—All had been prepared to make the Pharaoh comfortable when he passed from the mortal world. But no one could possibly prepare him for what could happen to you in the afterlife. . . .

"To See Beyond Darkness"—Could a cat league with a god to save the Pharaoh and his kingdom from an unseen evil which threatened to consume all life?

PHARAOH
FANTASTIC

More Imagination-Expanding Anthologies Brought to You by DAW:

VENGEANCE FANTASTIC *Edited by Denise Little.* From a young woman who would betray her own faith to save her people from marauding Vikings . . . to a goddess willing to pull down the very heavens to bring justice to a god . . . to a deal struck between Adam and Eve and Lucifer himself . . . to a "woman" who must decide how to rework the threads of life . . . here are spellbinding tales that will strike a chord with every reader. Enjoy seventeen unforgettable tales from some of fantasy's finest, including Mickey Zucker Reichert, Michelle West, Nina Kiriki Hoffman, P. N. Elrod, Jody Lynn Nye, Elizabeth Ann Scarborough, Mel Odom, Kristine Kathryn Rusch, Gary A. Braunbeck, and more.

FAMILIARS *Edited by Denise Little.* Here are fifteen original tales by such top writers in the field as Kristine Kathryn Rusch, Jody Lynn Nye, P. N. Elrod, Andre Norton, Josepha Sherman, and Michelle West, stories ranging from a humorous look at the role played by the Clintons' cat, Socks, in the troubles that occurred during Bill's administration . . . to the challenge a minor wizard faces when he seeks a way to save his own cat familiar and stop the mysterious enemy who has been targeting familiars for death . . . to the desperate battle for survival and justice waged by a warlock and his dog when Cotton Mather targets them for judgment . . . to the incredible odyssey of a college student who undergoes past life regression only to discover that he was not even human in his past life. . . .

APPRENTICE FANTASTIC *Edited by Martin H. Greenberg and Russell Davis.* Thirteen weavers of words—including Michelle West, Charles de Lint, Esther Friesner, Jane Lindskold, David Bischoff, Tanya Huff, Fiona Patton, Mickey Zucker Reichert, and more—have crafted thirteen magical and memorable stories for your enjoyment. From the poignant tale of a young girl learning to "paint" the future . . . to a young man who "apprentices" himself to the devil . . . to a nephew whose great-aunt teaches him to understand the "spirit gift" they share . . . to the way in which Will Shakespeare really learned his trade, here are unforgettable portraits of apprentices attempting to master their highly unusual talents.

To Michael,

My hero, my love

B. K.

CONTENTS

INTRODUCTION

by Brittiany A. Koren

R ECENTLY, I learned to treasure my family and the time spent with them more. Not that I didn't enjoy being with them before—after all I do love them very much—but quality time with them was always put off to the next day . . . and that day rarely came.

The pharaohs of Egypt knew their time was limited from the beginning of their kingship. Whether it was because the current ruler was murdered by someone who wanted the throne or merely died at the grand old age of forty, time was short for the godlike pharaohs. To make up for their mortality they accomplished great feats like building the pyramid tombs, erecting numerous statues of both the Egyptian gods and themselves, and seeing to their people in times of need.

To some people putting up statues of themselves at

every corner might seem arrogant, and perhaps some pharaohs were. But possibly they just wanted to be remembered, and isn't that a common hope of all of us? We all want our family and friends to remember us in a good light. And most of us want to know that our life mattered, that it meant something to others, and that we won't be quickly forgotten.

But then it is hard to forget pharaohs like Ramses and Tutankhamen even after all these years. After all, Ramses the Great is in every Bible story with Moses, and King Tut's tomb was the archaeological find of the twentieth century.

Still, pharaohs were much more than statues and pyramids. They led lives of greatness and glory. They also had lives of love and simple pleasures. The stories herein show a deeper, richer side to the pharaohs, bringing to life their families, close friends, servants, and enemies. In Susan Sizemore's "That God Won't Hunt," a pharaoh's fiancée helps solve the mystery of one of the palace's prize hounds. Rosemary Edghill tells us of a servant's loyalty to his pharaoh in "A Light in the Desert." And in "The Voice of Authority," Jody Lynn Nye shows us an unexpected pharaoh who turns to his father for guidance while learning all about the trials and tribulations of being a pharaoh.

Our families need to be cherished. This was as true of the pharaohs as it is for us today. One can only hope that they, the pharaohs of ancient Egypt, are looking down and smiling hand in hand with their loved ones right now.

SUCCESSION

by Tanya Huff

Tanya Huff lives and writes in rural Ontario with her partner, four cats, and an unintentional chihuahua. After sixteen fantasies, she wrote her first space opera, *Valor's Choice*, the sequel to which, *The Better Part of Valor*, is now out from DAW. Currently she is working on the third novel in her *Keeper* series, which began with *Summon The Keeper* and *The Second Summoning*. In her spare time she gardens and complains about the weather.

HE ruled over an Egypt combined because of her. She had seen him in a vision as though he were the heart spring of the Great River itself and out of his beginning would stretch a long line of pharaohs until they ended, finally, in the Great Green Sea. For the sake of this future, she had come to him, offering herself in marriage.

He had been wise enough to know he needed her, to ignore her age which, equal to his own, made it very probable that she would never give him sons. *Other wives may give me sons*, he'd said. *You give me what they cannot.*

She had given him the *deshret*, the Red Crown of Lower Egypt. Hers by right. His by marriage. Joined now to the *hedjet*, the White Crown of Upper Egypt. One country, united in them.

He had been wise enough to acknowledge her power, to take her counsel, to recognize that although he was pharaoh, Horus incarnate as king, they ruled together.

He had been wise enough to court her friendship. He had even come, a time or two, to her bed and seen to it that the experience was pleasant for them both.

"But now, Menes, you are become a fool," Neithhotep sighed. She had been standing at the window long enough, the stone had warmed under her bare feet. The last of the *dahabeahs* had finally docked, the dowry and the bride unloaded, and the procession readying to wend its way to the palace.

The builders, pulled from their usual tasks, had been working day and night to finish the way of the procession, leaving several other more important parts of Memphis to stand uncompleted. As little as she approved of the pharaoh's sudden obsession, she had to admit it was pleasant to have some part of this new island city actually finished. She was sick to death of the slam of chisels and the shouts of the overseers.

There. The procession was moving.

Neithhotep stepped away from the window and held out her arms. The two slaves who dressed her hurried forward, one with the nearly translucent overshift, the other with the heavy collar of onyx and gold that held it in place.

"You have decided to attend, my queen?"

"No, Hemon, I have decided to wear my best so that I may sulk in splendor." The overshift had been designed to cover her arms while leaving her shoulders bare. Age did not show on a woman's shoulders—and that was very nearly the only place the years had not kissed. Matching gold-and-onyx cuffs held the billowing sleeves in place, matching sandals, matching band about the short full wig. Her face had already been dusted, kohled, and hennaed. A touch of scented oil, and she was as ready as she could be. "How do I look?"

"Regal, my queen." The scribe inclined his head. "Gracious."

"Gracious? More than I had hoped for. Let us only hope Methethy is as impressed. I want no more whispered words falling into the ears of the Great Menes."

"The queen is jealous of your new bride, Great Pharaoh. Jealous of her youth and beauty."

Oh, please. As though there hadn't been young and beautiful brides before, not to mention concubines and

catamites, and she had been jealous of none of them.
Well, a little jealous perhaps when Hathor gifted their
young bodies with new life and softened their eyes
with a mystery she would never know—but that was
personal, not political.

The difference today was not with the bride but
rather with the way the girl had been presented. And
by whom. The pharaoh's vizier thought that by providing a young beauty for the old king to prove his
virility upon, it would move him closer to power. That
the girl he had procured would be able to influence
the pharaoh to give her a queen's power—
Neithhotep's power—which he would then control as
he controlled the girl.

*"The queen is jealous of your new bride, Great
Pharaoh . . ."*

The young were never subtle when they made their
play—could his intentions be any more obvious?

Did he honestly think she would allow such a
thing? Especially as the only way the pharaoh could
remove her from power without throwing Upper and
Lower Egypt into civil war, would be to remove *her*.

The girl could clasp the wrinkled body to her young
bosom as often as she could stand it, but it would not
bring her one step closer to the throne.

Three attendant slaves, two guards in *her* ceremonial
armor, and a boy to carry the large fan of peacock
feathers—more of an escort than she would normally
require within the grounds of the palace but large
enough to please her husband, who would assume she

came in state to honor his new bride. Large enough also to remind her husband's vizier that she had resources of her own but not so large he could convince anyone she was a threat.

Politics. If it destroyed fewer lives, she would enjoy the game more.

After so many years, Neithhotep knew to the moment when her husband would arrive in the throne room—this time, she subtracted a few moments for desire, arrived earlier than she would normally, and still barely made it to her place before the Great Menes entered, nearly treading on the heels of his guards in his haste. He frowned slightly when he saw her, then smiled and crossed toward her with his hands outstretched, the gold that trimmed his robe whispering secrets against the marble floor.

"Methethy said you would not come."

"Not come?" She smiled as though the matter had never been in doubt and allowed him to catch up her hands in his. "As your first wife, Great Pharaoh, it is my duty to welcome your newest wife to her home, but it is also my pleasure to be with you to share your joy."

He was honestly pleased; she could see it in his eyes, in the way the tight creases at the corners relaxed under the lines of kohl. His mouth opened—he was about to ask her advice, she knew the expression, had seen it a hundred times, and thanked the gods she was seeing it now. If they could just have a chance to speak without his vizier or his vizier's spies in attendance. . . .

The gods were not so kind.

The bridal procession had reached the palace.

Menes spun about so quickly, he knocked his wig askew. Neithhotep gently straightened it as she ascended the dais behind him.

Methethy entered first—as she'd known he would—and considerably ahead of the actual procession. He was far too astute to leave so critical a meeting to chance. His eyes flashed when he saw her already in place, the expression gone too quickly to read, but she knew he was not pleased to see her. Hardly surprising as he'd made it quite clear that this new queen would become first in Egypt. Neithhotep could almost see his mind working as he crossed to the double thrones.

"Great Pharaoh, Berner-Ib comes, and she is more than everything she was declared to be."

Berner-Ib. The girl's name meant Sweet-heart. Could the situation become any more cloying? Yes. Merely wait until Egypt's first wife welcomed the newest wife to the family. Neithhotep had every intention of greeting the girl with open arms and overwhelming her with kindness. As she had told the Great Menes, it was her pleasure to share his joy—it was also her intent to remove the vizier from the equation, to give the girl someone new to rely on.

The vizier's voice pulled Menes to the edge of the throne. "More beautiful? More graceful?"

"Yes, Great Pharaoh. The most beautiful girl in the length of Egypt, from the First Cataract to the Great Green Sea. The most graceful. The most gracious. And yours."

"Mine."

He was besotted and hadn't even met the girl yet. Had heard only Methethy's honeyed words over and over until his desire, his need for this girl had overwhelmed all other senses.

There's no fool like an old fool.

An observation she had no intention of applying to herself.

Berner-Ib would have been told she was her enemy. Which was true.

Beware the first wife; she will poison the pharaoh's heart against you. You are young, you are beautiful, you should be first, not her. She could hear the words as clearly as though she'd been standing beside Methethy as he said them. And she could hear Berner-Ib's words to the pharaoh even though they had not yet been spoken. *If you want me, Great Pharaoh, you must be rid of her.*

She had to capture the girl's self-interest before those words were spoken. Once a man began thinking with his body, intelligent decisions came few and far between.

The bride's dowry entered before her. It wasn't large—Mutardis, the Nubian wife, had arrived with twice her weight in gold and ivory, four hunting leopards, a fully trained and outfitted war elephant, and a legion of Nubian warriors to add to the pharaoh's guard. The elephant had made rather a large mess during the festivities. In contrast, Berner-Ib's dowry consisted of two dozen large baskets of grain—symbolic of what would now be sent yearly from her father's lands to Memphis—six pure black hunting dogs, and three burly young men who all bore the marks of stonemasons. A clever dowry, Neithhotep granted. In a city still half built, the stonemasons alone did much to make up for the lack of gold, but not by any means a pharaoh's dowry. Her husband was besotted indeed to accept so little.

Berner-Ib entered in a gilded litter, enclosed behind linen draperies imprinted with the pharaoh's cartouche.

"Shall I bring you your bride, Great Pharaoh?"

Methethy's smile was all gentle deference but Neithhotep could see his eyes glittering in anticipation of his triumph. She turned her head in time to see the pharaoh nod. The others would see him incline his head regally; she saw he couldn't trust himself to speak.

The vizier held his hand at the break in the draperies and a small hand emerged to lie like a fallen flower petal upon his. A tiny foot in a golden sandal followed and Berner-Ib emerged from her litter like a butterfly emerging from a cocoon.

She was undeniably beautiful and she moved like a breeze across still water, but she was not the practiced seductress Neithhotep had expected. In fact, if the girl had even had her first blood, she'd be very surprised.

"Is she not everything I promised, Great Pharaoh?"

Neithhotep could hear Menes' heart beating beneath his heavy gold-and-faience collar.

"She is."

The child flushed. The color touched her cheeks like the kiss of Ra, making her more beautiful still.

"And you have my guarantee, Great Pharaoh, that she will bear you a son."

The guarantee of a son. He had spoken the words to her husband, but he had also thrown them at her like a challenge.

It was much, much worse than Neithhotep had feared.

"I could not get near to her." Neithhotep sank down on a gilded bench, and began to pull off her court finery. "In the one moment that could have been mine, my feet were trapped in shifting sand and I could only watch mouth agape as my husband and the vizier swept the child away."

"I don't understand why this child is so much more dangerous than the temptress you expected, my queen."

"Then allow me to gift you with the details, Hemon." She all but threw her collar at the slave waiting to take it. Would have thrown it had she not been so tired and it so heavy. "The child is a pawn in this game, her unfortunate fate to be born with beauty and grace and a *ba* so pure it lights her from within. She is as trusting as an ibis in the reeds. Methethy has probably been searching for one such as she for as long as he has been at the court of the pharaoh—one of the right face and form to enchant an old man who needs to be

reassured of his physical power and of the right age
and innocence to be used in enchantment."

"Magic," the scribe breathed.

The Great Menes believed in science and had constructed his capital around a massive temple to Ptah.
His court welcomed doctors and astronomers, artisans
and scribes, but there were no wizards.

Until now.

"Magic," Neithhotep agreed, removing wig and
band both in one irritated swoop. "He will use her
youth and her purity, he will bind it with the first
blood of her body, and he will bring our husband to
her when the auguries are right, bring her somewhere
hidden from the eyes of Hathor, and he will give the
Great Menes a son."

"Your pardon, Great Queen, but is that such a bad
thing?"

She stared at the scribe for a moment, then shook
her head. "For the pharaoh to have a son? No."

The pharaoh had, in point of fact, seven sons—and
twenty-two daughters—but they were not the issue at
this time. All seven of his male children had been born
of concubines or slaves; not one of his wives had given
him a living son although two had died trying.

"It is the way of the having," Neithhotep continued,
pulling an offered shawl around her shoulders. "If we
ignore, for a moment, the magics; who do you think
will control this son when he is born? And when
Khepri comes in his own good time to carry the

Pharaoh's *ba* to the underworld, who will hold power in this son's place?"

"The vizier."

"Indeed. The girl will not be able to stand against him. In fact, she will turn to him, for he is all she knows in this strange place. He will wed the son to the mother to gain the sovereignty and will, in point of fact, rule Egypt. Will likely rule in truth the moment the child names him heir."

"But for that to happen, he must ensure your death before death takes the Great Menes," Hemon protested, brows drawn down into a deep vee.

"While that is not likely to be a great problem for him, we have more at stake than my life alone."

"Great Queen!"

"What is at stake, Hemon, is the life of Egypt. We *cannot* ignore the magics, not even for a moment. For the son of Osiris made King to allow his divine body to be touched by the dark arts; to place in time upon the throne a pharaoh born of such darkness . . ." She shook her head, staring off into the memories of a thousand rituals to honor the gods and keep the land strong.

"The gods will turn away from us?"

The voice of her chief scribe returned her to the present. "We will be fortunate if in their anger they only turn away. Too much attention from the gods can be worse than none at all."

"Then you must expose this wizard to the light of Ra!"

"And place myself in opposition to the plans of the pharaoh? Force the people to choose between the White Crown and the Red? Divide us into two countries again? Place us once more at each other's throat? Is that what you would have me do?"

Her voice had grown sharper with every word, and she spit out the final question with force enough to drive Hemon to his knees.

"No, Great Queen."

Neithhotep watched him for a moment, saw how he trembled, and suddenly sighed, all the anger leaching out of her. "Get up, Hemon. You know how I dislike speaking to the top of your head."

"Yes, Great Queen."

"And you were right, I must do something." This was not the time to be old and tired even though she was undeniably both. "Methethy's plan rests as this stool does, on three legs. If I can remove one, the plan collapses. There is no point in speaking to the vizier, and I am certain he has a thousand perfectly legitimate reasons why I cannot see the girl—all of which I could counter in time, but time is on his side." She stared down at the stool, at the three legs ending in gilded copies of the hooves of the sacred bull. Without the bull, there would be no calf. "I will speak with the pharaoh."

"Your pardon, Great Queen, but do you actually think that the vizier will not have given the Great Menes an answer for everything you might say?"

"I think the vizier does not know everything I might say."

"Great Queen, the vizier has said no one is to see the King of Two Lands without his authorization."

Neithhotep lengthened her stride so that Kenamun, the pharaoh's chief scribe, had to scurry like a fat scarab to keep up. "I am not here to see the King of Two Lands."

She could feel the frown against her back. "But I thought . . ."

"I am here to see my husband who is in his private quarters. Does the vizier rule my husband's entire life?"

He did. And they both knew it. But the walls of the palace had ears, and the route she'd taken—from the farthest entrance to the Women's Quarters—led past many who were listening. Kenamun could no more answer in the affirmative than he could say what he truly thought of her making a eunuch her chief scribe.

"No, Great Queen, but . . ."

"Has my husband left instructions he was not to be disturbed?"

"No, Great Queen, but . . ."

"But what, Kenamun?" She stopped at the entrance to the pharaoh's private quarters and spun around on one heel, spearing the officious little man with a look.

"But . . ." Kenamun glanced around. Realized the amount of attention their progress had attracted and sighed in surrender. "The King of Two Lands is not expecting you, Great Queen. His slaves will not have prepared a welcome suitable for one of your rank."

It was a pitiful protest, and he was well aware of it.

"I appreciate your concern for my rank," Neith-hotep told him, smiling as he shivered slightly. "But the only welcome I desire is from my husband. Stay here." Her attendants bowed and stepped back as she swept regally forward and between the closest pair of guards.

The vizier has said no one is to see the King of Two Lands . . .

The changes have been made by the orders of the vizier . . .

. . . as I was instructed by the vizier, Great Queen.

She frowned as she walked, trying to remember when Methethy had gained so much power. He had been assistant to the old vizier—she remembered a sleek-haired young man who watched and listened and learned. Toward the end, he was doing the vizier's job and doing it very well. When the old man died suddenly, Menes gave the position to Methethy over the sons of the old vizier. What had happened to the sons? It bothered her that she didn't remember. And how *suddenly* had the old vizier died?

Why had no one ever noticed that Methethy was studying the dark arts?

I am becoming old, she sighed silently. *I had intended only to knock the wind from Methethy's sails by befriending the girl he thought to put in my place. Now, I find myself all that stands between Egypt and the wrath of the gods.*

Next time I will remain sulking in my chambers like the sensible woman I am supposed to be.

"Great Queen, the pharaoh is not . . ."

"Expecting me. I know." Neithhotep barely glanced at the slaves as she passed. There had been no priests lingering in the corridors. That was a bad sign.

Menes was sitting in a spill of sunlight, his head propped on one hand, a scroll in his lap he didn't see. He was asleep. Where others might think he was merely thinking deeply, she knew him so well she could see sleep resting on his shoulders. And not only sleep, in softened lines of muscle and in the angle of bone through oiled skin, she could see every one of his sixty-three years.

He had been a great king once. Would it hurt her more to discover he was, like the girl, a pawn in Methethy's plans or that he willingly defied the gods and risked his people?

She stopped far enough away so that he could wake and still deny he'd been sleeping. The conversation they were about to have held pit traps enough, they need not begin with him on the defensive. "Great Menes."

He started. Sleep fled. Clutching the scroll, he turned toward her, his eyes half-hooded. "Methethy said I should not allow you to see me alone."

"That comes as no surprise."

"He says that you are jealous of how I favor him."

"Does he?" Neithhotep snorted, moving around so that she could look the pharaoh squarely in the eye.

"He also says that I am jealous of your new bride. He seems to judge the emotions of others based on his own. I am jealous of neither."

"And yet you clearly labor under strong emotion," Menes murmured, smiling a little.

He knew her well after so many years and it seemed the time they'd shared had weight enough to pierce the fog Methethy wrapped around the pharaoh's mind.

"I am concerned," she admitted, beginning to hope.

"That when I have a new wife and son you will fall to nothing in my court?"

Those were Methethy's words. Hope died.

"I am concerned," she snapped, "about the consequences Egypt will suffer if you allow Methethy to use magics to get you a son."

Menes' lip curled. "What consequences?"

He knew. Not a pawn, then. To her surprise, she felt relief. Better Great Menes be rash and stupid than helpless.

"The gods will not . . ."

Fingers white around the ebony arms of his chair, Menes surged to his feet. "I am a god!"

"Then you should know better!" Not the most politic of responses, particularly said in a tone she used when she lost her patience with children and slaves. Still, a retreat here would not help the situation. "Great Pharaoh, I have been a priestess of Hathor in all her many beauties my entire adult life and there are writings that warn against this, against the *guarantee* of a son or a daughter. Great Hathor is the Mother of all Pharaohs and children are her gift, not Methethy the vizier's."

"And the goddess has not gifted me."

"She has gifted you twenty-nine times!"

"But never a son from a queen." He leaned forward, his eyes glittering. "There will be a son from this queen—it has been promised me. Methethy gives me the dynasty you foresaw so long ago in your dream."

"Do not bring my dreams into this," she warned. "A son by the dark arts . . ."

"A son by any means!"

"Will prove you are still vital and strong?" She saw the answer in his eyes and continued before he could realize he'd given so much of himself away. "What of the girl?"

"She is the greatest treasure in my kingdom and once she has had her first blood, she will be mine, the mother of my son, and much exalted. You have no choice but to suffer that!"

"This is not about *me*. Will you allow a queen of Egypt to be used so? Used as nothing more than a vessel for dark magic?"

He was angry now. "Do not pretend to me you care about the girl."

"I care about Egypt!"

"I will allow a queen of Egypt to be fed to the crocodiles if it gets me my son," he growled. "Do not doubt me in this, Neithhotep."

They were both breathing heavily.

"I do not doubt you, Great Pharaoh." More was the pity. "Once your mind is made up, the years have taught me that it is futile to attempt to change it."

More than futile, the attempt would only hold him more stubbornly upon his course.

"You have been to see the pharaoh, Great Queen."

"I am leaving his private chambers, am I not?" She should have kept her voice carefully neutral, knew better than to give rumor and gossip any fuel at all, but not even she, with years of experience to draw upon, could hide her new dislike of the pharaoh's vizier.

Motioning that the chief treasurer should go on without him, Methethy fell into step by her side. "It is not fitting that you walk the halls unescorted, Great Queen. Allow me to return you to your attendants."

"Is the pharaoh not expecting you?"

"The Great Menes will be happy to wait while I do my duty by you, Great Queen."

"The Great Menes will be happy to wait for me, old woman." Neithhotep could hear the words beneath the words.

A crocodile smiled in much the same way.

She slowed her pace, forcing him to shorten his stride as she had earlier forced Kenamun to lengthen his. Petty, but she had asked neither of them to walk with her.

"I hear that you worry about Egypt, Great Queen."

"Your ears are fleet of foot if they had time to tell you that," Neithhotep snorted.

"My ears . . . ? Ah, yes, my ears. The pharaoh's security is my concern."

"Because I cannot get to you unless I go through him?"

This new smile had honest amusement about it. No, not honest, but Methethy was definitely amused. "Plain speaking, Great Queen. I will gift you with the same—as you cannot go through him, you cannot get to me."

The backs of the pharaoh's ceremonial guard were an arm's length away. Beyond them, her attendants and the constant, ever-changing crowd of nobles, merchants, artisans, and slaves. They must not know, must not be forced to choose sides. The Red Crown could not be seen in disagreement with the White. The union of Upper and Lower Egypt was too fragile still; war still too possible.

She turned and saw this knowledge reflected on Methethy's smiling face.

"I am tired," she sighed. "You may gloat tomorrow."

He bowed deeply and murmured for her ears alone. "I am sorry you take this so personally, Great Queen, but you cannot stop me."

"If he had said nothing in the throne room, if he had never mentioned a son—no, if he had left me out of this altogether, never started that stupid 'the old queen is jealous of the new,' I wouldn't have been in the throne room." Rubbing her temples, Neithhotep dropped down onto the bull-legged stool. "He wanted me there.

He goaded me into going so that I would see the girl and he could let me know exactly what he is doing."

Frowning, Hemon froze, a scroll half unrolled. "But why, Great Queen?"

"Methethy is not the type to hide his lamp under a basket—what is the point of orchestrating such a clever coup if no one knows? He needs someone to appreciate the full magnitude of what he does—but not just anyone. It must be someone worthy of knowing."

"So your life is not in immediate danger."

She thought about that for a moment. "No, I suppose it isn't." Her lips twisted into a self-mocking smile. "A little joy in every life, it seems."

"He must have known you would try to stop him."

"He is young, he is powerful—he doesn't think I can. The Great Menes will not listen to reason, the people cannot be made to choose between us, and both the vizier and the girl are in a circle of the pharaoh's guard, six guards deep. Not literally, Hemon," she added catching sight of the scribe's expression. "I merely mean they are so well protected by the pharaoh, I cannot prevent this insult to the gods without causing the very war I am trying to avoid."

"You cannot reach the pharaoh, the vizier, or the girl, Great Queen."

About to snarl that he should tell her something she did not already know, her mouth closed with a snap as he did.

"You *can* reach the gods."

* * *

Although Hathor had a temple within the city large enough for all of Memphis to attend her many festivals, Neithhotep preferred the small wooden temple within the palace complex. As First Queen and High Priestess, she had spent half her life in this quiet sanctuary. Built to her exact specifications, it matched the temple in which her mother and her mother's mother had served the goddess. She waved away the attentions of a lesser priestess and walked slowly toward the enclosed sanctuary, the painted eyes of the goddess' many faces following her.

On the back wall of the sanctuary was a painting of Hathor as the Great Mother, her cow body stretched across the sky, Horus suckling at her teats, Ra held in safety between the spread of her horns.

You can reach the gods.

She should have thought of that herself.

But what to say?

Perhaps, she thought, laying the lotus blossoms she'd brought as an offering down before the goddess, *this is when I should listen.*

But the goddess stared out at her with wide eyes and remained silent.

Sighing, Neithhotep stepped back to the bench her age had granted her, and sat. Behind her, in the main part of the temple, she could hear a priestess—who was also a wife of the pharaoh although she couldn't at the moment recall her name—casting auguries over a child.

I am old, Great Mother. She glanced down at her

hands, at the way the skin wrapped loosely around the bone, at the marks of age across the wrinkled backs. *And I am used to knowing what to do. This wizard seeks to twist a child from your son, Horus made King, to raise up not your child as pharaoh but his. If I stop him, I break apart the unity I have lived my life for. If I do not stop him, how can my country survive the just retribution of the gods so denied?*

Again, the goddess remained silent.

Neithhotep felt her mind begin to drift. She had always found this aspect of Hathor comforting. The Great Cow, the Mother of all Pharaohs . . . Her thoughts slid over the little distance from the Great Cow to the Sacred Bull and from the bull itself to how she had thought of Menes as the Sacred Bull and from there to a memory of the first time she'd given Hathor's blessing as a priest collected the sacred seed into a clay cylinder corked tightly in its narrow end.

She snapped out of memory so quickly she couldn't catch her breath and had to sit, one hand clutching her chest while possibilities tumbled around in her head.

"As a queen of Egypt, Berner-Ib becomes a priestess of Hathor the moment she finishes her first blood."

The pharaoh flicked his fingernails against the arm of the throne. "She has not *had* her first blood."

The Great Menes was sounding sulky, tried of being denied. Good, that could only make him more susceptible. "Then—in Hathor's name—I must know when she begins so that the preparations for her ritual may be properly timed."

Lip curled, Methethy leaned forward to capture the pharaoh's ear. "Great Menes, did this 'ritual' occur with your other wives?"

"As Great Menes is aware," Neithhotep answered before the pharaoh could, "his other wives were older. The ritual occurred, but there was no need to know of the queen's blood or to have you involved."

"Then why am I now involved?" Menes demanded.

Neithhotep bowed as gracefully as her back would allow. "Your concern for your new queen's safety has made it difficult for me to deal with her directly."

If Berner-Ib does not have this ritual, then she may not be perceived as truly a queen. That could disrupt the smooth transfer of power later on.

No need to read the vizier's thoughts, she could see them flowing like the Nile in flood across his face.

You are up to something, old woman.

He was not much of a wizard, or he would have used the dark arts to scry her purpose. She had begun to suspect he was merely an ambitious man who stumbled upon one spell in his studies and now looked to use it to his advantage.

Momentarily startled by the rude gesture she made, hidden from the rest of the court by the wide sleeve of her overdress, Methethy recovered quickly and smiled. "I suggest, Great Pharaoh, that one of your new queen's women gift Queen Neithhotep with the information she desires when it occurs. I also suggest that

Queen Neithhotep be granted access to the new queen for the duration of the ritual only and that it be held in the small temple in the palace—so that she be from your side for the least amount of time."

"Let it be so."

"They appear to be slender vases."

"They are." The cork was well hidden within the narrow end. It hadn't been difficult to find artisans able to create what she needed—a potter for the narrow cylinders, a metalworker for the stands that held them erect and hid their true function. She had him create two dozen only to confuse the vizier's spies. "The girl has begun to bleed. Have you found the next night the stars will align as Methethy needs?"

"It was not easy, Great Queen. The magical texts are complex and with no wizard to guide me . . ."

"Do you have the night?"

"I believe so, Great Queen."

"You believe so?" When he nodded, his eyes miserable, she spared him a comforting smile. "Do not worry, Hemon. We deal with the gods, belief is everything."

Neithhotep saw Methethy's eyes widen as he took in the pharaoh's wives and daughters behind her. It was one thing to know their number, it was another entirely to see them gathered together in a small temple—all wearing robes identical to the girl he escorted. He would have more trouble keeping her in view than he had anticipated.

The wives and daughters were a smoke screen only. Neithhotep had told none of them what she intended, allowing their curiosity about the new, isolated queen to draw them from the Women's Quarters.

She had made the vizier wait outside the temple, a lesser priestess purifying both the new queen and her escort with lotus blossoms dipped in scented oil and droning out the longest blessing in the history of the Two Lands. When Neithhotep saw his patience reach the breaking point, she stepped forward and held out her hands for the girl.

Berner-Ib was as lovely up close as she had been from a distance. Neithhotep could almost understand how an old man could risk so much so foolishly for one melting glance from her dark eyes ... her eyes ... She glared at the vizier. The girl's eyes were clouded and dull.

"I am taking no chances, Great Queen," he murmured as he placed the chill hand on hers. "If you had planned to appeal to her directly, I'm afraid you'll get nothing but placid agreement and mindless cooperation."

"She has been drugged."

"Relaxed," he corrected mildly. A hand waved back at the pharaoh's guard suddenly surrounding the temple. "The Great Menes wishes for nothing to disturb your ritual and has sent guards to keep the curious from all your doors. He requests that you return his queen to me the moment the ritual is complete. And I will examine her," he added, "to ensure there has been no barrier placed in my way." Bowing mockingly, he stepped back through the temple door and stood, arms folded, at the edge of Hathor's domain.

By the time two of the pharaoh's daughters led Berner-Ib unresisting into the sanctuary, Neithhotep was as heartily tired of the whole thing as the waiting Methethy had to be and was becoming concerned that the drug would wear off too soon. She was prepared with drugs of her own but would rather not have to use them.

Finally, as she was beginning to despair, a warm, damp, yielding packet was pressed into her hand. Turning, she met the gleaming onyx eyes of Menes' youngest concubine.

The concubines had a good sideline going selling the pharaoh's seed to the better apothecaries to be used in charms against impotence. Neithhotep refused to speculate on what the lesser apothecaries used. Concubines not high in the pharaoh's favor lived as good a life as the first wife allowed, and, today, she had called in the debt.

"The goddess intercedes directly?"

"Perhaps she fears that time is running out and the new queen is his last chance—I do not question the will of the goddess."

Pouting a little, the girl twisted a shining strand of hair around her fingers. "Great Menes has not called me to him since the new queen arrived."

"Neither has he been to the new queen," Neithhotep said

pointedly. The old woman and the young exchanged a
speaking glance. "You must go to him—I would not pre-
sume to instruct you on how to proceed from there, but it is
vital you lie with him so, if I may, I suggest you convince
him that you fear he is no longer strong or vital enough to
please you and then let him prove you wrong."

"The vizier . . ."

"Will be escorting the new queen to the temple. You must
begin the moment he leaves the pharaoh's side and use him
as an excuse to leave quickly when it is done."

Neithhotep had wasted no strength on worrying
whether the concubine could slip past the pharaoh's
guard into the temple—after all, the girl had been
trained to wrap men about her tiniest finger. Now, as
she slipped into the sanctuary, she pulled the slender
clay tube from under her robes. Warmed by her body
heat, it would not chill the prize poured into it.

The girl lay on the bench staring up at Hathor's gentle eyes.

"I miss my mother," she said suddenly.

"I know, child." Neithhotep folded dimpled knees
to make room and sat as well, replacing the girl's legs
across her lap. "There are days I miss mine."

In three months there were rumors the new queen
would bear the pharaoh's son. By five months the rumors were celebrated as truth—all the auguries in
every temple said the baby was a boy. The celebrations
lasted for days. Great Menes was like a man reborn.

He worked the words "my son, Djer," into every speech. He forgot aches and pains. He ate and drank like a young man.

The apothecaries did a growing business in impotence charms.

He even took up hunting again.

The ruling of the country was left to the vizier as the pharaoh rediscovered his youth—which was not a situation Neithhotep had anticipated though it had come as no real surprise.

She knew she lived only so Methethy could gloat.

Great Menes' protection continued to surround him like an army.

Berner-ib came to Hathor's temple when ritual demanded. Heavy with the pharaoh's son, she was strong and healthy and willingly joined the prayers to Taurt, the hippopotamus Hathor wore as the protector of pregnant women and infants. As she prayed, Neithhotep prayed beside her.

They were together in the temple, the old queen and the young, walking slowly to the door where Methethy waited, when a young guardsman covered in mud stumbled toward them, wet sandals slipping against the polished floor.

Pushing past the vizier, he dropped to his knees, gasping for breath. "Great Queen, the pharaoh . . ."

"To me!" Methethy snapped, yanking him around. "Talk to me!"

". . . something went wrong during the hunt,

Great Lord! Great Menes has been killed by a hippopotamus."

As one, the two queens turned to stare at the statue
of Taurt.

"Killed?"

"Carried off, Great Lord. But we retrieved the body."

Neithhotep turned again, and met the vizier's eyes.

Methethy stiffened, suddenly realizing no army surrounded him now. Leaping forward, he grabbed the
young queen by the arm.

To his surprise, she screamed.

Did she scream because he hurt her? Or because the
news of the pharaoh's death had that moment pene-
trated the fog of her pregnancy? Neithhotep neither
knew nor cared.

"He tries to injure the pharaoh's son! Stop him!"

She wore the *deshret*. She could command when she
had to.

Menes had been a great king once. And her husband.

But she could not get to the vizier unless she went
through him.

Although she had kept Egypt from the consequences,
he had willingly dishonored the gods and they had
turned their faces from him. Or toward him. Too much
attention from the gods can be worse than none at all.

Pushing the girl into the arms of a priestess and
waving the half circle of guardsmen back, she lowered
herself carefully to one knee beside the bleeding body
of the vizier. Mortally wounded, he was not yet dead.

"I told the Great Menes not to hunt the hippopotamus. I told him I knew his age as well as my own and he should leave this foolishness for younger men. I told him that a son would not return to him the strength and speed of his youth. I told him *not* to hunt the hippopotamus." Others would hear her words as mourning, but she saw that Methethy understood and leaned closer still. "You were wrong," she told him softly. "It wasn't personal; it was always politics."

She ruled over an Egypt combined because of him. Honored the man he had been and ruled as the Pharaoh Iti crowned with the Red and the White in one crown in the name of his son, Djer, the second in a long line of pharaohs destined to end finally in the Great Green Sea.

For the sake of this future, she had gone to him.

THE VOICE OF AUTHORITY

by Jody Lynn Nye

Jody Lynn Nye lists her main career activity as "spoiling cats." She lives northwest of Chicago with two of the above and her husband, author and packager Bill Fawcett. She has written twenty-two books, including four contemporary fantasies, three science fiction novels, four novels in collaboration with Anne McCaffrey, including *The Ship Who Won,* a humorous anthology about mothers, *Don't Forget Your Spacesuit, Dear!,* and over sixty short stories. Recent books are *The Grand Tour,* third in her new fantasy epic series, *The Dreamland,* and *Applied Mythology,* an omnibus of the *Mythology 101* series.

"**Y**OUR Highness," whispered Mumsatra.

"Go away," mumbled Prince Hekamaatre-setepenamun.

"But it is time for you to rise. The priests of Horus are here." Hekamaatre-setepenamun's hand crept out from under the thin gold-woven coverlet and felt around for something to throw, but he knew from experience that Mumsatra had backed out of range. Two things he hated were getting up early and being nagged.

"Tell them I am indisposed."

A commotion arose in the outer hall. Hekamaatre ignored the muffled whispering back and forth. Mumsatra's footsteps withdrew hastily. Heka had almost gone back to sleep when they returned.

"It is General Khaurmene."

"What? Chariot practice is not until the afternoon. Tell him I will see him then."

Mumsatra went away, but came back at once. He knelt beside the couch.

"He says you must come at once," Mumsatra paused. "Your Majesty."

That made Heka sit bolt upright. Mumsatra beckoned to a cluster of shadowy figures who hurried in and threw back the shutters of the bedchamber. They descended upon the prince, who could only stare at a point of light on the wall as they washed, shaved, and dressed him in court clothes, wig, and jewelry.

* * *

Heka alighted from the lead chariot and hurried into the palace-temple of Medinet Habu as General Khaurmene signaled the others to go back to the stables. Inside the vast building, men and women clutched one another in fear. Servants went about their tasks with their heads bowed. An incredible number of priests were clustered in the hall outside the royal bedchamber. Most of them regarded him with a mixture of awe and astonishment, as wide-eyed as the gods painted on the walls. Heka drew himself up, straightening the turquoise-and-gold pectoral on his thin chest. He knew he did not cut an imposing figure, being shorter and slimmer than his great father, and possessed of a nose somewhat too long for his face, but he was a prince of the royal house. Had they been talking about him?

His mother, the great royal wife, came to clutch his arm, then withdrew, her hands shaking. He put an arm around her, and she nearly collapsed.

"Mother, what has happened?" he asked.

"The unthinkable," she said, tearing at the fine linen of her dress, which he could see was rent already. She had shaved off her eyebrows. So this had not just happened. He noticed several of his brothers and sisters were already present and dressed in mourning clothes. A few of the men gave him dirty looks, which they quickly veiled. "He had gone to lead the sunrise ceremony in the temple of Amon-Re when he was taken ill."

Hekamaatre shook his head. "He did not have to

rise for that," he said. "His ancestors, may they exist eternally in the sunshine of the gods, allowed the priest to greet the sun in his stead."

The old woman shook her head. "You know your father, may he have life, prosperity, and health." Then she burst into tears.

"Come see the great one, may his *ka* be in comfort throughout eternity," said the vizier, To. The old man appeared before Heka and his mother, and bowed, gesturing to the great carved doors at the end of the corridor.

Heka allowed himself to be herded along through the brightly painted hall, but he was suspicious. The vizier, who had served throughout his father's long reign, had never made secret how little he thought of the king's eldest surviving son. During the campaigns of his father's early reign Heka had been a general and an adviser, but the Dual Kingdoms had been at peace for many years. Three of his brothers had died, and still Ramses had not named him or anyone else as heir. Heka's father had made it clear many years before that he thought none of his sons worthy to succeed him. The relief work on the walls of the very palace in which he stood showed no name in the cartouche of first royal son and heir. Heka had resented the omission for a long time, then decided he saw no reason why he should not enjoy his forties in comfort, since he would seem to have no other duties. He lived his life to please himself, within guidelines allowed by the living god, who only occasionally stated his displeasure. But all Heka's pent-up resentment fled when he saw what was waiting for him in the king's chamber.

The wailing of the servants increased in volume as the doors were drawn open. Heka hardly dared approach the great, gilded bed. His father had ruled Upper and Lower Egypt for thirty-one years. Heka had begun to think of him as huge and imperishable as one of the countless temple pylons that he had commanded to be built. The body that lay shrouded under a gold cloth seemed shrunken, diminished, too small to be that of his father. When the life force had fled, it had deflated the corpse to the bones. Heka gently turned back the linen. The face was that of an old man. Surely this could not be the great Ramses, third of the name? He turned away, overwhelmed by grief. To was still talking.

". . . He had only a moment to speak before he died, when he named and confirmed thee, Hekamaatre-setepenamun, as the heir. We asked him if he was certain. He must have been vouchsafed a vision from the god, for he said only, 'he has the promise.' And then he was in the arms of Osiris. Your name was the last thing on his lips, may you live eternally, so we dared not question his will. . . ."

Feeling stunned, Heka turned back toward the hall. To followed, his long back bent so the top of his head did not rise above that of Heka, who was a handspan shorter than he. The priests of the House of Eternity who would oversee the embalming and burial were already moving in closer. Automatically, Heka made room for them, but then noticed that they were ducking out of his path.

"We will all understand if you wish to pray alone, Majesty," To said, smoothly cutting off the advance of Sekhemptah, high priest of Amon-Re, who appeared to be beside himself with woe. Talk would already be spreading that it was in his temple that the pharaoh had died. Donations and sacrifices might be falling off during the next few months. There would be more talk; the scandal that had erupted over twenty years ago would surely resurface, when an attempt was made upon Ramses III's life by his own officers and women of the harem. Heka thought there might be fresh gossip of foul play. Indeed, there might! It would have to be investigated, and it would undoubtedly be up to him to initiate the investigation. He hated politics and wanted to stay out of the whole mess. How he wished his father was alive!

Who could have foreseen such a swift death? Only the year before had been the Sed Festival celebrating thirty years of his father's reign. His many-times grandfather upon whom Ramses III had styled himself had lived to be ninety-six. Heka assumed one of his countless, hard-working younger brothers or his own eldest son would become pharaoh. Why could one not take over now? He liked his life. He saw no reason why he needed to change. Perhaps they had heard his father wrongly.

"You will need to prepare yourself for the acces-

sion," To said, bowing him toward the chariot that
awaited him on the steps.

"So soon?" Heka asked. "Why?"

To came close, his heavy-lidded eyes peering closely
into Hekamaatre's. He kept his voice low. "Why? Because the gods have called thy father to them. He
could not depart for the Hereafter without naming the
new Horus-on-Earth. Why the gods had wished to
keep thy divinity secret from thee, only they know. I
regret it because it prevented thee from receiving in-
struction that thou will need at once."

Heka frowned. "When?"

"Tomorrow morning. Thou must be ready before
the sunrise. The accession must take place at the appearance of the day's eye, to prevent any mischance.
There must be no gap in the kingship. That, at least,
thou must know."

Heka groaned. Up before sunrise! He was too old
for this. "Very well," he said.

To hesitated. "Thy name . . . must be determined by
the priests. Would thou be . . . another Ramses? Or are
the gods speaking another name in thy ear?"

Heka goggled at him. "I . . . yes . . . Ramses. Of
course." He strengthened his voice, though he quaked
inside. "I will be another Ramses."

Following To's suggestions, he did not permit any
audiences during the rest of the day, and had guards
stationed at every doorway. His household was not
idle, though. For a prince and official for whom no one

had much time before that day, Hekamaatre eaves-
dropped frankly upon the countless courtiers who arrived in his outer hall and tried everything from bribery
to threats to enter his presence. Heka took advantage
of not being expected to appear anywhere; he spent
his hours pleasantly, leaning on his favorite cushions,
listening to musicians and poets, eating delicate dishes
and drinking good wines. His chief wife babbled in his
ear of the new gowns she would wear, and the exotic
plants she would put into the garden of the Queen's
House. Heka paid her little mind.

It was his last idle moment. He was awakened before dawn by a procession of priests, Chanting, they
washed and robed him, then escorted him into a regal
palanquin that carried him over the long and bumpy
road to the temple of Amon-Re. The priest, Sekhemptah, and To walked beside him.

It was one of those perfect days when the lightening
sky was like lapis lazuli and a faint breeze cooled the
hot air. He had never seen so many people lining the
streets. No one bore a torch except those guiding his
bearers. The temple, too, was packed with more than
priests and pure ones. Every noble within a day's ride
or sail must have traveled all night to be there. Heka
shuddered. Imagine traveling the deserts at night!

Inundation was under way. All the common folk
who would, in the other two thirds of the year, be concerned with farming were now occupied with building projects on the heights and in the cities and
temples. It was actually a fortunate circumstance, if

one could call it that, because it meant thousands of
workers, builders, painters, and stonemasons were in
the capital city when Ramses III died. Most of them
were hastily pulled off whatever projects they'd been
employed on for the sake of finishing the old king's
tomb in the Biban el-Moluk during the seventy days of
embalming rituals. Since those could not be delayed,
they must finish with all haste what remained to be
done. Ramses IV's coronation would take place the
day after the interment. The priests and astrologers
were not best pleased. The most auspicious dates
would have been on the new year or the beginning of
the Season of Coming Forth, but the one had just
passed, and the other was more than six months away.

Since the old king had reigned for such a long time,
his elaborate tomb had many chambers, including
chapels and even painted reliefs of a kitchen and sailing vessels. The sarcophagus was a marvel in itself,
being carved from the trunk of a single cedar from the
Lebanon. In the funerary temple, the most sacred rites
to preserve the body would already be underway.
Hekamaatre realized that he, too, would have to begin
building his own house of eternity. Too soon to think
about dying, he thought hastily.

Hekamaatre followed the priest into the holiest of
holies, the central shrine. He was a little nervous. Only
the king himself was permitted to enter the small
chamber. Heka felt eyes on his back. He wanted to
glance over his shoulder, but that would not be fitting.
Sekhemptah chanted the words of the morning ritual.

That at least sounded normal. Heka began to relax.
Nothing out of the ordinary was going to happen, after
all. He began to think about how it would be to be king.

With a quick glance at the prince beside him,
Sekhemptah recited the common formula. "I am the
priest. It is the king who has sent me to behold the
god." That reminded Heka that his father was dead.
He sobered at once.

At the conclusion of the daylight ceremony, they
emerged into the outer sanctuary. Music and cheering
greeted Heka as he came forth. The high priests took
the roles of Amon and Horus to purify him, chanting.
"Welcome, welcome, O son of Amon. Behold thy law
and order in the land. Thou arrangest it, thou puttest
to rights what is faulty in it . . . We acknowledge the
descent of him who created us . . . Thy soul is created
in the hearts of thy people so they say, 'He is the Ka-
mutef's son whom the gods love.'" Heka was shown
to the double throne before which stood the Imhutef
priest. He made as if to sit down, but Sekhemptah, in
the role of Amon, held him back.

"Not yet, Majesty," he whispered. "There is more to
accomplish."

Heka glared at him. "Why did you not instruct me
in this before?" he hissed back.

Sekhemptah sighed. "I was not permitted until you
were confirmed in your divinity, Great One. But you
will find this is ever the way of kingship: you must do
first and learn how afterward. Follow my lead. I will
not fail thee, I swear."

Pure ones carried in censers from which clouds of fragrant smoke arose. Temple dancers threw themselves into the timeless sacred patterns, creating a holy, inviolable space around the prince and the dais. Priests in the brightest white linen brought forth the golden circlet with two feathers affixed, kneeling before Heka as the priests continued their litany. More of them swirled around him, removing his attire and replacing it with beautiful, transparent raiment embroidered with the symbols of Horus and other gods. A heavy pectoral that he recognized as his father's jubilee necklace was clasped around his neck. The crowns were placed on his head. He scarcely felt them as he floated upon a sea of words.

Three more priests, representing the scribe-gods Seshat and Thoth, came forward. For the first time Heka heard his new name stated to the gods: "Thou art Horus, Divine of Forms, Divine of Births, Horus of Gold, Who becomes King of Upper and Lower Egypt, He of the Sedge and the Bee, Ramses the Fourth, the *Kas* of Re appear in Glory; Son of Re, Hekamaatresetepenamun, All that the Sun enriches, granted life and wealth eternally." Heka, feeling like an awkward youth, recited after the Amon priest a formula of homage to the god and to his late father. More priests and some of his kinsmen, in the roles of ancestral spirits acclaimed him.

As the living god, he had to oversee the translation of his father as Osiris, leading prayers and personally interceding to ensure that his father passed through the trial of his heart. Placating Sobek, the crocodile god, not to eat his father's heart, made him quail. The sharp-toothed god had always frightened him. When he was an infant, his nurses had cautioned him to be good lest that happen to him one day. Now he was supposed to believe that he stood as Sobek's equal.

The assembly was reenacting the seeking for Osiris. He commanded two priestesses, in the roles of the goddesses, to search in the waters of the Nile for the body thrown there by Set, the murderer. The litany became engraved upon his heart. The words, as ancient as time, ought to be no more real than a story, but the opposite was true. He would have said automatically that the gods accepted his sacrifices, but he seemed to *know* it in his heart as never before. Every time he spoke as He Who Gives Life to the Land, he felt gods all around him. Not only that, but he sensed that his father was not far away. In his role as Horus, bereaved son, he seemed to hear his father's voice in his head, telling him what to do, what to say, before Sekhemptah told him.

He stopped in the middle of a recitation to pay attention to the voice. He heard nothing, but he felt *impatience* from the very air. Quickly he began speaking again, but it felt as though his tongue was not his own, his movements belonging to someone else. Puzzled, he continued with the ritual.

Thoth, chief scribe of the gods, stated, "I establish for thee, then, thy Crowns of Re, and thou livest eternally on the throne of Horus like Re." He turned to the crowd and proclaimed the new king's titles aloud.

There was an outcry of joy and relief. Egypt was now safe from evil because Horus-on-Earth had been restored. Hekamaatre—no, he corrected himself—Ramses sat first on one throne, then the other, remaining on the throne of Horus. Then he was presented to men he had known all his life: nobles, friends, courtiers, chiefs, who bowed low as his gaze swept over them. He heard the acclaim of the crowd.

At the conclusion of the traditional *hetep* meal he remained in his place, rigid, his arms and legs strangers to him. He felt as though he was flying. Everything he touched seemed to tingle. He looked toward the priests for help. They rushed to assist him from the throne and down from the dais.

Sekhemptah's face was full of satisfaction. "Thy flesh is gold, Your Majesty," he said, and looked smugly at To.

"Very well, very well, you told me he was the one," To grumbled, but he continued to support the pharaoh to his palanquin. Ramses was grateful for the seat. He could not have supported himself in a chariot at that moment.

The feast that followed Ramses' return to his father's palace was the most sumptuous since the Sed Festival the year before, but he got to eat little of it. From the moment he entered the great Hall of Truth, everyone came to kneel or bow before him. Foreigners, who had not been permitted to attend the accession, crowded behind To, waiting their turn for an audience.

Ramses took his place on the twin thrones of Horus

and Set to receive his visitors. When they knelt before him, he *knew* what was in their hearts. It overwhelmed him so much he could hardly speak. To and Sekhemptah stood at his elbow to send each petitioner away in turn. They had to be satisfied with a gracious nod.

"What is happening to me?" Ramses demanded in a low voice. "I am seeing each of their lives stretched out behind them like unwinding papyri!"

"That is the gods' power bestowed on behalf of your father, may his *ka* survive eternally," explained the priest, "but now you are taking it unto yourself."

Ramses was astonished. He held up his hands. They almost glowed in the torchlight. When he concentrated upon them, he could see every sinew, every vein, suffused with their own light. "I knew my father wielded great power, but I always assumed that it was rhetoric."

"Not so," Sekhemptah assured him. "The power is real. Did thou not feel it when they placed the crowns upon thy head?

"I thought I was light-headed from my grief," Ramses said. He clutched his brow where the golden circlet rested. "It confers my power?"

Sekhemptah shook his head. "Not so," he repeated. "It merely confirms it. You are the divine channel, the reincarnation of Horus-on Earth. I, as priest of Amon-Re, have experienced this before the face of that god, but you have ties to them all. You are Pharaoh. These powers are yours, Majesty, and whatever you do with them is right."

"I am too old to learn this," Ramses said. He looked

desperately around him for a means of escape, and knew just as surely there was none. All he wanted to do was go back to his quiet life of being ignored. "I can't learn this. Tell them all to go away. This is too great a responsibility. I need time!"

"There is no time, Majesty." To looked surprised. "The priests and I must discuss the most propitious time in which to hold thy coronation. In the meantime, we depart in two days' time for Edfu."

"Why?" Ramses asked.

"Why, to repeat the accession in the temple of Horus. Thou must confirm thy power from the god who confers it directly to thee."

"Very well," Ramses said, thinking hard. It had been so long since he'd dealt with the day-to-day governance of a nome, let alone a kingdom. He needed rest. "Then we will return here, and I can begin my rule."

"Certainly not!" To looked shocked. "From there we travel to Kom Ombo. The Two Ladies must be given thanks for your names and crowns. And there is Heliopolis, Tanis, Bubastis . . ." To ticked them off on his fingers.

"You are naming every major temple in Egypt!" Ramses exclaimed.

"But of course, Majesty," the vizier replied. "Thou must walk thy kingdom and claim it as yours. Thou must proclaim thy devotion to the gods, and in return they will support your kingship. And, as it is in the afterlife, so it becomes here in the Two Lands."

The queue of courtiers suddenly looked endless.

They all *wanted* something from him. Ramses hastily signaled for more wine. "But there is tomorrow," he said, clutching at the vizier's earlier words. "You said I could rest tomorrow."

"No, Majesty. Alas, you may not." That was the old voice of authority. Hekamaatre automatically flinched, but Ramses IV found the courage to challenge it.

"No?" he asked, looking full in the old man's face. To stepped back. Ramses read surprise, fear and, surprisingly, admiration in the scroll of his life.

"There will be time in the future to learn and understand thy power," To assured him. "But tomorrow thou have ahead of thee the greatest task of the year. Alas, because of thy father's will, there is no time to learn the lessons thou would have had in interim times. Thou must cease Inundation so that planting season can begin. Thy father began it, but alas, did not live long enough to end it."

Ramses blinked. "Pharaoh does that? He called the *waters?* By himself?"

"Every year. It is a divine gift. Thy father was most adept at it, as was thy grandfather. Before that, I cannot say, but we could consult the records. It is a shame thou will not be crowned, but thou hast been confirmed in thy godhood, and that should be enough." To did not look certain of his assertion. "Tomorrow, thou will drive back the river Nile."

"Drive back the Nile?"

"Tomorrow," Sekhemptah said. "In the meantime, enjoy the feasting."

They withdrew and signaled forth the next in an end-less file of courtiers. Ramses' mind was only half on them and not at all on the food or musicians or dancers in the hall. How could he enjoy himself after that ser-pent's egg was dropped in his lap? Drive back the river?

The Nile was a blinding silver sheet that stretched al-most from cliff to cliff. Ramses, dressed in finest linen and gold and with a braided wig upon his head, stared out at its vastness. His twin shadows, To and Sekhem-ptah, stood behind him in the courtyard of great Kar-nak. Around them waited a vast procession of priests and nobles, all watching the river and the king.

The Nile cried out to Ramses that it needed to rest. The land underneath it pleaded to see the sun. Afraid of the voices, Ramses turned to his advisers. "I can't do this. You want someone as strong as my father."

"Thou are as strong as thy father. Thou are thy father, and thy grandfather, in a right line that leads back to the gods," To said. "The power is in thy hands."

Curiously Ramses looked down at his hands, seeing the golden pulse in his flesh as he had the day before. Such a thin pulse! "It's not enough. How could it be?"

Sekhemptah put a kindly arm around his shoulders. "I told thee thou must do first and learn later. Your hands do not plow every field in Egypt, but it is by thy command it is done. Thou cannot pull every seed out of its shell to grow, yet by thy command it is done. Go into the waters and give thy command. They will obey. Divine Utterance is in thy mouth," he said, speaking the ancient form. "Understanding follows thee, O Sovereign, life, health, and prosperity be yours, and thy plans come to pass. I have never broken a promise to thee, have I?"

"I'm an ordinary man," Ramses said miserably.

"Thou art Egypt," Sekhemptah said soothingly. "*Be* Egypt. Close your eyes. See the path where you must walk."

The Amon-priest's soft voice helped Ramses to calm down. As the sun warmed his skin, he felt his body turning to gold. The sacred metal melted and ran. He felt himself spread out over the land. He was the moonlit waters lapping up to the feet of cliffs. He was the rich, fertile silt that lay within them, soaking into the dry soil, which he also was. He knew every part of the land he ruled—and served. Knew the people within it, all of them, those with clever hearts and those with foolish ones, those who were honest and those whose villainy was undoubted. He knew their names, and knew at that moment that was how his father had given such clear and fair judgments when cases were brought to him. He knew the truth of the hearts of all Egyptians, and he loved them. That surprised him. He thought he should hate wrongdoers, but they were Egypt, its living and moving component. *He* was Egypt. They were all him, and all drew life from him.

"Now, roll back the waters," the priest said, his voice coming from far away.

Ramses laughed. As tall as the heavens, he bent down to the silver ribbon of the Nile, as small as a toy.

It was so easy! He gathered the water like a man taking up handfuls of jewels, and patted it into a line.

"Too narrow!" the priest exclaimed, and Ramses knew he was right. With one huge finger he felt the empty edge of the deep channel. It should still run with water during the spring and summer months. He sprinkled jewels that ran through his fingers until they filled in the gap. When he was through, there was still a great deal of the glittering treasure piled up. Leaning to the south, he pushed it with both palms, up past the first and second cataracts, up past Nubia, where another set of hands, these dark as ebony, took the burden from him. He felt the dark skin touch his, and knew he had made contact with another avatar. That surprised him, too. He should have to speak to the emissary from Kush and find out if the king of the lands which Egypt did not rule in Sudan also spoke to gods.

"Now, come back," the priest commanded. But Ramses did not want to. He was in his glory. He truly did walk with the gods! He took a step into the air. He wanted to see the chariot of the sun, to ride with Amon across the sky.

"You do not serve Egypt if you are not among us. Come back!" To exclaimed, his voice alarmed and very far away. "The real task of kingship is not to wield power, but to know when to stop."

But Ramses had heard a voice above him. "Well done, my son."

The sun should have blinded him, but it did not. Clad only in a kilt and the sidelock of youth he ran beside the glowing white-gold chariot, laughing. Two figures rode behind the horses, not one, also glowing white gold, and he knew them.

"Father!" he cried. A strong hand reached out to help him inside.

"I knew you could do it, my son, Horus-on-Earth." Ramses III looked as tall, handsome, and vigorous as he had on the day he was crowned. Old age had been burned away from him. Hekamaatre Ramses bowed to him and the god. Old feelings and resentments rushed to his mind. He knew at that second that his father could hear all of them as he did the heart of any courtier at the feast.

"This has all happened so fast, Father!" he cried. "Why did you never name me as heir? I needed to learn all these mysteries long ago."

Ramses-Osiris bowed his head. "You must recall the attempt on my life."

"That was twenty years ago!"

His father looked grim. "It was a magical attack, instigated by men I trusted, to attack my name and that of my heir. One's most vulnerable spot, apart from the inaccessible and imperishable _ka_, and your _ba_, which serves you and no one else, is your name. If those were known to all, you would be open to the attack that nearly brought down my kingship twenty years ago, and perhaps would destroy you, too. Egypt would have been thrown into turmoil while the priests waited for a new king to arise. I had a vision from the gods, at Amon's direction, that if my heir remained unnamed, he would be safe. It left you unprepared, but I knew you had the clever heart to pick up at a moment's notice." Ramses-Osiris hesitated. "Do you understand and forgive? I still require you to protect and defend me, to proclaim my deeds and my victories. I am not yet a god."

As Horus had embraced Osiris, Hekamaatre embraced his father and laughed for joy, his resentment quelled, his heart at peace. He felt light and young again. "I forgive. I rejoice!" He turned to kneel on the chariot springs to the great god. Amon towered above him, his noble face radiant under the aegis of the sun disk. His flesh was gold, and his eyes blazed. Ramses bent his head humbly. "I vow that, in thy name and his, I will be a good king. I will pay homage to all the gods, but especially to you."

"Thou art my son," the great voice boomed. "Return!" Every word shook the very bones in Ramses' body.

Suddenly, he realized that his body was being shaken in truth. He opened his eyes. He was an adult again, dressed in royal finery, and the glory of the god had receded. To knelt beside him, white-faced. Ramses stood and glanced across the broad courtyard to the banks of the Nile. They were shining and wet. Beyond them, the gleaming ribbon had narrowed into its springtime channel.

"It is a divine gift," Sekhemptah said simply.

"Thy Majesty has a natural talent," To said, his voice now trembling with awe as well as age. Ramses looked at him in surprise. He'd spent his life being afraid of the vizier, but now the old man was afraid of him, or that which he commanded. In that moment, Ramses forgave him, too. His father wished him to show honor to To. The vizier had saved the honor of the house more than once. Ramses smiled upon him, and had the pleasure of seeing the old man relax.

"Seeing the withdrawal of the waters always overwhelms me," Sekhemptah said. "And now, thou know the truth of thy station. Thy tongue commands the universe."

"And now the festival of planting begins," To said, his wits recovered. "There will be a great feast tonight."

"I shall enjoy that," Ramses said, leading the way back to his waiting procession. The servants who had witnessed the dismissal of the Nile gazed upon him awestruck and flung themselves to the ground. The nobles present were already kneeling, not daring to look him in the face. "I think," he said with pleasure, "I shall sleep late tomorrow. We shall depart for Edfu at my will."

"Whatever thou command, Majesty," To said, without a trace of disapproval.

Ramses grinned and followed the incense bearers back into the temple confines. Absolute power was his. He was pharaoh. He was the living god, no longer subject to anyone's whims or orders. He could do the important work of keeping Egypt prosperous, and delegate that which was not appropriate to him. All was going to be well. He was going to enjoy his authority.

*   *   *

The feasting lasted well into the night. He felt as though he had barely closed his eyes when he felt a hand shaking him roughly. He opened his eyes, thought he saw Mumsatra's silhouette.

"Majesty, wake up. It is time to call forth the sun."

"I did that yesterday." He rolled over.

"And must do it today," the voice boomed. Ramses really woke up now. That was not his servant. The man beside him seemed to be glowing with pink-orange light, like the rising sun. Ramses scrambled to sit up. Where were his bodyguards? How had this stranger got into his royal chambers?

"I am not a stranger," the tall figure boomed in a voice that echoed within his mind as loud as thunder but did not so much as set the strings of his small harp whispering. "Behold!" The man threw out his arms, and the faint light issuing from him blossomed into white-gold glory. "I am the living disk of the sun."

By that time Ramses was on his knees. "My lord Amon-Re! What . . . what do you wish of me?"

The god looked amused. "What? Have you forgotten your vow so quickly?" The figure made a gesture toward the east. "Go to my temple! Bring up the sun-disk so that our children do not live in the darkness all the day. Get up. Such behavior is not fit for a king. Get up and do your duty."

"But I haven't slept!" he wailed. "Sekhemptah is your priest!"

"What of that? *You* are Egypt. You do what she needs, or she suffers."

"And when you have finished with that, go to my temple," said a handsome, blue-skinned man wrapped in mummy cloths, close behind Amon-Re. It was Osiris. "Your father, whose *ka* has been judged to be pure, was always a devotee of mine. He wishes you to make a great sacrifice to me in his name."

"And you must go also to mine," grinned crocodile-toothed Sobek. "As the waters have withdrawn, you must praise those of my children who will bless the fertility of the fields."

"And speaking of fertility," said a cow-headed female, "you never gave thanks in my temple for your last daughter's birth. I've been *waiting!*"

"And do not forget," said hawk-headed Horus, with a glint in his black eyes "you leave for Edfu today. I await you, son and brother."

Ramses rolled over with a groan, wanting just a moment's peace from the clamor. All things were commanded from above—including him. Now he could be nagged in two planes of existence at once. Praying for strength, he rose and called for his servants.

BENEATH THE EYE OF THE HAWK

by Jane Lindskold

Jane Lindskold is the author of eleven novels, including *Wolf's Head, Wolf's Heart, Through Wolf's Eyes, Legends Walking,* and *Changer.* She has published over forty short stories and a variety of nonfiction pieces. A full-time writer, she resides in New Mexico with her archaeologist husband, Jim Moore, with whom she sometimes goes on digs. Although they have yet to find either a mysterious tomb or a treasure hoard, they have not yet lost hope. Lindskold is currently at work on a third novel in her "wolf" series, and plans to follow this with one featuring the further adventures of Neville Hawthorne and Eddie Bryce.

TWISTING around on his galloping camel and glimpsing the pursuing Bedouin resolving into form within the dust cloud that had been stirred into life by their own pounding mounts, Neville Hawthorne spared precious breath to curse the day Alphonse Liebermann had come to Egypt.

"Alphonse Liebermann is a cousin of Prince Albert," Colonel Reginald Sedgewick explained to the tall, broad-shouldered man standing in front of his desk. "A German, of course. Something of an archaeologist and theologian."

Colonel Sedgewick smiled rather deprecatingly.

"Or rather I should say Herr Liebermann fancies himself an archaeologist and theologian. If my reports are correct, he is a hobbyist more than anything else."

Neville Hawthorne, captain in Her Majesty Queen Victoria's army and currently assigned to the diplomatic presence in Egypt, didn't permit his lips to twitch in even the faintest of smiles. He knew such wouldn't be appreciated.

Colonel Sedgewick—in civilian life a lord and knight—might feel free to comment on the foibles of his social betters, but Lord Reginald Sedgewick did not think his junior officers—at least those without honor or title—should share that privilege.

Indeed, there were times, Neville mused, that Sedgewick probably thought that those without appropriate social rank and fortune shouldn't be permitted to hold officers' commissions.

However, snob or not, Sedgewick recognized talent and ability, and it was for both of these qualities that he had called Captain Hawthorne—rather than one of Hawthorne's more socially advantaged subordinates—to him.

"As a courtesy to our queen's German relations, I'm assigning you to Herr Liebermann as a nursemaid. Won't call it that, of course. Bodyguard and translator. Liebermann will need the latter. Understand he doesn't have much in the way of Arabic, though he's fairly fluent in French."

Neville Hawthorne nodded, hiding his sudden interest behind a properly impassive face. Fluency in French was not only useful, but fairly necessary in some circles of Egyptian society. France, like England, had numerous interests in Egypt. Indeed, the reforms instituted by Muhammad Ali and continued with more or less enthusiasm by his heirs meant that French remained an important language in both society and government.

What tantalized Captain Hawthorne was that his commander had singled out Arabic from the slew of languages spoken in modern Egypt, a mixture that included—in addition to English and French—Armenian, Greek, Coptic, and Turkish.

Most Europeans didn't have much Arabic. Nor did they need it. Even if this cousin of Prince Albert's was interested in archaeology and theology, he could research to his heart's content without ever speaking a word to the Arab population. Indeed, the majority of archaeological matters were still administered by the French.

"Then Herr Liebermann wishes to travel outside of the usual areas, sir?" Neville asked.

Colonel Sedgewick nodded, his eyes narrowing appreciatively as he reconstructed the course of deductive reasoning through which his subordinate had reached this conclusion.

"That's right," he said, glancing down at a letter on his desk. "Says here that Herr Liebermann wants to do some desert exploration. That's why he needs you to ease the way for him. Wouldn't be necessary if he was staying on the usual tourist routes."

"Very good, sir," Hawthorne replied. "When do I meet Herr Liebermann?"

"He arrives in Cairo two days from today."

A stack of papers, including Liebermann's original letter, were pushed across the desk and Neville gathered them up. He was careful not to so much as glance at the documents until his commander had finished speaking.

"To enable you to be at Herr Liebermann's disposal any time day or night, you're to put up at whatever hotel he chooses. If he has no preference, use Shepherds. They're accustomed to Europeans. My clerk will have expense vouchers for you. Make reservations, just in case."

"And my staff, sir?"

Colonel Sedgewick looked momentarily irritated,

obviously thinking that Captain Hawthorne should be thanking him for his generosity. Then he reconsidered.

"Yes, I suppose you'll need help if Prince Albert's cousin wants to go out in the desert. You can hire natives to handle the baggage and camels, but I'll give you a sergeant to wrangle the lot. Any preferences?"

"Sergeant Bryce, sir. Edward Bryce. He knows Egypt well, speaks Arabic, and has a way with the natives."

"Bryce . . ."

Sedgewick frowned.

Captain Hawthorne held his breath, hoping Sedgewick would have forgotten recent events.

"Wasn't Bryce just brought up for something?"

"Disorderly conduct, sir," Neville replied stiffly. "Drinking. Brawling."

Whatever Reginald Sedgewick's snobbery regarding the proper social class from which officers should be drawn, he was a seasoned veteran of the battlefield and no great advocate of the stricter patterns of behavior some of his colleagues tried to enforce off the field.

He snorted.

"Disrespect to officers?"

"No, sir. Bryce took exception to how a lady was being treated. Got into a fight."

"Did he win?"

"Yes, sir, but he'd had a bit too much, got rather battered, and consequently was late getting back to quarters. His uniform was wrecked. Officer on duty wrote him up."

Colonel Sedgewick shook his head in disbelief.

"You can have Bryce. If anyone protests that he's being rewarded for unbecoming behavior with soft duty, send them to me. I'll tell them a few hard truths about just how soft a bed of desert sand actually is."

Alphonse Liebermann proved to be short, wiry, and somewhere into his fifth decade. Bald as an egg, he sported the most magnificent eyebrows Neville had ever seen—bushy, sweeping gray specimens that leaped to punctuate their owner's every exclamation. They completely intimidated the German's perfectly unexceptional mustache and, indeed, made it hard for one to remember that he had any other features at all.

Liebermann was accompanied by one servant: Derek Schmidt, a tall, thin man with bristle-cut graying hair. Schmidt possessed a soldier's erect posture and a distinct limp to show why he was no longer in active service. He took charge of the baggage with such efficiency that Neville was unsurprised to learn Schmidt had begun his career in the Prussian equivalent of the quartermaster's corps.

"I have a secret, Neville," Alphonse Liebermann confided several days after their initial meeting. He kept his voice low and his English was so heavily accented that the phrase sounded rather like "I haff'a seekret."

Neville Hawthorne nodded, not certain how to respond to this strange confidence. However, he liked the little man—who had insisted immediately they place themselves on a first name basis—so he replied encouragingly,

"I'm not at all surprised, Alphonse."

Neville had not needed to be a great genius to figure this out. In the three days since Neville had met Herr Liebermann, the German's actions had been focused and purposeful. Alphonse had avoided all the usual tourist attractions—although he had looked longingly to where the Pyramids at Gizeh loomed over the city and audibly promised himself a visit after their return from the desert.

"I am preparing to make," Alphonse continued in the same portentous tones, "a discovery that will set my name in the pantheon of archaeology, alongside Winckelmann, Belzoni, and Lepsius. I have finished my preparations here in Cairo. You have our tickets?"

"I do," Neville said. "Tickets for a steamer to Luxor. From there we will change to a *dahabeah*. Sergeant Bryce has gone ahead to make arrangements for camels and a few native servants."

"Very good." Alphonse returned to his prior topic of conversation. "Neville, mine will be a landmark discovery. It will make a turnover of archaeology, reveal things about not only the days of the pharaohs, but about our entire conception of reality—about the relationship of gods to men."

Neville nodded, trying to match Liebermann's serious intensity. It was difficult. This crazed German seemed so like something out of a stage play that bouncy music hall tunes kept playing across Neville's inner ear.

For a fleeting moment Neville wondered how Prince Albert's family actually felt about this cousin. Perhaps Alphonse was an embarrassment. Perhaps he was supposed to get lost in the desert. Maybe that was why Neville had been picked for this honorable duty rather than one of Lord Sedgewick's more socially advantaged cronies.

Alphonse lowered his voice still further, "When we are away from Cairo, then I will confide in you what— and who—we are seeking. For now, I do not wish attention drawn to us. Would it be too much trouble for you and Sergeant Bryce to wear civilian clothes?"

Neville cocked an eyebrow, but forbore from requesting clarification.

"It will be no problem at all."

On their first evening aboard the steamer, Alphonse invited Neville to his cabin for brandy and cigars.

Although the weather on deck was pleasant and several of the young ladies taking the cruise were not nearly as snobbish as Colonel Sedgewick, Neville reported to the German's spacious stateroom. He found Alphonse poring over a sheaf of closely written pages.

"Captain Hawthorne," Alphonse said with more formality than he had shown since his arrival, "my great thanks for your coming to me. I have given Schmidt the evening off so that we may speak in confidence."

Neville nodded, accepted the brandy offered, declined a cigar, and leaned back in the well-upholstered chair across from Herr Liebermann.

Full from dinner, the engine rhythmically thumping in the distance, Neville had to fight a tendency to drowse.

"In Cairo I told you I had a secret," Alphonse began. "Now I will reveal this secret to you. You will become the second European alive—or so I believe—to know a great mystery."

"I am honored," Neville said and hoped that his suppressed laughter would be taken for British stuffiness.

"Very good."

Alphonse swirled the brandy in his snifter and settled himself more deeply into his chair. Although he kept his notes spread nearby, he never once consulted them. Clearly this was a tale he knew by heart.

"Some years ago," Alphonse said, "when I am doing research into the historicity of Moses, I hear an amazing tale from a Bedouin rug merchant."

"Wait," Neville said, raising an inquiring finger. "I thought you didn't speak Arabic."

"I do not," Alphonse said cheerfully, "but this merchant spoke French. Now, I must tell you that I do not think I was meant to hear this tale. The Bedouin was very old, and when I asked him about Moses, calling him 'the Lawgiver,' the Arab began to speak of another lawgiver, one from long ago. His lawgiver was a pharaoh named Neferankhotep. This name means 'Gift of a Beautiful Life.'"

Or "complete" or "perfect," Neville thought. He didn't

read hieroglyphics, but he had worked his way through some of the modern commentaries and found the material fascinating.

"Now even in ancient times," Alphonse continued, "Egypt possessed an excellent legal system, one that—in theory—protected the commoner on equal terms with the highest noble."

Alphonse grimaced, those amazing eyebrows lowering and then rising once more.

"But, Neville, we know that theory and practice are very different. In practice those with title and property are treated far better than the peasants who have little or nothing."

"True enough," Neville replied a trace sourly, "even today."

Alphonse's gaze was so penetrating and sympathetic that Neville was embarrassed by his own petty grievances.

"But not when Neferankhotep reigned," Alphonse went on, waggling an admonishing finger. "When this good pharaoh reigned, there was perfect justice, such perfect justice that all his people loved him. They wished that his mortuary complex would be finer than any pharaoh had ever known. The good Neferankhotep would not have this.

"He indicated an outlying valley, far from the fertile lands and said, 'Give me only a simple rock tomb, make my *shabati* figures from clay, my amulets from common stones. If these charms and honors are enough to serve my people in the afterlife, then they will be sufficient for me.'"

Guess we won't make our fortunes in gold and precious stones, then, Neville thought and poured himself a touch more brandy.

Alphonse's voice fell into a singsong, storytelling mode in which his German accent become oddly, pervasively musical.

"Eventually, Neferankhotep's life upon the earth ended. The mortuary priests immediately began the arduous process of embalming the pharaoh's mortal remains. On the very day that they began their work, a terrible sandstorm arose in the humble valley wherein the pharaoh had requested he be entombed. Watchers claimed that they could see towering forms moving purposefully within the clouds of sand and grit. The sandstorm raged with unabated fury until the very day that Neferankhotep's body was ready for burial. Then, as the last seal was set upon his sarcophagus, the storm vanished.

"Within the once barren valley stood the most magnificent pyramid that anyone had ever seen, complete with a complex of temples, chapels, and long avenues of guardian beasts. The decorations on the buildings and on the sarcophagus that awaited the pharaoh's mummy were of gold, silver, electrum, and precious stones, more and richer than had ever been seen before. Magnificent alabaster statues, one representing each of the myriad gods and goddesses of ancient Egypt, stood silent watch over the compound.

"The message from the gods was clear. Therefore, here in this complex crafted by the hands of his sibling gods who loved him, Neferankhotep was entombed. A community of priests was established to watch over the pharaoh's sacred person and to offer sacrifices at the appropriate times.

"All proceeded in honor and grace for many years, then thieves—some say greedy or jealous priests—attempted to loot Neferankhotep's pyramid. They did not manage more than to cross the threshold. As they made their nefarious intent clear, an enormous sandstorm arose from nowhere, although elsewhere the day remained still and clear. For seven days and seven nights the storm raged, a red glow as of divine fury at its heart. When it died away, the entire compound had vanished.

"What remained was an empty valley. Towering statues of the greatest Egyptian gods, armed as for war, stood at the four cardinal points. A warning against future desecration was deeply etched into the cliffs surrounding the valley. From that day forth, the Valley of Dust—for so it came to be called—has been a shunned and sacred place, although rumor says that there are those who, to this day, are sworn to protect its treasures."

Herr Liebermann concluded by bowing his head in a manner that would have seemed affected had it not been clear that he was deeply moved by what he had just related. Neville didn't want to admit the truth, not even to himself, but he, too, had been swept up in the tale.

Therefore, Neville forced himself to sound casual as he asked, "So, can I take it that you have a line on this Valley of Dust?"

Alphonse smiled a trace thinly, disapproving of the jocularity in Neville's tone.

"I believe I do," he said dryly. "Would you care to hear another tale?"

Neville reached for the brandy and poured himself a touch.

"I would be fascinated," he said with sincerity.

Alphonse accepted the unspoken apology, swirled his own brandy once more, and began.

"The tale of Neferankhotep was very interesting to me, even more so when I realized that I was apparently alone in having heard it. True, archaeologists have not translated all the texts from those tombs and temples they have found, but it seemed to me that I had come across something wonderful and unique. I began to research the sources of the tale, actively soliciting travelers' accounts and legends, looking for any hint that might lead me to Neferankhotep and the Valley of Dust. For a long time, I met with little success.

"Then one day a tightly wrapped package was left for me at my hotel. All the concierge could tell me was that it had been left by a woman, a desert Arab, or so he thought. He said she had asked in very bad French if this was where the German gentleman who was collecting legends was staying. When the concierge had confirmed this, she insisted on leaving the package. The concierge thought she seemed nervous. We were both surprised that she had left no way to contact her, for surely she expected payment.

"I thought about seeking the woman, but how to tell one woman from so many? I decided that she would return in her own time, perhaps after I had opportunity to inspect her offering and would be more prepared to pay her. Clearly, her menfolk didn't know she had come to me. Perhaps she wanted to keep the money for herself. So relieved of anxiety on that point, I retired to my room and unwrapped the package."

Alphonse placed his hand on a slim journal bound in faded and cracking leather.

"The package contained this journal written by an explorer who calls himself Chad Spice. Much of the contents are of little interest—at least from an archaeological standpoint, though as an account of a wandering life there is some amusement value. Let me read to you directly from the salient portions."

Neville nodded, fighting an impulse to lean forward like a child anticipating a treat.

"Please do."

Again the German's voice shifted, this time becoming not so much singsong as clipped and terse.

I was a fool beyond mortal knowing when I attempted to win the favor of Sheik Azul's daughter. In the dark of night, warning came to me that the sheik would have my life. I stole a horse and fled. At the ris-

ing of the sun, I saw that I had compounded my crimes. The horse I had chosen at random in the darkness proved to be the second favorite among the sheik's mares.

Terrified, I fled and with God's help managed to elude my pursuers. Yet I feared their wrath would follow me even into neighboring villages. Thus, I turned my course into the desert, for Sheik Azul rules a riverside town and in this way I thought I might bypass him and his allies. In the desert I came into an area where cliffs and broken ground barred me from returning on a straight line to the river. I was forced to push deeper and deeper into the sandy wastes.

After some days, the lovely mare I had stolen died from the harsh conditions. Without her blood to sustain me, I nearly perished from lack of water and the punishing force of the sun. On what surely would have been my final day on Earth, I glimpsed a towering solitary rock jutting from the sand. Spending my fading strength mercilessly, I stumbled into its shade and there slept until the cool of the night.

When I awoke, my tongue had swollen to fill my mouth. My eyes and lips were encrusted with sand. Maddeningly, I imagined I heard the musical trickle of falling water. Staggering to my feet—though I believed myself insane—I followed the sound. Moving as in a dream or delirium, I descended the slope until I came upon a tiny spring welling from the rock. I drank my fill and slept, waking only to drink again.

When dawn came, I saw I had come to an oasis populated only by goats and lizards.

I stayed in this oasis while I regained my strength. As my senses returned to me, I realized that I had stumbled into what must have been a holy place to the people of this land. Four gigantic statues—one of which had been the "rock" under which I had first sheltered from the sun—flanked the gentle vale and picture writing, marvelously fresh, adorned the rocks.

Although the sun's passage made clear which way east (and the Nile) must be, I feared to depart the oasis. Yet as I grew stronger, I became both restless and fearful. Goats are not common in the heart of the desert. Who had put them here? When might the goats' owners return?

One exceptionally clear day, I saw to the south and east a shape like unto the head of a monstrous hawk crested in green. Further study revealed it to be a vast rock. The greenery seemed to promise water, so I resolved to make this Hawk Rock my new goal.

After killing several goats—for they were as tame as pets and offered no struggle—and making bags for water from their innards, and a rough cap for my head and slippers for my feet from their hides, I ventured across the sands to the Hawk Rock. The distance was greater than I had imagined, but, once there, I again found water and so recovered my strength. While I recuperated, I noticed inscriptions like unto those I had seen at the oasis. From the Hawk Rock I made my final push to the Nile.

Worn and near mad, I stumbled at last from the sandy wastes. Joyfully, I plunged my head into the silty waters. The natives of that place looked at me as if I were insane. I fear I did not help myself to gain their regard, for as soon as I recovered enough to stand, I stood and saluted the Hawk Rock and invisible beyond it, the Oasis of Statues that had saved my life.

Alphonse closed the journal.

"Chad Spice records that as soon as he recovered from his ordeal—and the villagers treated him with the kindness that all Muslims are enjoined to offer beggars and madmen—he made his way to Luxor. There he found European allies who, hearing of his ordeals, took pity on him. Initially, Spice relaxed, but then he began to feel uneasy—as if he were being watched. At this point, he decided to depart for Cairo. As far as I can tell, Chad Spice never arrived. If he did, then he lost this journal along the way."

Neville frowned. "You mean his account ends?"

"That is correct, my friend. The last entry tells that he had signed as deckhand on some vessel and planned to depart the next morning. He was in high spirits."

"Odd."

"Very." Alphonse put the journal aside. "However, what happened to Chad Spice does not interest me. What does interest me is this Oasis of Statues he describes. It could well be the Valley of Dust. It is isolated from the usual burial grounds—as Neferankhotep wished to be. It is guarded by four statues, as legend says the Valley of Dust was guarded."

Neville couldn't quite accept this leap in reasoning. Egypt was riddled with burial grounds, temples, and other ruins. He sought for something encouraging to say.

"Even if it isn't the Valley of Dust, Alphonse, you certainly seem to be onto something. Are we hoping to find this Hawk Rock? Spice's journal seems to indicate that it can be seen from the banks of the Nile and it must be in the vicinity of Luxor if he went there as soon as he recovered his strength."

Alphonse's eyebrows shot up. He looked both amused and smug.

"Neville, I have already located the Hawk Rock—at least I believe I have. Using Luxor as a starting point, I have spent the last two winters traveling up and down the Nile shores, venturing into the fringes of the desert. Last winter, using the most powerful telescope I could transport with me, I sighted a feature that could well be the Hawk Rock. Summer was too close to wisely venture into the desert, but now . . ."

Neville Hawthorne raised his snifter in a toast.

"To the Hawk Rock!"

"I had a devil of a time getting camels," Eddie Bryce reported. "Seems like everyone had promised their beasts to someone else. Finally managed by catching up with a dealer before he reached Luxor. Camels and drivers will be waiting for us when we get off the boat."

Lean and sun-browned, handsome in a rough and ready way, Edward Bryce did not seem old enough to have fifteen years of honorable—if not always distinguished—service behind him. However, at age eight Eddie had run away to become a drummer boy, thus escaping a life of drudgery as a younger son in the great brood of a Sussex farmer.

In those fifteen years, Eddie had seen much of the Empire. Early on, he had discovered a liking for both languages and people. The first interest had thrown him and Neville together. Then Neville had learned that though Eddie spoke over a dozen languages quite well, he could hardly read, even in his natal tongue. Neville's determination to teach Eddie to read—over the younger man's initial protests—had cemented the friendship.

"The *reis*," Eddie continued, using the Arab term for a ship's captain, "says he is prepared to sail whenever Herr Liebermann is ready."

"Tell the *reis* tomorrow morning," Neville replied. "Herr Liebermann is impatient to be off."

The voyage up the Nile was—except for crocodiles and hippopotamuses in the waters, and aggressive merchant *fellahin* along the shores—uneventful, restful, and lovely.

Neville drowsed beneath the on-deck canopy and engaged in long discussions about archaeology with Alphonse. The four Europeans played whist almost every night. After hearing how Eddie had acquired the bruises that, though faded, were still greenly visible, Alphonse took a liking to the sergeant.

"You are a knight errant," Alphonse announced, greatly amused. "Like Parsifal or, since you are English, maybe Galahad, yes?"

Bryce, who was about as far from a virgin knight as was possible, grinned, but he didn't disabuse the German. "Let him keep his illusions," his grin seemed to say.

Camels and drovers were indeed waiting for them at the appointed spot, but Neville could tell from the storm cloud that settled over Eddie's features as the *dahabeah* came into shore that something wasn't right.

"Problem?"

"Too few camels. Looks like about half—and the worst half—of what I ordered. Can't tell about drovers."

Neville frowned.

"Find out. I'll keep Herr Liebermann busy unloading gear."

"Right, Captain."

Later, Neville headed to where Alphonse and Derek were checking items off a list.

"Bad news, Alphonse," Neville reported somewhat later. "Seems that we have about half the camels for which Eddie contracted. The man who stayed—along with his son and daughter—claims that his partner left after the local sheik started telling stories about some curse out in the desert."

"How many camels do we have?" Alphonse asked.

"Seven," Neville replied. "Solid beasts. I'll say that for them. All are trained to take either riders or gear."

"Seven is enough," Alphonse said. "My gear is not

so much. This will make carrying out artifacts difficult, but then we have no assurance we will find any. If you are willing, Captain Hawthorne, I will still go on."

"Your gear may not be 'so much,'" Neville reminded him, "but one camel at least should be reserved to carry water and fodder."

"But there is water at the Hawk Rock!" Alphonse protested.

"So that old journal said," Neville replied. "Things might have changed. That might not even be the right rock."

Alphonse nodded and turned to his assistant.

"Derek how may we repack? You are a very magician at this."

Schmidt looked thoughtful. "I'll have a word with the drovers, sir. See just what weights the camels will carry and repack accordingly."

Neville surrendered.

"Sergeant Bryce is with the drovers," he said to Derek. "Ask him to translate for you."

Dawn was barely pinking the horizon when they set out. In addition to the four Europeans, their party had been augmented by three Bedouin: Ali; Ali's son, Ishmael; and Ali's daughter, Miriam. Miriam was mounted on the camel which carried the water, riding lightly despite her enshrouding robes.

"She weighs hardly more than a feather," Eddie confided to Neville, his eyes bright with interest as he glanced back at the graceful figure. "She's the reason her father stayed when his partner left."

"I suppose," Neville said, thinking of his own sister, "Ali needs a dowry if he wants a good marriage for her."

"I don't know about that," Eddie said, "but from what I overheard, Miriam's got more pluck and character than the men. She won't run off from nothing. Won't let them run off neither."

It would turn out that Eddie was wrong about this, but when the time came, no one blamed Miriam at all.

As Chad Spice's journal had mentioned, distances across the open, featureless desert were very hard to judge. After one day's steady travel, the only reason Neville felt certain they hadn't been marching in place was because the village along the Nile had diminished into tiny shapes that vanished from sight as the ground over which they traveled became more and more uneven.

By the end of the second day's travel, however, Neville began to entertain a quiet certainty that Alphonse Liebermann had been correct in his assumption that the distant shape he had glimpsed from the Nile was the Hawk Rock. By the end of the third day's march, Neville—and everyone else—was certain.

They began their marches at dawn and continued until the heat of the sun became unbearable. Then they would pitch pavilions, rest until the heat began to lose intensity, and then resume. Had their goal been larger or more certain, they might have navigated by the stars at night, but as it was, even the eager Alphonse preferred to have their goal visible before them. Then, too, pitching tents and tending to camels by starlight were tasks that none of them cared to undertake.

On the night following the third day's march, Neville had wandered a short distance from the camp, seeking peace and quiet to cool his mind as the darkness cooled his body. No one would ever say that Alphonse Liebermann was a dull traveling companion, but his intensity scorched nearly as much as did the sun.

Neville soon became aware that he was not the only person out in the darkness. Three voices, speaking Arabic, caught his ear. Within a few phrases, Neville recognized the voices of their camel wranglers: Ali, Ishmael, and Miriam.

Miriam's voice, more high-pitched than those of her brother and father, carried clearly.

"Allah will keep us safe. Have you forgotten the creed? There is no God but Allah! How can you fear these ancient curses? They are the credulous beliefs of credulous people."

Ali replied, "But, my brother, your uncle said . . ."

"Uncle is more than half pagan!" Miriam nearly spat the words. "I thought you were wiser than he."

She certainly does have her share of pluck, Neville thought, remembering Eddie Bryce's description with amusement. *I wonder if Eddie realizes just how much.*

It hadn't escaped Neville just how frequently his sergeant found excuses to exchange a few words with the girl. Bedouin tribes varied greatly in how much liberty they gave their women—and a camel merchant like Ali might be forced to give his daughter much more freedom than would a wealthy man who could afford a fully isolated harem.

Nor had Neville missed how often Miriam's dark eyes—all of her face that could be seen over her modest veil—followed Eddie as he went about his duties. Doubtless, Ali had noticed as well, but it was becoming apparent that Miriam was more than a match for her father. Clearly, as long as she did nothing untoward, Ali would avoid scolding her.

"Besides," Miriam continued scornfully, "would you have us on foot into the desert? The English will not lightly let you take the camels."

Ali muttered something that Neville did not catch, and Miriam's reply did nothing to clarify the matter for him.

"Are they, then?" she said, and Neville could imagine the toss of her head. "Well, then, run if you are afraid of a big rock. I am not."

"You will obey your father!" Ali growled.

Neville decided that, unless he wanted to have a mutiny on his hands, he'd better interrupt this disturbing conversation.

He cupped his hands and called out in English: "I say! Ali! Ishmael! Where have you got to, damn it?"

He repeated the same, leaving out the emphasis, in Arabic.

He heard a muttered exclamation, then Ali called out in a mixture of Arabic and English:

"We are here. We were only praying."

The three returned to the camp soon after, and Neville saw no reason to make an issue of their absence, but over the evening game of whist he warned his companions of the possibility of mutiny.

"I don't think Miriam is at all for it," Neville concluded, "but the men are both frightened of the Hawk Rock. Frightened men do foolish things—but I don't think they'll attack us. Sneaking off in the night with as many of the supplies as possible seems more likely."

Eddie suggested a rotation that would "accidentally" keep their camels and gear under watch at all times. Neville agreed and, when Eddie volunteered to watch, suggested instead that rather than doing anything overt, they merely have Derek Schmidt doss down near the camels.

"I shall complain about your snoring," Derek agreed with a wry grin, "if anyone asks and perhaps even if they do not."

These arrangements must have been satisfactory, for dawn found their company and their gear intact. By the following night, they knew they would reach the Hawk Rock by midmorning of the next day.

The Europeans remained alert that night, but when Eddie rose shortly before dawn, Ali and Ishmael were gone. They had taken nothing but their own gear, some food, and water. The camels—and Miriam—remained.

"They are cowards," the girl said. "They fear this rock so much that they abandon me and even the camels."

"How will your father and brother survive a four-day journey across the desert?" Neville asked. "Four days, that is, by camel. It'll take more time on foot."

Miriam paused rather longer than Neville thought necessary before answering.

"They are Bedouin!" she replied proudly. "Not soft Europeans. They will have no difficulty."

Neville didn't doubt that the Arabs were tougher than he was, but he'd seen how ready both Ali and Ishmael had been for the afternoon's rests. He kept his suspicions to himself.

"Miriam," he said gently, "do you want to follow your father or go on with us?"

"I go with you," Miriam replied without a pause. "I am not a coward to be afraid of a big rock, and you are men of honor."

"Thank you for your trust," Neville said. When Miriam returned to her tent, he added in a soft voice to Eddie, "Make certain we live up to that trust. Do you understand me, Sergeant?"

"I do indeed, Captain Hawthorne," Eddie replied crisply, but the light that had entered his eyes when he discovered that Miriam had not fled didn't diminish in the least.

The defection of Ali and Ishmael did not change Alphonse's plans. He put himself on point when they departed and insisted Neville ride at his side. This close, the rock no longer resembled a hawk. The lines that had seemed to define wings and other features were revealed as crags, cuts, and the work of erosion.

"You and I, Neville, will look for any paths or trails," Alphonse said happily, "and for the water of which Chad Spice wrote."

Neville nodded, though his choice would have been to ride along the group's flank, watching for signs of trouble. He'd moved Miriam to the center of the group, Eddie to the rear. Both Derek and Eddie had been cautioned to keep alert for anything out of the ordinary, but he feared that Eddie had eyes for nothing but the pert little Arab girl perched atop her camel.

She's hardly more than a heap of cloth, Neville thought, *but Eddie's transformed her into a princess.*

As they came closer to the rock, Alphonse spotted a steep trail that led toward the top. Despite Alphonse's eagerness to begin exploring at once, Neville insisted on circumnavigating the rock before taking any other action. They found no evidence of any other human presence, but Neville noted several places where the rock could be climbed if the climber possessed sufficient patience and rope. Ample animal tracks—from small jerboa to what looked suspiciously like jackal— raised hopes that water was still available.

Alphonse's trail proved to be too steep for the camels, but a small, sheltered box canyon tucked in the hollow of the hawk's eastern "wing" provided an ideal place to pitch camp.

Neville assigned this task to Derek and Miriam, insisting that Eddie take a rifle and stand watch near the canyon's opening.

"But Miriam can't understand either German or English!" Eddie protested.

"Derek can make his needs clear with signs," Neville replied. Then he lowered his voice, "Get hold of yourself, man! She's a Bedouin. You have no idea what she looks like under all that cloth, and I'm not at all convinced that her men have abandoned us. Their best survival strategy would be to follow us, get hold of our gear, and leave us stranded."

Eddie nodded, a trace of stubbornness still in his eyes.

"Think of what you're doing as keeping Miriam safe, if you must," Neville offered. "Do you think her father will believe we left her unmolested? Unless this entire thing is her plan . . ."

He bit his lower lip thoughtfully.

"Never!" Eddie said and stalked off to his post.

Great, Neville thought. *I wonder just how much Alphonse is to blame for this? Him and his damn Parsifal!*

Slinging a rifle across his back, and checking the load in his pistol, Neville went to escort Alphonse up the trail. Both men carried axes in case there was heavier vegetation above.

"Surely you do not think you will need a rifle," Alphonse asked, his eyebrows taking flight in surprise. "A bucket perhaps. I have put a collapsible one in my pack."

"Hunting," Neville said shortly. He and Alphonse had already debated the need for the party to carry more weapons. "Where there is water, there may be game."

Alphonse nodded approvingly, and without further discussion they began their climb. The steepness of the trail was the least of their difficulties. The sandy soil proved to be permeated with small pebbles that rolled underfoot. Each step must be carefully tested. The occasional rocky stretches, though more challenging to climb, at least provided reliable footing.

Eventually, the trail spread out into a more-or-less level area, sheltered on all sides by rocky outcroppings, the highest of which, facing to the south, must be the head of the "hawk." The entirety of this upper canyon was lightly covered in bristly vegetation. Some of the shrubs clustered along the edges were as much as waist high. Ferocious-looking thorns testified how they had reached that height in such a barren region.

"Good fodder for the camels at least," Neville said, poking a narrow-leafed bush with the butt of his rifle. "Now let's see if we can find water. Check where the vegetation is thickest."

Alphonse nodded absently. He hadn't heard a word.

"This is the place," he announced rapturously. "It must be. I can feel it. Somewhere, Chad Spice wrote, there was an inscription . . ."

Neville sighed. Clearly, necessities like water and food took second place to archaeological finds on the German's list of priorities. However, the canyon wasn't terribly large. Unless trouble came down from the rocks, he could cover the area with his rifle.

"Keep an eye out for snakes . . . and scorpions," was all he said, but he was thinking about human vipers, not natural ones.

Neville easily located the spring welling up along the eastern edge of the canyon. He was beginning to hack away the shrubs that crowded around the spring when Alphonse cried out.

"I have found it!" he said, executing an impromptu dance of victory.

"Ye gods, man!" Neville exclaimed. "I thought you'd been bitten by a cobra."

"It is here," Alphonse said, pointing to the southern wall of the canyon. "Incised into the side of a rock."

He knelt and started brushing at something with his sleeve. Despite his own responsibilities, Neville crossed to examine the German's find.

"It looks like an obelisk," Neville offered a moment later, "fallen on its side. I bet it was erected where the taller rocks would protect it from the weather."

"I agree," Alphonse said, bending closer to inspect the writing. "Hieratic, rather than hieroglyphic. I would guess New Kingdom period."

"That's a good deal later than I imagined your Neferankhotep," Neville said, frowning.

"True."

Undaunted, Alphonse rummaged in his pack until he came up with a rolled sheet of paper and a chunk of drawing charcoal.

"I will make a rubbing," he announced, "so that I

may make my translation in the camp. Derek will assist me."

Neville wasn't surprised to learn that Alphonse's servant possessed the training to assist his master with this task as well.

"Very well," Neville replied. "I will finish freeing up the spring. Judging from the steepness of the path, I hope we can lower water directly to the camp rather than carrying it down the trail."

By that evening, Alphonse and Derek had worked out a rough translation of the inscription. As Alphonse read it to the assembled company, his measured cadence was accented with theatrical flourishes of his eyebrows:

> *Remember that Anubis will bring you before Osiris.*
> *Remember that your heart and your soul will be*
> *   weighed against Ma'at.*
> *Remember that the monster Ammit waits to devour*
> *   the wicked.*
> *The son and the self flies as the Nile and the boat.*
> *The mother and the wife follow as the Nile and the*
> *   boat.*
> *Under the watching Eye of the Hawk, the homecoming*
> *   is joyous.*

"Nice," Eddie said judicially when Alphonse concluded, "but what does it mean?"

Alphonse replied happily, "The first three lines are

traditional warnings or cautions, but the latter portion is not so clear."

Neville tilted the page Alphonse had handed around so he could read it more clearly in the firelight.

"I wonder," he said slowly, "if the boat mentioned here isn't an actual boat. Didn't the ancient Egyptians envision the sun as a boat? A boat on which a bunch of gods sailed?"

"Sometimes," Alphonse replied. "Another common image was of a flaming ball being rolled by a dung beetle—this is one reason the scarab beetle was sacred and used for amulets."

"Slow down," Neville insisted. "Sometimes too much knowledge is counterproductive. What's caught my eye is the way these people go 'as' the Nile and the boat. If the boat was a usual type of vessel, why 'fly'? I assume you didn't employ poetic license in your choice of words?"

"I did not," Alphonse said stiffly.

"I didn't think you would," Neville replied soothingly. "Now, here we have an inscription dating from a lot later than the legend you're tracking down, right?"

Alphonse nodded, still frowning.

"What if it offers some sort of directions?" Neville continued, excited by the picture that was building in his mind. "Directions written down later, for those who might have forgotten the way to the Valley of Dust but who might need to go there to make offerings? If the boat is the boat of the sun, then it travels from east to west. The Nile travels south to north—

contrary to just about every river I know. It's stretching some, but what if traveling as the Nile and the boat is traveling northwest?"

Alphonse's frown was replaced with a grin.

"If this is so," he said, "then the reference to a homecoming makes sense. It is a coming to the Valley of Dust—the final home of Neferankhotep's mortal remains. And the Eye of the Hawk . . ."

"Confirms our guess," Neville interrupted, too enthused to remember his manners. "There are only a few directions from which this Hawk Rock would resemble a hawk. We came from the southeast. The other angle that would provide the same general orientation is looking back at the rock from farther to the northwest."

Eddie Bryce thumped him on the back.

"Maybe you're stretching, Captain," he said, "but it's a nice bit of work nevertheless. What do we do now?"

"Tomorrow," Alphonse said, "I will go atop the Hawk Rock and study the land to the northwest through my telescope. Perhaps I will see something. Even if I do not, I would wish to journey some distance in that direction to see if we can find evidence to confirm Neville's reasoning."

Derek interjected, "We may run short on provisions, sir."

"Nonsense!" Alphonse replied with an airy wave of his hand. "Captain Hawthorne has found both fresh water and camel fodder. With the departure of our guides, we have extra provisions as they did not take their full rations. And the Valley of Dust was said to be populated with goats."

Neville didn't say anything about that last comment. He knew if he did Alphonse would merely point out that Chad Spice's journal had been correct on the matter of finding water at the Hawk Rock. Besides, if he was in the least honest with himself, he had to admit that he, too, was curious as to what they might find. Being part of a major archaeological discovery could only do good things for his reputation, both within the Army and in wider circles as well.

"I think we would not be imprudent," Neville said, "to continue our journey at least a bit farther northwest. Tomorrow morning, while Alphonse makes his telescopic survey, we will finish replenishing our water and cut fodder for the camels."

"Very good," Alphonse said, rubbing his hands briskly together. "Everything is perfectly in order."

Jackals barking in the small hours just before dawn offered the first sign that everything was far from in order.

"That doesn't sound right," Eddie said to Neville, after the captain shook him awake. "Too many. Too scattered. I might believe it of a wolf pack, but jackals . . ."

"My thoughts exactly," Neville agreed. "I'm going to wake the others. I'll send Derek to help you ready the camels. Muffle the harnesses. We'll take the gear but leave the tents set up."

"Are we leaving?" Eddie asked, stomping into his boots.

"I want to get out of this canyon," Neville replied. " 'Box' seems too apt a description for it. Let's make certain the box doesn't turn into a coffin."

Neville woke Alphonse and Derek, warning them to keep both light and sound to a minimum. Then he crossed to the small tent Miriam occupied. He'd half-expected to find it empty, but the girl was waiting, dressed and alert.

"Those are not jackals," she said as soon as she saw him.

"I thought not," Neville replied. "This canyon is too close for my tastes."

"I understand," Miriam replied. "I will help with the camels."

"Good. Send Eddie Bryce to me. I want him on guard."

Since their gear had been ready for a morning departure, loading the camels didn't take long. The jackals' barking had nearly ceased, but Neville wasn't fooled into complacency. Earlier, whoever was out there must have been getting into position. Now they were probably waiting for better light.

By the time Derek reported that the camels were ready, Neville had made his plans. Open desert was hardly preferable to the box canyon, but it did offer a faint hope for escape.

"Form up," he told the others. "We'll get out and head east toward the Nile."

No one spoke. No one protested, though the glimpse Neville had of Alphonse's expression demonstrated more eloquently than any impassioned words that Neville would pay dearly if this proved a false alarm.

It isn't, though, Neville thought, and moved his camel forward.

Camels' feet are soft and made for traveling across sand. They are quiet, but not noiseless. Equally, though Neville's band carried no lights and the moon had set, the darkness was not absolute. Starlight is quite enough for eyes accustomed to its glow. Even so, Neville hoped they might get away with it.

But whoever it was who had raised the jackals' call in the darkness did not wait for daylight to attack. Perhaps someone noticed that though the tents kept their places the grumbling shapes of the camels were no longer picketed at the camp's fringe. Perhaps the attack had been planned for earlier in any case.

For whatever reason, before Neville and his band had traveled far from the Hawk Rock, a shrill cry of rage and disappointment pierced the clear desert air. Neville knew that their enemies would seek them to the east—for there was nothing but desert to the west. Speed, then, rather than deception was their only chance.

He thumped his camel and the creature reluctantly stretched out its limbs in an undulating run. The others followed suit without prompting. Indeed, the shrieks from where the Hawk Rock bulked behind them were prompting enough.

It's five days back to the Nile, Neville thought despairingly. *If they have camels or horses, we're sunk. Maybe we should have fought it out back there.*

But he knew his small group wouldn't have had a chance. He and Eddie were in training, but Derek was a disabled quartermaster, not a crack shot. Alphonse didn't even carry a gun. Miriam would also be useless in a fight. Indeed, Neville expected that if he looked back he would see that her camel—and perhaps one of those bearing their supplies—was gone. What better way for the Bedouin girl to win back her father's support?

Thus Neville was surprised out of all proportion when Miriam's camel drew alongside his own. The girl called out to him.

"Follow me, Captain Hawthorne. I know a place where, Allah willing, these superstitious dogs will not follow."

Neville did not so much permit Miriam to take the lead as she pressed her camel to the front. The beast—not the water carrier this time—lightly burdened by no other weight than her slender form, took the lead easily.

And Neville followed. What else could he do? Miriam was offering some hope, slender as it might be, and if her offer proved to be another trap—well, they were already into it up to their necks. Glancing back over his shoulder, he was certain he saw a fair-sized dust cloud occluding the stars and knew that at least some of their pursuers were mounted.

Miriam led them to an area where the desert was broken and rocky. A rise—nothing like the Hawk Rock but at least higher and more substantial than sand dunes—

appeared from the surrounding area. When they drew closer, Neville realized that the rock showed signs of having been carved and shaped. He was not surprised when Miriam drew her camel to a halt and announced.

"It is a necropolis of the old kings. My father and his brothers have come here to rob the dead, but they never have trusted the place. Their fear may slow them long enough for us to make a defense."

Neville saw the wisdom in her words. Unlike the box canyon, where they could be surrounded on all sides, here they could claim the high ground. His and Eddie's rifles were likely to have better range than whatever the Arabs carried—at least he hoped so. Even Derek and Alphonse might be able to be of some use—and he no longer felt a desire to dismiss Miriam out of hand.

"Can you use a rifle?" he asked her as they herded the camels within the most sheltered perimeter of rocks. Derek forced the beasts to kneel and efficiently began unloading the most necessary supplies.

"I can," Miriam said, "but I can do more than that."

Moving with a lithe grace that demonstrated more clearly than words that she had no fear of this city of the dead, Miriam showed Neville several openings into the tombs.

"We can shelter within," she said, "if needed."

Neville nodded.

"Eddie!" he called back to his sergeant. "I'm going to do some scouting."

"Right, Captain," came the jaunty reply. "The

Bedouin have stopped just outside of rifle range. I borrowed the professor's binoculars, and it looks like they're arguing."

Neville wasted neither breath nor time in reply. Lighting a candle, he ducked into the first opening. This led to a dead end, but the second opening led to a well-preserved chamber. He was about to penetrate more deeply when Miriam's voice came echoing down the corridors.

"Please, Captain Hawthorne, Eddie Bryce is calling and someone is hit!"

Neville was outside almost before the Arab girl finished speaking. Derek was wrapping a length of fabric around his employer's left forearm. Alphonse was pale and so shaken that even his eyebrows seemed to have lost their customary exuberance.

"Report, Sergeant!" Neville snapped, flinging himself down behind their makeshift bulwark and readying his rifle.

"Not all of them are scared of ghosts," Eddie replied, "but a whole lot more are scared of my rifle now. Alphonse was clipped by a ricochet, not a direct hit."

"Where are they now?"

"Pulled back out of range. We've got the drop on them, though, and a clear line of sight all around."

"Problem is," Neville replied, "you and I can't watch everywhere. If we are forced to start shooting . . ."

Eddie shrugged noncommittally. The matter wasn't worth spelling out.

"Please, sir," Derek said. He'd finished wrapping

Alphonse's arm and was belly-crawling to join them.
"I can watch."

"I can watch," Miriam said breathlessly in Arabic.
She might not understand English, but Neville had already accepted that she was no fool. "And shoot."

Neville nodded. He shared out both rifles and side-
arms, posted Derek and Miriam so that the group now
possessed an overlapping field of vision in all directions, and felt completely hopeless. From what he
could glimpse through Alphonse's binoculars, the
Arabs outnumbered them four or five to one. Even su-
perior weapons would not compensate for those odds.

Favoring his lacerated arm, Alphonse crept up beside Neville.

"Captain, this is a ruin, yes?"

Neville tried to manage a chuckle. "But not likely
the Valley of Dust, I'm afraid."

"No. Not likely. However, I understand ruins where
I do not understand warfare. With your permission, I
shall continue the scouting you had undertaken."

"You have my permission," Neville said. "All I ask
is that you make the rounds from time to time with
fresh water. It's going to get damned hot out here."

"Of course!"

And it did get damn hot. The Arabs launched the
occasional charge, but were driven back without much
effort, sometimes dragging a wounded comrade.
Around noon, Miriam confirmed what Neville sus-
pected.

"They can wait. Why risk shooting and harming the

camels? A day or two is nothing, especially with water near."

Periodically, Alphonse made the rounds with water and food. Each time he gave Neville a report of his finds. The ruins were extensive, though thoroughly looted, at least where Alphonse had reached.

"But there is much the vandals did not take," he said. "Wood, broken furniture, cloth, even mummies destroyed beyond all recognition by those who stripped the amulets from within their wrappings."

Neville thought on this and as the boat of the sun began to sink in the west, he developed a plan.

"Wrap me so everything is covered," Neville ordered, "everything but my eyes and mouth and don't restrict my movement."

"I still think," Alphonse said, ripping a sheet into long strips—the linen from the tombs which had inspired Neville was far too brittle, "that I should take your place. You are a better shot."

"But you are wounded, and I'm not going to risk anyone else in such a jackass plan."

"You're risking Miriam," Eddie grumbled.

"Miriam is risking herself," Neville countered.

To be honest, he didn't feel good about Miriam's addition to their plan, but he had felt he must accept her suggestion—no matter the danger to which it exposed her. Miriam's diversion meant his outlandish imposture would have a better chance of succeeding without getting him riddled with bullets. He couldn't let false chivalry make him reject her offer.

Miriam's robes had been disheveled, the fabric artfully streaked with blood harvested from a protesting camel. She was ignoring Eddie's displeasure—but Neville had no doubt she was aware of it, and flattered by his concern.

"Right," Neville said when his mummification had been completed a short time later. "Everyone knows what to do?"

Nods and a sullen "Yes, sir," from Eddie answered him.

"Start shooting."

Eddie and Alphonse aimed at a sandy patch and let loose a barrage.

"Now, Miriam," Neville commanded.

The girl loosed a piercing scream and bolted across the desert in the direction of the Arab camp. At the same moment, Derek released three of the camels. They'd guessed that the Arabs might shoot at a woman, but not if they risked hitting a valuable piece of livestock.

Neville pursued the fleeing girl. He moved fairly rapidly, but kept his gait stiff and motions jerky. He must follow close behind the girl, but not too close. Behind him, the shooting had ceased and their besieged camp was as silent as death.

He heard Miriam's wails and screams as she burst in among her countrymen. Despite himself, Neville held his breath. One word from her would destroy them in an instant.

"It came from the tombs," Miriam sobbed. "One of the old kings, avenging ancient wrongs. It tore the English to shreds and comes for us! Look!"

She screamed theatrically, collapsing into the arms of the nearest Arab—one who just happened to be one of the Bedouin's best shots.

Neville moaned loudly and made a furious, throwing gesture in the direction of the nearest Arab. The man collapsed as if shot, not surprisingly, for he *had* been shot. Eddie Bryce had followed Neville, keeping to the shadows and trusting that misdirection and the fire-blinded eyes of the Arabs would keep him from discovery.

The Bedouins' reaction was all Neville could have desired. Those nearest to the fallen man leaped back, shunning the body. Neville gestured again and a second man fell.

The crack of the rifle was clearly audible, but no one paid attention. They were too busy scrabbling for the nearest mount or—more often—fleeing on foot into the desert. Derek had crept around and untied the horses and camels.

A few of the braver Arabs reached for brands from the fire, but an unearthly wail from the direction of the ruins froze even Neville's blood. The wail rose again, and Miriam shrieked:

"Another! Another! What demons have we unbound!"

That was more than even the coolest head could take. They hardly paid heed to the fact that the mummy nearer to their camp had produced an artfully wrapped pistol and was adding to the death toll. Within minutes the enemy was scattered. Neville didn't plan to wait for them to get over their fear. His band could navigate by the stars and Alphonse was holding their camels ready.

Neville offered no protest when Eddie swung Miriam onto the saddle in front of him, only smiled.

When they were safely on a steamer bound for Cairo, Alphonse Liebermann explained that he no longer desired to search for the tomb of Neferankhotep.

"I have found a tomb now," he said, cradling his wounded arm tenderly. "A good one, if I choose to excavate. However, perhaps playing at pharaonic revenge has ruined me for archaeology. It no longer seems so good to disturb the dead."

Neville nodded. "I understand."

Alphonse laid a hand on Neville's arm.

"I will be writing several letters when I return to Cairo: to the museum to register my find, to the Army and diplomatic corp to warn them of the restless Arabs in this part of the desert, and . . ."

He paused and smiled, his eyebrows dancing.

"And to praise a certain valiant Captain Hawthorne. I shall write my cousin, Albert, too. I think, 'Sir Neville' would sound very fine indeed."

Neville had to agree.

A LIGHT IN THE DESERT

by Rosemary Edghill

Rosemary Edghill is the author of *Speak Daggers to Her*, *The Warslayer*, and many other books. Her short fiction has appeared in *Return to Avalon*, *Chicks in Chainmail*, and *Tarot Fantastic*, among others. She is a full-time author who lives in the Mid-Hudson valley.

YES, I believed he was the Son of God. How could I not? When he came out of the desert after forty days spent in prayer and fasting, the light of revelation shining on his brow, his eyes as clear as the sky itself, what man could doubt that my lord had touched the face of God?

The answer, of course, is many. When he first began to bear witness to his new teaching, to tell those who

gathered to hear him speak of the new way he had
found, many did not wish to hear. The temple priests,
in particular, spoke against him and his doctrine of
oneness and love, of an eternal Father who cherished
all His children equally, and watched over them without the need of paid prayer and bought sacrifice.

But he was pharaoh, and they could not move against
him openly.

Even Nefertiti was silent, perhaps biding her time,
for she well knew that a sister-wife might easily be replaced at the pharaoh's pleasure, nor was she even co-
ruler with him, for that honor was reserved for his
younger brother, Smenkhare. She understood my lord
as little as her daughters did—I, who loved him best,
say this: my lord was as true and unchanging as the
Sun, his Master.

There were those who listened—the Twelve whom
he gathered around him to impart the inner teachings:
the poet, the philosopher, the farmer, the musician, the
builder . . . a master from every art in which A-ten had
seen fit to instruct his peoples. My lord taught them
A-ten's mysteries even as he began to build a symbol
of the Heavenly Truth upon Earth. Akhetaten, City of
the Sun, was to have been Wisdom in stone, built large
so that any man could read it. Would that it had survived! But perhaps Truth does not need stone, when it
may be written upon hearts: for truly it was the common people who loved my lord best, for the message
of love and comfort he brought, an end to exacting ob-
servances and petty quarrels in the halls of Heaven.

A-ten, the Light-Father, was supreme over all, the other gods of our divided land no more than His aspects, tiny parts mistaken for the whole. A-ten was as loving as Isis, as gentle as Hathor, as just as Ma'at, nor did He demand aught in sacrifice, but poured out His love upon his people as the sun pours its light upon the land. The people came from great distances to hear the words of my lord regarding A-ten, and to receive his charity.

It was a time of sweetness and plenty in the land, for when he received his revelation, my lord stopped the payment to the temples of the masks of God, and the bounty that had once gone to fatten the priests now went to feed and clothe the people, even the poorest among them. They would never see the inside of the temples, but they saw well the loaves and fishes, the linen and beer, which my lord's bounty represented; the tangible symbols of A-ten's love.

I was his steward, and so the disbursement of these riches fell to me. I never grudged the work, nor did I hold back any of the wealth that passed through my hands. It was all for them, for him, all for the glory of A-ten. I was the son of a desert people, sold into slavery in a famine year, but by Pharaoh's love I became the highest of all his servants, his right hand, the hand of the Son of God.

He could never have won the priests, but soon he had the army and the people, and all could see that the favor of the Sun was upon him. If events had gone well, perhaps what the priests thought would not have mattered, for with time my lord could have hardened the bonds of custom about the land, until those who would not follow A-ten for love must follow Him out of tradition and habit.

But the years he would need for this, my lord was not to have. One day a traveling magician—from Crete, or so he said—came to the court. He said he was a magician, and I have no reason to doubt it. They worship the Earth-Serpent on Crete, for its coilings beneath the ground are a great trouble to their land, and the mage could turn his stave into a snake so mighty that the whole court trembled with fear to see it.

But my lord did not tremble, saying that A-ten's love protected him from all magic, and so the mage grew angry, and prophesied the coming of seven plagues to teach my lord humility. The priests of the Old Gods were quick to turn this into a warning of the gods' displeasure at the new ways, but my lord discounted it, saying there were no host of gods, only One Who loved His people as a kind Father. And the magician departed the court before I or any could think to have him detained and questioned, to discover who had sent him to my lord, and why.

But though he was soon gone, his visit was long remembered, for that year the Nile again ran red, as it sometimes does, but this time the scarlet tide was more abundant than any man could remember, turning the water to very blood. It killed the frogs that bred along the river's banks and the fish that swam in its waters, and from their corpses was bred such a plague of flies as stung every man in Thebes and the Seven Cities into a festering knot of open sores, killing children, the old, and the sick with their poison. With the river corrupted, there was no water fit to drink, and thousands died of thirst as well.

It was easy to turn away from the new religion then, and many did, but others held fast to my lord's promise in A-ten's name: that through His love, we would become like A-ten, and though trouble and darkness might beset us, we should not die, but go down to the Land of Death as He did and be reborn anew, to walk with Him in His Heavenly Paradise, never to fear the Darkness nor the Halls of Judgment.

But whatever the future might hold, the time of plenty and ease in the Two Lands was past, and many blamed my lord's new teaching for our troubles, and thought that his death would ease the travail of his people—especially if no man's hand could be seen to compass it. In the dark night hours the priests of the Old Gods came to me and offered me thirty silver shekels, the price of my freedom, the price of a man's life, if I would bring my lord to death.

But I refused.

When I told my lord of this new treason, he gathered the Twelve about him secretly to give them the guidance of the Light. He said to them that they must depart to their own lands once more, bearing A-ten's wisdom, but that first, some one of us must kill him, and his name pass away from men, so that A-ten would know those who loved Him from those who merely feared Him, and so that the priests of the Old Gods would be satisfied, and cease to oppress the people.

But through love and fear, none of us would do as he asked, and so in the end it was my lord himself who gave his life up to the priests, walking alone in the palace gardens at night where they could take him easily. And so they slew him in his thirty-third year of life, and set his brother Smenkhare to rule as pharaoh in his place, tearing my lord's name from the rock and the temple walls, despoiling his burial chamber and destroying A-ten's name wherever it was written. Work was stopped upon the Heavenly City, and the temples to the Old Gods were reopened once more.

I who had been his closest friend was sold into a far harsher slavery, but there also I kept faith with my lord, for who remarks the thoughts of slaves? And many of A-ten's followers among the common people who had loved him best remained true as well—we would meet, at night, among the tombs in the City of the Dead, and tell each other of all we had heard and seen in Akhenaten's reign, for so we hoped to pass the memory of the One True God and His martyred Son to our children, and to our children's children. In the rejoicing of the priests, we were overlooked, for a time.

But Smenkhare died after only a handful of seasons, and his younger brother took the throne, a new pharaoh who was but a child, and so even more firmly beneath the hand of the priests. As their tool, he sought for enemies everywhere, and settled upon us, who had not renounced the Sun, nor the Son of the Sun. My people would not swear by the Moon, or pour incense to the Old Gods, and so we were easily singled out for persecution, and those of us who were still free were made the meanest of slaves, all of us now forbidden by pharaoh's decree to bear living children. I knew then that if A-ten's holy name were to survive, we must flee Egypt itself.

Though I had been born a shepherd of goats to a tented people, and now spent my days as a common laborer, I had once been cupbearer to pharaoh, and I still knew all the secret ways into the palace. If we were to leave behind all we knew, we must have swords and gold to ease the journey, and so one night I sent word that all who loved A-ten were to gather together in our secret place, and when they had done so, I led my lord's people into the palace that had once been his, there to despoil he who was now pharaoh and leave Egypt before the dawn.

All went as I would have it go, for I was not foolish enough to fling words of defiance in the face of the boy-king or his priest-guards. Silent as mice to the granary we came, praying to A-ten to send his servant-aspect Bast to guard us, for she, like all cats, loves the hours of darkness, and all games and trickery. Silent we came, and silent went, in the darkness of night, with only Thoth and Anubis to see what we did.

South we went, garbed as desert wanderers, across the Sea of Reeds. We were A-ten's people now, free of all earthly masters, bearing the treasure of His Light along with Egypt's gold, and strong bronze spears and swords to defend our flight. We were few—only a handful, out of all the teeming peoples of Egypt—and I did not think that Tutankhamen would send soldiers after us for golden cups and arm-rings and strings of beads, even should he discover the theft and know which way we had gone. Yet what little we had taken of all Egypt's great wealth would be riches enough in Canaan to buy goats and land, and in that far country we would make a place for our altars, and tell our children of the One True God, Whose Light is too bright to see, and Whose unknowable form is like fire at noonday; He who came to my lord, and spoke with him, and gave him His love.

I, Ahmose, cupbearer to pharaoh, who have looked upon the face of the voice of A-ten, who have felt the clasp of his hand and seen his smile, say these things, and say that all will be done as my lord would have wished it done. In that green and pleasant land we will make of ourselves a new people, a nation ruled not by priests nor kings, but by the living voice of Truth.

And always I will tell the story of that day, when the Light came to me out of the desert, garbed in the flesh of a living man. My pharaoh, the Son of God.

THE SCROLL OF WISDOM

by Josepha Sherman

Josepha Sherman is a fantasy novelist and folk-lorist, whose latest titles include *Son of Darkness, The Captive Soul, Xena: All I Need to Know I Learned from the Warrior Princess* by Gabrielle, as translated by Josepha Sherman, the folklore title *Merlin's Kin*, and, together with Susan Shwartz, two *Star Trek* novels, *Vulcan's Forge* and *Vulcan's Heart*. She is also a fan of the New York Mets, horses, aviation, and space science. Visit her at www.sff.net/people/Josepha.Sherman.

*T*HE walls of the tomb were all about him, the air close and dusty as Prince Khamwas carefully dug by the glow of one magical globe of light. This was the tomb of the long-dead Prince Na-nefer-ka-ptah, and buried here, as well, if all the tales were true—

They were! With the lust of a true scholar for knowledge, Khamwas snatched up the scroll said to have been written by Thoth, God of Wisdom Himself. Very gingerly, he unrolled it. The magics inscribed on it must be wondrous—

Ptah help him! They blazed at his mind, too strong for any mortal. One spell burned its way into his brain before he managed to seal the scroll again with hands that shook. Gods, no, he should never have come here, magician-priest or no, never—

She was a slender figure in the darkness, clad only in gleaming gems and her own long, dark hair, and she was beautiful, so very beautiful. . . .

"Tabubu," he murmured, knowing her name without knowing how he knew.

"Come to me, Khamwas. Do with me what you wish. Come to me."

He burned for her as though he were a boy after his first woman, with a lust away from all logic, and something was wrong, this wasn't a woman—illusion, sent to madden him, sought to destroy his mind, all so that he would lose the scroll. And he—

No! This was wrong! This was the past. There was no Tabubu, there never had been anything of her but illusion, and—

The image shifted. She was a slender figure in the darkness, clad in a gown of purest linen, glowing softly white by her own light. No longer Tabubu but Ahwese, the true guardian of the scroll.

"Hail, O Darkness!" she wailed. *"Farewell, O Light! That which was here has departed!"*

"You have the scroll, Ahwese. No need to mourn. Or to haunt me."

"That which was here has departed!" she insisted. "Seek it, seek!"

Prince Khamwas, fourth-born son of divine Pharaoh Ramses and magician-priest of Ptah, woke with a start, shaking with shock.

I thought I was free from it, from my—my stupidity.

Clearly, I am not.

The corridor was narrow and dusty, sloping ever downward, so dark that their torches made the time-worn reliefs of men and gods carved into the walls seem to dance. The place smelled faintly of frankincense, and more strongly of death.

Not surprising, Khamwas thought. It was, after all, not the place for mortal men. Not even a man who was both of royal birth and the high priest of Ptah—the god who probably wasn't approving of him being here at all.

Rituals of purification shall be performed, he promised Ptah silently, *my word and honor on it.*

Khamwas glanced over his shoulder at Inarkos, whose narrow face bore a look of resolute terror. They were both about the same youngish age, but he was taller than Inarkos by a head, broader across the cheekbones, as handsome as his divine father the pharaoh, while Inarkcos was, well, pleasant-faced. Despite the differences, Khamwas didn't doubt that Ramses, who seemed well on his way to siring a hundred or more offspring, had sired Inarkos as well.

At any rate, Inarkos wouldn't abandon his foster brother. But that wasn't making the man any happier about being in a tomb that had been ancient when the land of Khemt was first being born.

But we must be here. Or at least I must. After that dream, what sort of magician-priest would I be if I didn't heed—

He broke off the thought with a hiss of disgust: His torch, which had been flickering badly, had just gone out.

"Enough," Khamwas said. He held out his hand, palm up, and murmured a Word under his breath. A cool globe of fire formed on his palm, lighting up the corridor with a steady glow.

"Nice," Inarkos muttered. "Nicer if it wasn't green."

"Critic," Khamwas retorted without heat.

He and Inarkos had shared years of easy jests and stingless barbs. But that he had been here before, in this tomb of the long-dead Prince Na-nefer-ka-ptah, was a secret he would never share with Inarkos.

"You have returned," a voice whispered.

There was a gasp from Inarkos: He, with no magic, had heard and seen nothing strange, but he would have felt a sudden chill stirring of air and known only that something eerie was occurring.

But Khamwas saw truly, and knew. "Ahwese."

She could almost have been mistaken for a living

woman, slender and sloe-eyed. But she had been the wife of Na-nefer-ka-ptah, and her ghost stayed here now, with that of her husband, to guard the tomb, and the scroll. She might seem but a slim and delicate being—but power fairly radiated from her.

"I am not here to steal this time," Khamwas assured the ghost hastily. "I had a dream that warned—"

"It is already gone," she cut in.

"It— No!" Stunned, he lost control of the globe of light, which vanished in an instant.

But Ahwere glowed softly white on her own. "Ah . . ." she breathed. "Truly, you did not know. This time you are honorable."

Khamwas ignored that backhanded form of compliment. "Who?" he gasped. "Who had the power?"

"Tabubu."

"B-but there is no Tabubu! I mean, she is but an aspect, illusion, a shade of a ghost—"

"No longer merely that, not after she met you and strove with you," Ahwese said with absolutely no tone in her voice. "No longer merely that once she knew of the scroll, and where it was reburied, and could take the scroll and slip through time. You know what is written on it, you who read that spell and opened the way for her."

And here I thought it was over, and my guilt absolved. Bah, things are never so simple when magic is involved.

If Tabubu was now a real being, with the mind and will of the Underworld, the mind and will to read and control the scroll but without a *ka*, without any sort of

a soul—gods, she would have no mortal sense of justice, no pity—she could use the power in the scroll to
destroy all Khemt! Khamwas had a quick, terrible
image of Tabubu erasing the names of all mortal souls
so that no one would have even existed.

Yes, he reminded himself, and she was a being who
would not have even come into existence if he hadn't
been knowledge-hungry enough—no, make that *stupid* enough—to steal the scroll in the first place.

Where has she gone? "Slip through time . . ." *It cannot be
the past, or I would not be here at all. The future . . . ?*

Was there such a thing as a tangible future? How
could it already be formed when it did not yet exist?

The scholarly side of Khamwas took over. Some saw
time as a linear flow, like that of the sacred Nile. But
others did speculate on it being more fluid, like the
Nile's waters. Could it be?

Perhaps. Perhaps he would simply be torn apart
into nothingness, with no body left for mummification
or a place in the Afterworld.

But . . . my land . . . my people . . .

Yes, he was terrified. But as magician and as priest—
yes, and as a prince of Khemt—he could not turn
away. "Let your heart not grieve," he told Ahwere as
steadily as he could. "I will follow her and return with
the scroll."

How?

The spell, a corner of his mind prodded. *Think of it.
Think of what it held.*

The power of day and night—ha, yes, the power of time itself.

"Go back," Khamwas told Inarkos. "Go back to my home and wait for me."

"But I—"

Khamwas caught him by the shoulders. "Inarkos, brother, I will need you there to be an anchor for me. Now, *go!*"

It was said with magical force. And Inarkos went.

Khamwas closed his eyes, calming his mind with all the disciplines he knew. *Forgive me, Ptah, if you can, and guide me if you wish. Only, let my* ka *not wander homeless, or become nothingness!*

No. He was calm. There were no doubts. There was no fear. There was . . . no . . . fear.

He began the spell, letting the words come free as they would, focusing on the scroll, only on the scroll, and doing nothing else but that. This was not a magic to be controlled or shaped by mortal man. The scroll . . . the scroll . . . the scroll . . .

And . . .

. . . it . . .

HURT! The magic blazed through his body and mind like Ra's fire, tearing at his sense of self, hurling him from the solid world to—

Gods, not nothingness!

Somewhere.

Somewhere solid.

Someone solid—yes! He and someone had just collided as he materialized, sending them recoiling off each other and crashing to the floor—thank the gods, yes, there was a floor, and walls, a room, a recognizable one.

For a time, he could do nothing but stay where he'd fallen, getting his breath back, and his senses as well. To his relief, Khamwas realized that, yes, he still had a body (a little bruised by the rough arrival), and, yes, he still had a mind. But . . . where was he? When, rather?

Shivering, he struggled to his feet. A room, yes, strewn with what looked like piles of pale papyrus and proving that wherever, whenever, he was, they still had recognizable architecture, and presumably some form of writing. It was far colder here than in Khemt, enough so to make him regret being clad only in his noble's kilt of pleated linen.

The other person with whom he'd collided lay in a crumpled heap. Wonderful, in this time for only a few moments, and he'd already managed to kill one of the local people. He hurried to his—no, to *her* side, gods, he'd killed a woman, a young woman, brown-haired, fair-skinned, clad in some exotic blue tunic and some odd kind of blue leggings, and—

At that moment, she opened her eyes, widening them in astonishment, staring up at what he guessed from her expression must have been a truly bizarre sight to her: A bronze-skinned man in a collar of gold and colorful enamel and a linen kilt bending over her. But at least she didn't scream. Instead, she scrambled back in alarm, snapping something that sounded angry and like so much gibberish to him.

This grows better with every moment. A foreign time, a foreign land, and now a foreign language as well.

He held up both hands to show he held no weapons, and backed up from her, giving her a chance to recover from the initial shock, and taking advantage of the chance to glance around. A table, a chair, unfamiliar in design but not really that strange, one chair on its back, presumably from the force of his sudden arrival, sheets of . . . papyrus? . . . everywhere, and rows of shelves holding—what? Some manner of bound scrolls? Including the scroll? He had a sudden wonderful image of grabbing it and being instantly whisked home again.

Of course. It'll be just as simple as that. And then I'll go out and single-handedly conquer the Hurrians.

And . . . his senses told him that it wasn't there. Had the spell misdirected him? No, he dared not believe that.

The young woman seemed to have recovered her breath and composure. He'd knocked the wind out of her, then, not badly hurt her, thanks be to Ptah. Khamwas said, "I mean you no harm."

Instead of the blank look he'd expected, she frowned slightly. Getting to her feet, she gestured at him, clearly telling him to keep talking.

"Very well. I am Prince Khamwas, fourth son of the divine Pharaoh Ramses."

She opened her mouth, closed it, swallowed, then tried again, very, very carefully, "*What* . . . said?"

"You speak my language!"

"It . . . not . . . can . . . be! Who? How . . . here?"

"I am, as I said, Prince Khamwas of Khemt, fourth son of the divine Pharaoh Ramses."

"Not . . . pos'ble."

Her accent was terrible, but at least it meant that something of the language had survived. It also seemed to be keeping her intrigued enough not to call for aid.

"I mean you no harm," he repeated more slowly.

She exclaimed in her incomprehensible tongue words that sounded like, "Whoa, wait." In his language, more or less, "*The* Khamwas . . . schol'r?"

She'd heard of him! Flattered in spite of himself, Khamwas agreed, "Yes, I am a scholar, among other things."

But she held up a hand: He was speaking too quickly for her. They stared at each other helplessly for a moment. Then she said, "Aha!" and signaled to him to stay just where he was. She hunted feverishly through the bound scrolls on the shelves. With a satisfied, "Got it!" she turned to him, holding one bound scroll out.

Khamwas studied it with a frown. Not papyrus after all, but something vaguely similar, perhaps the material they were said to make in the lands of Chin. On it, symbols were written in some form of ink—ha, this was a listing of the two languages, his and, presumably, hers!

"Excellent," Khamwas said. After some hesitation, since the listing was arranged by her language's ordering, he managed to find and point to hieroglyphs that told her, "I am, indeed, Prince Khamwas of Khemt."

She snatched the bound scroll from him, hastily leafing through it, carefully pointing out the message, "If you are who you claim, how did you get here?"

"Where is here?" he countered.

She gave him an impatient glance, then said in her own tongue words that she obviously couldn't find in the language of Khemt, "New York City. NYU. You know, New York University."

That meant absolutely nothing to him.

The woman frowned at his utter confusion. *Come*, her gesture said, *look*. Khamwas warily followed her to the room's one window. It was covered in . . . were those panes of clear glass? And outside—

"Ptah preserve me!"

No, no, he was a scholar, he should be analyzing what he saw.

And Thoth himself is going to rise up to guide me to the scroll—no, forget that thought. This is hardly the time for impiety.

The world outside was full of buildings, taller than any he'd ever imagined, all of stone, with those glass-paned windows. The streets were paved, though he could not have named with what. Some cement, maybe, as he'd heard they used in Mohenjodaro in the Indus Valley, and some black substance on which ran . . . metal . . . chariots without . . . horses. People, most of them young and strangely clad seemed to be everywhere, laughing or chattering or rushing along on their own business. The chill air had a weird, alien reek to it that made him cough, then sneeze.

Gods, what manner of land have I—

No, he already knew that this was . . . what . . . New York, En Why Yew. Whatever that meant. He wasn't even sure how to ask what year it might be, since their two systems of measurement would surely not be the same.

The young woman was still frowning, watching his reaction. She started leafing through the bound scroll, trying to find what she wanted. It took her so long that Khamwas gave a cry of sheer frustration.

"I cannot stay in this room forever!"

As the woman watched him in some alarm, Khamwas turned his mind inward, calming himself, and once again called upon the spell, hunting for one tiny bit of its immense power . . . yes. The smallest fragment of power . . . He let it come forth.

It hit with the force of a boulder. Khamwas opened his eyes to find himself flat on his back, with no memory of having fallen. The young woman, wild-eyed, was shaking him.

"What happened, what did you do, what—oh. Oh. My. God. What am I speaking—what—that was *magic*, the way you appeared, the way you just did that Universal Translator bit—"

"I don't think we are speaking my language," Khamwas said, hearing those strange words. He sat up, waiting a moment for his head to clear. "Whatever combination it may be, at least we can understand each other now." He paused, studying her. "I know that this has been a tremendous shock."

"A *shock?* I'm talking to a man from, what, the Sixteenth Dynasty—oh, God, I just said that." She got to her feet. "Look, I'm not usually so crazed, but, well, this isn't something that happens every day, not even in New York."

He got to his feet as well, asking, "This—this city?"

She nodded, a gesture that apparently meant "yes." "What makes it even weirder is that I am a grad student—you know, a graduate student—you do understand?"

"A . . . scholar?"

That rewarded him with the quickest, shakiest flash of a smile. "Almost. Anyhow, I'm a grad student of—would you believe it?—Egyptology. Uh, that's the study of Khempt—"

"Khemt," he corrected gently. "Your study is of my people?"

"Khemt. And, yes. But this—I mean, how often does a grad student of Egyptology get to meet an honest-to-God Prince of Egypt?" She stopped, shaking her head.

I have been taken to someone who has studied Khemt. This cannot be coincidence. "You believe me, then."

"I don't want to; I liked things the way they were, you know, the past in the past and— Yeah, I'm babbling again, I know it. But I don't really see how I can deny, well, everything! You read Ancient Egyptian—"

"It is hardly ancient to me."

"—and the right New Kingdom dialect, too. Hey, that could be a coincidence. But when you looked outside— if what was on your face was acting, it was award-winning stuff. And, uh, I feel like I'm in the *Twilight Zone* or something for even saying this, but, well, if you really are Prince Khamwas—"

"I am."

"—the tales about you say you were—are—a magician, and the way you burst out of nothing, and now, the, uh, language bit—God, there's no other explanation for it. That was m–magic!"

"It was," he said very gently. "I am real. And here. Out of my right time."

"Why?"

"This . . . isn't going to be simple to explain. Ah, first of all, have you a name?"

"Katharine Watson. Kath, for short. Go on."

With a sigh, he summarized the story of the scroll and its theft.

"Uh-huh," was all she said when he finished.

Khamwas didn't need the language to catch the skepticism in her voice. "I don't suppose I'd believe me, either," he said, "but there it is."

"Tabubu."

"So she is called. I cannot put a name to what she actually is, other than illusion that has become tangible. And with the scroll in her possession, she is truly dangerous."

"Then we should call the cops!"

"The—"

"The police, you know, the Law."

"Gods, no! This is not their affair."

"I, uh, guess not. Cops aren't trained in—in magic. O . . . kay. I guess the city's seen stranger things than a . . . whatever she is and a magic scroll. But why did she come *here?*"

"I wish I could answer that. If she is hunting something, I have no idea of what that could be. Perhaps she is here simply because she is not human and the scroll's power took her here at random. The same power," he added with a sharp glance at her, "that took me straight to someone in this future world who has studied my people."

"Oh, boy," she said without enthusiasm. "I just love it."

But Khamwas stiffened, suddenly aware of an eerie sense of . . .

Tabubu! She was somewhere in this building—and so was the scroll.

"Hey!" Kath moved to block his path. "You can't go anywhere dressed like that!"

"But she's somewhere nearby! I sense—"

"*I* sense you getting frostbite, or arrested for indecent exposure! Wait. I'll be as quick as I can."

She scurried off while he waited, trying not to pace. The sense of Tabubu was, maddeningly, growing more and more faint while he stood trapped in this room.

Kath suddenly reappeared in the doorway, arms full of fabric and voice breathless. "Had to . . . rob a dorm.

Hell, they already . . . think archaeologists . . . are nuts."

She tossed him the clothing and turned her back: a custom of modesty, apparently. Khamwas studied the unfamiliar clothing, but the clothing wasn't too bizarre: These were obviously for the feet, these were obviously leggings, this was . . . a very odd form of fastener, on some manner of metallic track . . . and this was a form of tunic.

All in all, the fit wasn't too outrageous, he supposed, though fashion wasn't exactly high in his mind just then. Suitably dressed for the realm, Khamwas raced out of the room—

Then came to a sudden stop.

"What's wrong?" Kath asked. "Lost the trail?"

"Utterly." He staggered, all at once feeling as though someone had cut all the strings of his body.

"Oh," Kath said, sudden pity in her voice. "And here I thought *I* was the one who felt overwhelmed. It's got to be a lot worse for you."

"I will survive."

"Hey, magic or no magic, you're still only human, right? Give yourself a break."

"A . . . break?"

"Never mind: idiom. Look, I don't care who or what she is, this—this Tabubu can't have gone very far. A priceless papyrus isn't the sort of thing you want to casually carry around Manhattan. That's, uh, where we are, part of the city, and—okay, now I think we both need a time out."

"Out . . . of what?"

She threw up her hands. "I rest my case."

"A . . . case of what?" he asked helplessly.

Kath sighed. "Coffee," was all she said.

He had no idea what that was, either. But in the next few minutes, as they stepped outside, Khamwas had enough else on his mind. Gods, the strangeness! Crowds were nothing new to him; he'd wandered through enough market days in Khemt. But everything, *everything*, from clothing to those terrifying metal vehicles—automobiles, Kath told him—to the towering buildings, the height of which he only now could see, was so undeniably *alien!*

But Kath, Ptah bless her for her kindness, got him through it, her hand on his arm, guiding him to what she called a "coffee shop," and calmly accepting that he would have no such modern thing as coins (foreign concept in Khemt, where all worked by standardized barter). Now he sat across from her, sipping a hot, slightly bitter but invigorating beverage—the mysterious "coffee," and rewarding her kindness by granting her whatever knowledge about his people her scholar's curiosity desired. She had, he thought suddenly, quite a charming face, so young and earnest, her skin slightly flushed and her eyes sparkling with the delight of learning.

Don't be a fool! he told himself sharply, and said, "We have lingered long enough. Can you show me what else there is to your NYU?"

Did she suspect why he had suddenly become so

abrupt? Possibly. The culture might have changed, but Khamwas doubted highly that human nature had changed that greatly. At any rate, Kath didn't argue, merely raised an eyebrow at him, got to her feet, and began showing him about the extended complex that was the university.

Maddeningly, Khamwas time and again sensed tantalizing hints of Tabubu or the scroll that would send him rushing forward—which was a definite peril in this age. Only Kath's determined grip on his arm saved him from being hit by the metal vehicles.

"Red light, death, green light, life," she scolded after the second near miss. "Got it?"

"Yes. Green is life and red death in my land, too. Forgive me. I suspect Tabubu is wandering in and out of the buildings, possibly to deliberately confuse the trail. But she does seem to be heading—" a quick glance up at the sun, "—north. What buildings lie north?"

Kath looked at him blankly. "I don't know."

"But—they are part of the university!"

She blinked. "That's funny. I can't remember."

Khamwas felt a chill steal through him. Kath could simply be absentminded. But then again, this could be the first warning that Tabubu was already using the scroll, working the slightest alterations. Clearly, she didn't have full control over it yet, but— "There! That is the northernmost building. And that's where—come, hurry!"

This time, he did manage to avoid the metal vehicles. With Kath clinging to his arm, Khamwas raced up the steps of—

"Whoa, wait!" she cried. "You can't get in without me! I have the ID!"

"Ah. Good point. You, then, are the student, and I am the odd foreign teacher who has forgotten his, um, ID."

"Exactly. Oh, geez."

"What?"

"I suddenly do remember this place. It's the Medical Sciences building. That's where they study dangerous microbes—ah, small, dangerous illness-causing things. How could I have forgotten?"

"Tabubu."

This was why Tabubu had been heading for this building, here, where she could do the most damage. With the power of the scroll, she could erase medical knowledge, create new disease-beings, warp and change and destroy reality.

But why do this? Why destroy the future?

Simple, he answered himself. *If she alters the future, there are none to remember our names. She has destroyed Khemt's reality: two realms destroyed in one.*

The guard barely glanced at Kath's ID. With the uneasy feeling that the man had already forgotten their appearance, Khamwas strode down a hallway, Kath hurrying at his side. A bend in the hall, and:

"Tabubu!" Khamwas hissed.

"That? No," Kath protested, "that's Professor Smythe, Ancient Literature!"

"No."

"Yes! I took a course with her!"

"You couldn't remember this building until a moment ago."

"Yes, but—"

"You cannot trust memory right now. Tabubu, I know you! I call you by name! Three times I call you, Tabubu, Tabubu, Tabubu!"

She turned to him, and even Khamwas had to admit that she looked exactly like a woman of this time, from the exotic clothing, a dark blue tunic and kilt, to the leather satchel she held in one hand. And for a moment he doubted himself . . .

"Professor Smythe!" Kath said hastily. "You have to excuse him, he's new here, and . . . and . . ."

Professor Smythe—no, no, Tabubu, held up the leather satchel and murmured, "Khamwas . . . come to me, Khamwas . . ."

No, curse it, no!

"You want to possess me, Khamwas . . . you burn to possess me . . ."

I . . . will not!

But it was true. He did burn with lust. His mind was still free, but his body fought to betray him, fighting his magician's will. Raging, Khamwas took a helpless step forward—

There was a blur of movement, two shrieks, and the lust vanished as suddenly as though he'd been dumped in the Nile. Kath had leaped between them and snatched away the leather satchel. "Got it! Get her!"

Tabubu's mouth was open, ready to unmake Kath's name and reality. Khamwas struck Tabubu hard enough to send her slamming back against a wall. Before she could recover, he began, "You are Tabubu. You are Tabub. You are Tabu."

She knew what he was doing and shrilled her rage, but he continued relentlessly, "You are Tab. You are Ta."

She shimmered like heated air.

"You are T," Khamwas concluded. "You are NOTHING!"

Wild wind tore at his hair and clothes, then . . .

. . . was gone.

"Kath? Kath!"

She had gone flat on the floor. Scrambling to her feet, wild-eyed and disheveled, she said, "I—I—I was right, wasn't I? This is *it*, right? In this briefcase?"

"Yes."

People, their memories returned, were rushing to investigate what the sudden weird noises had been. Khamwas took Kath by the arm and walked them away from the crowd.

"I . . . know I shouldn't," she said. "But . . ."

"No. You must not see the scroll."

She sighed. "Figured. It's safer that way. And—what?"

"Now I know why the spell brought me here. Not to the scroll, not to Tabubu—to you. What made you realize what was happening?"

"Oh, come *on!* You're a magician and a prince and all that, but you're still a guy. And my mind just couldn't accept anyone going mad with lust for Professor Smythe!"

"Poor Professor Smythe."

"Khamwas . . . I . . ."

"No," he said very gently. "You are of this time, this realm. And I am of mine."

"Oh, hell. Just my luck." She gave him a not quite convincing grin. "You sure know how to show a girl a good time, Prince Khamwas. See ya in some other era, maybe."

She turned and resolutely walked away.

"May your words be heard," Khamwas said softly.

Then, the scroll firmly in his grip, he let the spell take him . . .

. . . home.

(NOTE: *There really was a Prince Khamwas, or Khaemwasat, the fourth son of the very fertile Pharaoh Ramses II. Khamwas really was a scholar-priest, and later stories about him claimed that he was also a magician. However, the NYU in this story is not to be mistaken for the real university!*)

WHATEVER WAS FORGOTTEN

by Nina Kiriki Hoffman

Nina Kiriki Hoffman has been writing for twenty years and has sold two hundred stories, two short story collections, novels (*The Thread That Binds The Bones*, *The Silent Strength of Stones*, *A Red Heart of Memories*, *Past the Size of Dreaming* and *A Fistful of Sky*), a young adult novel with Tad Williams (*Child of an Ancient City*), a *Star Trek* novel with Kristine Kathryn Rusch and Dean Wesley Smith, *Star Trek Voyager 15: Echoes*, three R. L. Stine's *Ghosts of Fear Street* books, and one *Sweet Valley Junior High* book. She has cats.

IN the course of my life, I was a scribe under one pharaoh, a general under another, and finally I took the Crown of the Two Lands myself. These are some of my titles before I ascended to the double crown:

Foremost of the King's courtiers;

Fanbearer on the right of the King;

Master of the Secrets of the Palace;

Overseer of Offices of the King;

Overseer of the Generals of the Lord of the Two Lands;

Seal Bearer of King of Upper and Lower Egypt;

High Steward;

Mouth Who Appears in the Entire Land;

True Royal Scribe;

One Who has authority over the library;

Overseer of all Overseers of Scribes of the King.

As pharaoh, I had many other titles. I ruled after He Who Shall Never Again Be Named, and spent most of my reign righting that which had been unbalanced, restoring that which had been cast down and neglected. I cast out corruption in my government and punished those who mistreated slaves or cheated the poor. I led military campaigns to reclaim all the lands lost during the reign of He Who Shall Not Be Named.

At the end of my life, I looked back and was satisfied with all I had accomplished for the glory of Egypt and the honor of the gods. I had chosen my successor and trained him well; I left my kingdom in strong hands.

I lived long enough to prepare my tomb with all the things I would need in the life to come: spells and prayers on the walls, all the instructions and the maps I would need to navigate to the land of light; pictures of me and my chief royal wife making offerings to the gods that would renew themselves so we always had tribute to offer; images of food and drink, of the perfect garden full of trees ripe with figs and dates, of the finest blue pool with its stand of papyrus, its leaves and flowers of blue lotus, and the shadows of fish below its surface; pictures of all the things I most liked to do in life: hunting lions from my best chariot, bird-hunting in the marshes with my wife, our dead daughters, and our cat, a banquet with guests and musicians, sailing on the Nile.

Also within my tomb I put many *ushabtis*, statues of helpers who would do all labor in the afterlife; and fine furniture, jewelry, and clothes, perfumes and ointments, all the tools of the everyday; everything I could imagine needing in the life beyond.

My chief royal wife died before me. I saw that she had all the necessary ceremonies and preparations, and laid her to rest in my tomb, in hopes that we would meet again.

I set in my tomb statues of myself and my wife. I had our cartouches carved on the walls so that our names would live forever.

My priests performed all the necessary rituals for me after my death. Forty days my body lay in the pre-serving salts, and afterward my priests anointed it, speaking the right words, and wrapped it in pure linen, placing amulets among my wrappings where they would protect and aid me.

My priests spoke the Opening of the Mouth for me and touched me with the sacred adze to loose all my parts from the bonds of Seth so that I could use my senses after death. They sang the hymns that counseled my heart not to witness against me, and all the hymns that would let me change shape, and eternally make offerings to the gods in the afterlife. They placed my body within its three coffins and then into its granite sarcophagus. They closed my tomb and sealed it with my name.

In the underworld, I went before the Forty-Two Assessors in the Hall of the Two Truths with confidence, and declared my innocence of evil to each truthfully. As my heart was weighed on the scales of Ma'at, I did not worry that the Devourer of Hearts would eat it and cast me forever out of the afterlife. And indeed my heart balanced with the Feather of Truth, and the Devourer let me pass.

After the judgment, I went before the Throne of Osiris and was made welcome into the life to come.

In my tomb the six parts of my soul rejoined each other: the five names that combined to make my one name; my body, made to last forever by the attentions of my priests after my death; my shadow; my *akh*, that part of me from the realm of the gods, which is eternal; my *ka*, the vital force that gave me life and held my personality, the spirit that lived in my heart; and my *ba*, the part of my soul with the freedom to wander, which had left my body when I died and did not return until I had safely passed all the tests of the gods.

Then I knew paradise.

My wife had also successfully passed through the Hall of the Two Truths. She waited for me in the land of light, and even as our hymns had said, we were restored to greenness, to youth and vigor.

Every day the priests brought food to the altar in my mortuary temple so that my *ka* could feed. Every day chantresses and dancers came into my sanctuary and performed so my *ka* could watch and listen. My wife and I attended and enjoyed.

Between these devotions, we lived as I had planned, with all the images of the tomb made real, as fragrant and pleasant as anything I had known in my previous life. I hunted lions in the desert but did not suffer from the heat or sand. My wife and I hunted ducks in the marshes and brought them home for the *ushabtis* to prepare.

Each day we performed the rituals of offering to the gods. Each day we received the blessings of the afterlife. When my wife and I went sailing on the river, there was always a breeze, and always it was scented with the spices of the homeland. Every meal we ate, whether offered by priests or prepared by the *ushabtis*, tasted divine.

Each day was precious. Day piled on day, and I treasured them all.

Gradually, my wife and I stopped sending our *ka*s to

the mortuary temple, for gradually, there was less there to eat, less music to delight us, fewer people performing the funerary offices in our names. It did not matter, for we had everything we needed inside our house of eternity, which was a whole world of joy, forever.

And then the promise of eternity was broken.

"Where is your vulture pectoral?" I asked my wife one perfect morning.

She placed her hand to her breast. "I don't know. What has become of your golden flies of valor necklace?"

"Where are your carnelian earplugs?"

"Where is our blue faience senet set?" She set her hand against my chest. "What has become of your green jasper heart scarab?"

I looked away from my wife, gazed from our columned portico across the river toward the desert above the cliffs, where the sun was just rising, its light driving the stars before it from the sky.

"Our table," she said. "Our breakfast. Our servants."

I looked toward the inner court, where at this time every day the *ushabtis* set our breakfast, bread, beer, pomegranates and figs and dates. No table stood there, and there was not even the smell of bread in the air, only the scent of dust. I closed my eyes.

When I opened them, we were in darkness, and I stood on my head.

"Horemheb!" cried my wife.

"Mut!" I tried to reach for her. Oh, how weak were my arms! How dark were my eyes! How came we to be in the land of night? Had our shadows swallowed us?

She wailed, a high thin cry like a mourner in a funeral procession.

I reached for my beloved but found her not. After a moment, I fell. I lay on my stomach. I searched for strength, and found only a little. Never had I been so weak, not even when I had died.

I crawled toward my wife. "Osiris. Son of Nut. Ruler of Eternity. King of Gods. Lord of the Living, and King of the Dead! Help us, we pray," I said. I felt feeble and battered and older than I had in life, and my nose and mouth were full of dust. My wife's wail went on without interruption.

How had we lost our morning and our light? Had we done something to offend the gods?

There was a taste in the air, the sour taste of deceit and betrayal, desecration.

I found my wife's hand and gripped it. Her skin was dry and rough; I could feel all the bones beneath it. She stopped wailing and choked, then sobbed.

Then we were gathered up into the hands of the god. He set us back into our morning in our house on the west shore of the river. He did not speak to us, but left us there.

Mutnodjmet and I held each other. In the embrace, we felt as though we were still ourselves, but when I finally released her and we stared into each others' eyes, I saw that she was old, and her hair was white as it had never been in life, when we had recourse to our favorite wigs and all the powers of the dyers' arts.

"Horemheb," she whispered, staring at my left side below my ribs. She traced the incision the priests of Anubis had made to remove my inner parts. In all our life since death, that wound had been invisible; the priests had placed a wax plate incised with a *wadjet* eye over the cut, and made it go away.

I stroked her hair and studied her age in the lines of her face, the sag of her chin and breasts.

She smiled. Her beauty was still there.

Holding hands, we went into our house. All our treasures were gone: our games, our jewelry, our furniture, our servants.

On the back wall of the house, though, were the images I had had scribed onto the walls of my tomb: the loaves of bread that stood for a thousand loaves; the offering trays piled high with haunches of beef, plucked ducks, figs, grapes, lotus blossoms; stands with bottles of wine in them . . . there were our names, and there were our images, images of us doing things we loved.

I went to the wall and touched the image of bread, felt its crust come alive under my hand. I closed my fingers over it and pulled it from the wall.

I held a loaf of bread in my hand.

My wife touched it. She stared up at me.

I broke the loaf and handed half to her.

We ate.

The bread was not as fresh as that baked every morning by our *ushabtis*, nor even that the priests had left for us in the mortuary temple, but it was bread. It was sustenance.

My wife took figs from the wall and handed one to me. If it tasted a little dusty, still it was sweet.

Best of all, when we studied the wall after our meal, all the images were still there.

We had lost much, but we still had life.

We were old, but we grew no older.

The sun still shone on us; we still had the river, the desert, and each other. And so we lived, as day piled on day.

One day I woke and she was not there.

I knew before I opened my eyes. Her warmth, her breath, her presence, all aspects of her were gone.

I opened my eyes and discovered that *I* was gone.

Where I have gone, I do not know. The air tastes different, and the voices I hear speak in tongues I do not recognize. The world is cold. I am without the power of speech or movement; all my powers except those of perception have vanished. People I do not know touch me without my permission, and worse.

It comes to me after a short eternity in this place that they have violated what little of my soul is left.

My name is not here. My body no longer responds to me. My *akh* has fled, so that I cannot even approach the gods with a plea for help or mercy. The lights are brighter here than any I have seen before, so that my shadow is strong beneath me, but it cannot move unless someone moves me. My *ka* flickers. My *ba* has taken its outer shape: a human-headed bird, the form of exploration. It sits on my chest, staring into my face.

I see in my *ba*'s eyes that I no longer look like myself. When it can no longer recognize me, it will leave me and wander the earth, homeless for eternity.

Here comes the woman again, the one in a white tunic. She holds a knife in her hand. It is not the first time she has come to me with a knife.

My *ba*'s head lifts. It stretches one wing, then another.

As the woman leans forward and touches my side with the knife, my *ba* takes flight. It rises up through the vault of the ceiling and is gone.

The woman is the Devourer of Hearts.

I let my *ka* blow out.

Then I am flying, high above a city larger than any I have ever seen.

The world is so wide!

Who was I a moment ago?

It is gone. It is gone.

Below me sun gleams on the river. I fly south.

LET OUR PEOPLE GO

by Mickey Zucker Reichert

Mickey Zucker Reichert is a pediatrician whose fantasy and science fiction novels include *The Legend of Nightfall*, *The Bifrost Guardians* series, *The Last of the Renshai* trilogy, The *Renshai Chronicles* trilogy, *Flightless Falcon*, *The Beasts of Barakhai*, *The Lost Dragons of Barakhai*, and *The Unknown Soldier*, all available from DAW Books. Her short fiction has appeared in numerous anthologies, including *Assassin Fantastic*, *Knight Fantastic*, and *Vengeance Fantastic*. Her claims to fame: she *has* performed brain surgery, and her parents *really are* rocket scientists.

THE angular contraption of plastic and metal took up a quarter of Brody Williams' otherwise contemporary living room. To Jakob Binyamin, the matching couches, love seat, and chairs with their not-quite casually tossed blankets and pillows might grace the cover of *Better Homes & Gardens.* He turned to his partner, Khalil Abdel-Sahmar, only to find the squat Arab American studying a beautifully displayed collection of ceramic elephants.

Tall and wiry, Spc. Commander Williams got right to the point. "Koby, Khalil, you know why I called you here today?"

Jakob glanced at Khalil, who looked up from the elephants and shrugged.

"No idea, sir," Jakob said. He ran a hand through his short-cropped, sandy hair, the only nervous gesture he allowed himself to show. As volunteer operatives went, he doubted Brody Williams could have chosen any pair less experienced. Though a part of the team for more than three years, they had not yet gone on any mission, especially one involving the most significant and secret invention of the twenty-first century: the time portal.

Khalil stepped up beside his partner. Coarse-featured and swarthy with wiry black hair, he stood a good four inches shorter than Jakob's five foot eleven. "It has something to do with the wars in the Middle East, I'd wager."

Jakob nodded. It made sense. Though the special

volunteer operatives, the SVO, demonstrated a diversity as complex as America herself, no other team consisted of an Arab and a Jew, especially ones who worked so well together. When not on assignment, which was most of the time, they were neighbors who carpooled to the same job at the same advertising agency. Jakob finished the rest of the puzzle. "Don't tell me we're going back in time to stop the wars."

"Not exactly." Brody began to pace. "You guys haven't ever jumped, have you?"

It was not precisely true. "Only the standard training, sir," Khalil said. "Where they kill a bug, a mastodon, and a caveman to show that the future isn't so easily changed as sci-fi writers and the *Twilight Zone* would have us believe."

"Right." Brody's long legs carried him swiftly to the couch, and he turned to face his men again. "We've learned to travel back but not forward. We also know that, once lived, the past develops what we've called 'performance inertia.'"

Jakob remembered the comparison their drill sergeant had used. "It's like a person's weight. The body has a point set by genetics where it wants to be. Staying there is easy. Maintaining a lighter or heavier weight requires serious daily effort."

Khalil nodded again, living proof of the theory. A bit overweight, he had to diligently control his portions while Jakob ate freely of almost anything and managed to stay at a comfortable 160.

"That's right." Brody paced back toward them. "The

past tries to lock on a set outcome. Making permanent changes requires major interference. Even then, it's not unheard of for a later event to come along to balance the first. On the other hand, we can't travel to the future, but that's still malleable. So, ultimately, we want any effort we make not to affect now so much as the course of later events."

Khalil and Jakob focused on their leader, curious about their assignment. The SVO rarely got called up for anything. To decide to alter past events meant the president knew of a future catastrophe and had exhausted all of his diplomatic avenues. "What's about to happen?"

Brody lowered himself to the couch and studied the two men in front of him. "The Global Antislavery Act of 1964 freed those Jews who had not already escaped Egypt through the millennia. Unlike blacks in America, Jews in the Middle East never did assimilate into the Arabic societies."

Jakob shrugged. "Gotta expect some bitterness, and some prejudice, after more than 3500 years of slavery."

"Especially," Brody said carefully, "in societies entrenched a few hundred years behind the times." He glanced swiftly at Khalil. "No offense meant."

The Arab American smiled. "No offense taken. Don't mistake what I am. My mother is as American as apple pie and as Christian as you. They divorced when I was very young, and she raised me, so I'm not exactly a scholar of the Koran."

Jakob added, "And I'm a fourth-generation American with long roots in Europe. True, my family doesn't put up a 'Chanukah tree,' and I believe 'Jews for Jesus' is the ultimate oxymoron; but I know all the words to 'Silent Night' by heart, having heard it seventy million times over mall loudspeakers, and have eaten my share of ham and Swiss sandwiches."

"Got it." Brody gestured for the other men to sit. "You're not stellar examples of hyphenated Americans. But you can physically pass for Middle Easterners, and you understand the importance of stability in that region, which is enough for now."

Jakob shoved aside a pillow and sat on the love seat. Khalil perched on the edge of a chair, clearly concerned about dislodging any of the decorations.

"We and our allies are planning to re-create a Jewish state in the Middle East, to bring together a scattered people. It's a small piece of land, completely barren, without so much as a hint of oil. Nonetheless, the Arab countries have vehemently opposed it. Several have already massed nuclear and chemical weapons along the proposed border."

Jakob hid his shock with humor. "So, what I think you're saying, sir, is the Arabs aren't jumping for joy over this."

Brody ignored the joke. "It seems to me that, if we could emancipate the slaves at an earlier point in history—"

This time, Khalil interrupted, "Say, before the advent of weapons of mass destruction?"

"—and reestablish free Jews in a significant portion of the Middle East . . ."

Jakob finished excitedly, "We could get the Arabs and Jews to live in harmony there."

Khalil smiled.

Brody grunted. "Ideally. But, given the past's penchant to remain as it is, I think the best we can hope for is the successful establishment of a Jewish state in their homeland. And, if not mutual tolerance, at least enough balance of power that the Arabs can't just wipe out their new neighbors." The commander studied his two operatives, both nodding with thoughtful vigor. He continued, "There's a mention in the Bible, amidst all the begats, of a slave infant rescued from the Nile by the pharaoh's daughter. Supposedly, when he grows up, he discovers the secret of his past and leaves Egypt to become a simple shepherd and does some begetting of his own."

Not recalling that particular obscure verse, Jakob spoke carefully. "All right. So our mission is . . ."

"To overturn the simple life of this slave-born prince, and mold him into a savior."

Jakob stared over the vast plain of sand, scarcely daring to believe any land could look so barren. The sun beat down on his broad-brimmed hat, and he appreciated the SPF 40 sunscreen the commander had insisted they wear. Beside him, Khalil stared wide-eyed at the desolation, clearly as impressed by it as his companion. Both wore unadorned T-shirts and jeans shorts, and each carried a small pack of provisions, including a handheld device which allowed them to come and go at will. The SVO had promised them the full support of its labs, stores, and personnel, and Jakob found himself both appreciative and cowed. Apparently, someone foresaw desperate tragedies arising from the Middle East animosity; and it seemed nearly inconceivable that they would trust such an awesome mission to a couple of rookies. *Yet*, Jakob realized, *there aren't many experienced operatives when it comes to time travel, especially ones with Middle Eastern languages and ties.*

Of course, neither of them spoke the ancient dialects of 1628 B.C. either, but the inventor of the time portal had also come up with a solution to that dilemma. The gadget, which resembled a small recorder, could not translate any language into another; but it did neatly close the gap between ones of similar origin.

Khalil broke the awed silence first. "Are you sure we're in the right place?"

Jakob laughed. "I'm not even sure we're in the right century. It's all a guess when it comes to interpreting history that old chronicled as stories and sprinkled with folklore." He continued to study the landscape, watching heat haze rise like waves of rubber over the sand. "Let's head this way." He took a step, halted by Khalil's reply.

"Or that way."

Jakob looked at his companion, who pointed toward some blowing dust in the distance.

"That looks promising."

Jakob shrugged. One direction seemed as good as any other. "All right." He trotted after his companion, kicking up sprays of lightweight, tawny sand. Soon, scraggles of vegetation appeared amidst the vast plain of desert, and dunes interrupted its flat smoothness. They clambered up the side of one of these, gouging out hollows soon filled by shifting sand. At the crest, they looked down onto a placid valley. Sheep grazed the sun-withered plants, while an ancient shepherd dozed in the shade of an olive tree. He wore white linen wrapped around every part of him, and a soft hat shaded his head and neck.

"Ready?" Khalil asked.

Jakob nodded. If he had to face primitive men from Biblical times, he preferred ones who appeared old and docile. Together, they walked toward the man and his flock.

As Jakob drew nearer, he got a better view of the sleeping man. Sun had burned his face berry brown with deeply etched wrinkles. White hair flowed from beneath his hat to join with a mustache and beard tangled with sand. Age spots and calluses marred his hands. Jakob could not remember ever seeing someone who looked so old.

"Methuselah?" Khalil guessed.

Jakob smiled. "He could be in his forties. People didn't live as long back then."

"You mean back now." Khalil walked around the man, examining him from every angle. "I seem to recall reading about guys "begetting" in their hundreds and living four or five centuries."

"I'm eighty." The man's eyes opened, dark and shrewd, but tired. "It's customary in these parts to introduce oneself before making prying comments."

"They call me Koby," Jakob said. "And this is my friend, Khalil."

Now, it was the old man's turn to stare. He leaped to his feet, gaze wandering over their clothing in wonder. "Where . . . where . . . do you come from?"

"Uh, uh, uh." Khalil said in a singsong, not allowing the man to escape his own demand for manners. "Introductions first."

"My name," the old man said, never taking his eyes from the pair, "is Moses."

Khalil's eyes widened.

Jakob swallowed hard. "You? You're Moses?"

Cautiously, the old man nodded.

Khalil spoke from the side of his mouth. "Perhaps we should come back earlier."

Jakob silenced his companion with a wave. "Son of Amram and Yocheved?"

Moses stiffened, glancing swiftly between the two. "Those were the names of those who gave me life, yes. But I am no man's son, though once my father was Egypt's pharaoh."

"What?" Khalil said, brows furrowing.

"Shush," Jakob said. "Let me handle this." He addressed Moses again. "Didn't your mother fish you out of the river?"

"My sister," Moses corrected. "I was three months old when she rescued me from the Nile. My mother bore Pharaoh no sons, so they took me in, succored me, and raised me." He wrapped his hand around a gnarled staff leaning against the tree and clambered to his feet. "Why this interest in my childhood? Who are you two odd-looking strangers, and from where do you come?"

Khalil answered before Jakob could. "We're messengers of God."

"Which god?"

"*The* God." Khalil sneezed out a noseful of sand, looking affronted. "The one God. The God of Abraham, Isaac, and Jacob."

Moses nodded thoughtfully, "The Hebrew God."

"Yes, that one." Khalil sniffed, and his voice lost its grandeur. "The Hebrew God. *Your* God."

Moses turned away. "I'm an Egyptian, not a Hebrew."

Damn it, why didn't Khalil just say Horus. Even as the thought arose, Jakob understood his companion's motive. It did no good to work Moses onto the throne if he simply carried on the ways of the Egyptians. He needed to free the slaves, to rule as a Jew. "You are a Hebrew," Jakob corrected. "And an Egyptian. And God wants you to free and lead his Chosen."

Moses slid down his staff to a sitting position, clearly stunned silent.

Jakob and Khalil exchanged glances.

"Wh—" Moses finally managed. "Why me? How

can I understand the burden of slavery when I've never suffered it? How can I speak for a God I've never learned to believe in, a people who do not know me? I'm just an old shepherd. I . . ."

Jakob raised a hand to stem the tide of self-deprecation.

Khalil made a gesture to indicate that the man did have an undeniable point. "Hey," he said suddenly. "If you were the pharaoh's only son, shouldn't you have inherited the throne?"

Moses turned his deer-in-the-headlights look directly on Khalil. "Who are you that you don't know? The succession of Egypt passes through the eldest daughter. The man she marries becomes the next pharaoh."

"Really?" Khalil spoke their surprise aloud. It seemed odd to discover anything matrilineal from this long ago.

"It's the only way to assure the divine bloodline, which I could not have done in any case."

Having recently seen *The Mummy*, Jakob could understand the reasoning. In it, a pharaoh's mistress had an affair with his high priest. The only sure and certain bloodlines did necessarily have to come through the mother. "So, the current pharaoh is your sister's husband?"

Moses nodded. "Late sister. All those who knew and loved me have died. She did bear a son, my nephew, whom I've never met."

"Why?" Khalil demanded. "Why would anyone leave the life of a king's son?"

Moses closed his eyes. "It's not something I like to remember." He shook his head, berating his own stupidity. "When I became a young man, I asked about my circumcision, and my mother told me my story." He clapped his hands over his face. "I didn't want to believe it. Born one of . . . them. Then, I started noticing how we treated the Hebrews, how I had scarcely thought of them before. One day, I found a taskmaster whipping a man my age. I saw myself in the battered man's place, and I couldn't help myself. I killed the master, a crime punishable by death. Others saw what I did. I had no choice but to flee, to exile myself forever."

Suddenly, Jakob saw the significance of Moses' age. All those who might remember him, who might inflict punishment for his crime had died.

Khalil dumped sand from his running shoe. "And you never went back?"

"Never." Moses wept into his palms. "One by one, my family died, and I never returned to say good-bye, to comfort the survivors."

Several moments passed in awkward silence before Moses regained control. "I might have been able to help the slaves once. If I had appealed to my father rather than killing in a fit of rage . . . I—I might have freed them or, at least, eased their burdens." He wiped his eyes and leaned upon his staff again. "I was my parents' beloved son, in a unique position to dispel the suffering of others. They knew and loved me as a normal man in a way they never did the slaves. I could have used my origins to make them view the Hebrews differently, to see them as men and women rather than dangerous chattel and rivals. I could have been one of them—" His fists clenched, blanching around the staff. "I might have saved them. Instead, I did something brash and stupid. I ruined several lives and condemned many more to a lifetime of slavery." He rose again. "I'm not worthy of the attention of any god."

"Well, God thinks otherwise, and He's never wrong."

"I would feel better," Moses proclaimed, "if I heard it from Him."

Back on the other side, Khalil and Jakob relaxed in Brody Williams' living room with iced teas and their feet propped on the coffee table.

Khalil ran a finger through the condensation. "The way I see it, we need to go back to an earlier time, before Moses does . . . what he does . . . to mess things up."

Jakob shook his head. "Don't you see? First, that would require a whole new and expensive jump, not just a simple return. Plus, we can always do that if our later stuff fails. It's easier to go farther back in time to prevent something you muffed than to screw things up from the get go."

Khalil flicked sand from a fold in his shirt. "You sure about that?"

Jakob had no more experience than Khalil, just a

greater interest in the working details of the time portal. "Let's say we jump all the way back to before Moses kills that slaver and try to influence him when he's an adolescent. If we fail, we then have to deal with the effect our words have had on him and what he might have told others. He may seem willing enough at eighty to do things differently, but he's got sixty plus years of maturity and hindsight on him that he won't have at eighteen. If we work backward and fail, we can always jump farther into the past and get a whole new clean slate."

Khalil grunted out a grudging, "Maybe." He changed the subject. "So, how are we going to get the voice of God to Moses?"

Jakob had considered that very issue all that night. "A microphone and a speaker?"

"Duh." Khalil tipped backward in his seat. "But how are you going to get Moses to just the right place? God wouldn't miss when it comes to where he puts his voice." He sat up suddenly. "We need to focus his attention. And I've got just the thing."

Jakob had gathered a few toys of his own. "If you're going to play God, you can't be too prepared."

The open desert provided little cover, but Khalil managed to find a place hidden from the grazing valley by a dune. Jakob perched on top to serve as his partner's eyes. "He's coming," he announced into a palm-sized walkie-talkie.

"10-4," Khalil gave back, readying the microphone.

Jakob surveyed their handiwork. Not far from the tree where Moses had rested stood a plastic, battery-powered fireplace log, burning in holographic flickers of scarlet, orange, and amber.

Moses stopped, the sheep milling around him, and stared at a decoration Khalil usually reserved for Christmas.

The half-Arab's disguised voice boomed over the microphone. "Moses! Moses! Here I am!"

Moses went utterly still.

Jakob whispered into the radio. "You got his attention."

"Good." Not a hint of their exchange carried over the microphone. "What's he doing now?"

Jakob detailed Moses' actions. "He's just standing there. Oh, now he's heading toward the artificial fireplace." Worried the lack of heat might expose them, he added, "Probably shouldn't let him get too close."

"Stop!" Khalil's voice boomed. "Come no nearer! And take off your shoes, for goodness sake; you're standing on holy ground."

"Nice touch," Jakob whispered into the radio as he watched Moses scurry to remove his sandals.

"He buying it?" Khalil whispered back carefully, so as not to cross conversations.

"Hook, line, and sinker. He's got his shoes off, and he's just staring like a cat at a tuna."

"What . . . who . . . are you?" Moses continued to stare.

"I am the Lord," Khalil boomed. "The God of your

fathers. The God of Abraham, the God of Isaac, and the God of Jacob."

"How . . . ?" Moses began and stopped, averting his eyes from the artificial fireplace. "Why . . . ?"

"He wants to know why," Jakob said.

"Why what?"

"You are God. You figure it out."

"Very funny." Khalil returned to the microphone. "I have seen the suffering of my people in Egypt, have heard how the taskmasters hurt them, and I have come down to deliver them from bondage by sending you to pharaoh."

"Me?" Moses squeaked. "I'm eighty years old, feeble, and have never known the whip." He added, barely loud enough for Jakob to discern. "And when I get nervous, I tend to stutter."

The walkie-talkie buzzed. "What did he say?" asked Khalil.

"He wants to know why you picked him. And he says he stutters."

"Just frickin' great." Khalil went back to the microphone. "Don't be questioning the judgment of the Lord!"

Moses dropped to his knees, head bowed.

Jakob described the scene. "He's kowtowing, Khalil."

Khalil shouted. "Get up, Moses. Worshipers of false gods kneel. My followers stand proud."

Jakob nodded, impressed. "Very nice."

Moses scrambled to his bare feet. "Sorry, God. I just . . . I just . . ."

Khalil returned to the original question. "Don't fret, Moses. My servants, Khalil and Koby, will assist you. I will be with you, too, though you won't be able to see me."

Moses stood tall, barely leaning upon his staff. "When I tell the Hebrews that you have sent me and they ask your name, what should I tell them?"

Taken aback, Jakob asked over the walkie-talkie, "Did you get that?"

"I got it," Khalil muttered, clearly vexed. "Tell them: I am . . . what I am."

Jakob could scarcely believe it. "You're quoting Popeye?"

"Shut up! You try sounding divine when you can't even see the guy you're talking to." Khalil shifted uneasily, then his voice boomed out again, "Just call me the Lord God. That will do."

"The pharaoh is a stubborn man," Moses proclaimed. "I do not believe anything anyone says will get him to let your people go."

"*Your* people, Moses."

"But I wasn't—"

Khalil anticipated the question. "You are by blood and now by faith. Go. Go to pharaoh and ask."

"He will not listen."

"Then I will smite him and his people until he does. Go. Go, Moses. Go prepare yourself for pharaoh."

With a last look at the smoldering logs, Moses went. Jakob slid down the slope toward Khalil. "Exactly how much 'smiting' do you plan to do, your godliness?"

Khalil answered with a somber face. "As much as it takes."

While Moses got his affairs in order, Khalil and Jakob returned to Brody Williams' living room to discuss details with their commander.

Jakob sat on the couch, legs stretched in front of him and crossed at the ankles. "How many miraculous displays do you think it'll take, sir?"

"One or two, at the most." Brody paced between the furniture, his long legs striding across the carpet. "But we need to prepare for a dozen or so, each one more horrific than the last."

Jakob glanced at Khalil, who returned his stare with alarm. "Horrific in what way?"

"I'm thinking," Khalil said, "we could start with a few simple tricks. Say a remote control car."

Brody stopped in mid-pace and laughed. "Good idea. But they won't know what to make of a Pontiac. A remote control snake would work better. They had a healthy respect in those parts for cobras."

"Still do," Jakob said. "At least I know I do. And we don't even have them here."

Khalil piped in, "I've got a cousin who stocks fish hatcheries. There's one big type of fish that eats frogs. Once a year, he throws in this red powder. Stinks to high heaven and makes the water look like blood, but the fish love it. Within a few days, he's got a lakeful of tadpoles. In a few weeks, there're frogs hopping every-where."

Brody stroked his chin. "That sounds promising." He resumed his pacing. "The lab says to start vaccinating now. Get the Jews and whatever few herds belong to them, and then loose a couple of diseases. One takes out the Egyptians' animals, but the shots protect the Jewish ones. Bingo! Looks like divine targeting."

Jakob looked ahead, horrified. "You're not going to give those people plague or something. Are you?"

Brody paced back toward his men. "I was thinking more along the lines of chicken pox. Itchy. Leaves bumps, open sores, maybe a few scars; but it's rarely fatal. Protection only requires one shot, and it works pretty quickly."

Khalil nodded, finally getting into the spirit. "I'm thinking bugs. Japanese beetles reduced my garden to Swiss cheese last summer."

"*Japanese* beetles made it into *Swiss* cheese?" Jakob could not resist. "What did you plant? *French* fries, *Belgian* waffles, *Brazil* nuts, and *Turkish* taffy?"

Even the boss chimed in. "Next year, you ought to police the garden with *Siamese* cats while you play *Chinese* checkers."

"And plant them in a *Grecian* urn," Jakob added.

"Ha, ha, ha." Khalil stopped the game with sarcasm. "I still think my point's valid."

"How about lice, mosquitoes, and locusts?" Brody suggested, demonstrating that he did, indeed, catch and care about Khalil's point. "The bio lab can bring in plenty of those. We can apply delousers and repellents to the Jews. They don't own any land, so the crops the locusts destroy won't affect them directly, and we can supplement their food supplies."

"How about weather?" Jakob suggested, slightly jealous that Khalil had so easily come up with a bunch of usable ideas.

Brody made a dismissive gesture, his features crinkled in thought. "Not much we can do in that vein, as much as we'd love to make floods and droughts a thing of the past."

Khalil leaned forward. "Not to mention guarantee eternally sunny Super Bowl Sundays."

Brody sat, turning thoughtful. "I suppose if we timed things around the weather, we could take responsibility for some whopper of a storm."

Khalil's coarse features creased. "They've lived through plenty of storms. They know they happen naturally. Unless we get hold of some prehistoric weather report so Moses could predict something that came up at a weird time without warning, I don't think that would work."

So much mythology arose from attempts to explain weather that Jakob could not let it go. "An airdrop of thousands of golf balls on a rainy day might simulate some pretty godlike hail."

Brody bobbed his head. "Could be workable."

Taking his cue from Khalil's words, Jakob added, "The Connecticut Yankee managed to use an eclipse to his advantage. Maybe we could do something like that."

"Maybe we could do something *exactly* like that." Brody leaped to his feet with clear excitement. "A phenomenon like that can actually be dated pretty precisely."

"We might only get a few hours of sun or moon blot," Jakob continued. "To primitives, if forewarned in a regal-enough voice, that'll seem like a few days."

"Great," Brody said. "I'll get our men busy preparing. You get back there and deal with Moses. Sort Egyptians from Jews and start the vaccination program."

The remote-control snake and the nine plagues went off with barely a hitch, yet the Children of Israel remained slaves in Egypt. Each time, the pharaoh agreed to free them; and, each time, he revoked his word as the Hebrews prepared and the effect of the last affliction faded. Hearts heavy, Khalil and Jakob returned to their commander to report their latest failure.

Brody took the news in stride. As before, he paced the confines of his living room like a trapped animal, stroking his chin and muttering epithets. "That goddamned pharaoh is a rock."

"A fool, sir," Jakob corrected. "Goddamned, indeed, and too hardheaded to consider the well-being of his own people."

Brody sucked in a deep breath, and his eyes narrowed to slits. "It'll become a common attitude, I'm afraid. Men so entrenched in a warped belief, so fanatically emphatic that they would kill themselves and their loved ones for no better cause than hurting those of different faiths."

Jakob's gut clenched. Though he knew they could not yet perform future travel, perhaps not ever, Brody knew something they did not. "What happened while we were gone?"

Khalil held up a newspaper that Jakob had not noticed amid the papers on Brody's coffee table. It showed a picture of shattered buildings awash in flames, a massive crater, and a hovering mushroom cloud. "Crazed terrorists with some weird, warped version of Islam killed thousands of civilians. With nukes." He shook the paper. "That, my friend, is what remains of D.C."

"Oh, my God!" Shocked, Jakob found himself incapable of coherent speech, of even daring to believe. Months in ancient Egypt seemed less surreal than a newspaper in his own time. "How . . . ? Why . . . ? Really?" Unable to complete a sentence, he stopped and restarted. "Did . . . ?" His throat went painfully dry. "Did our meddling . . . cause that?"

"No." Brody put his hand over Khalil's, pushing the newspaper back to the table before they could read any more. "Your lack of success did. Though we didn't expect it quite this soon, this brutal, or in this manner, we all knew this was coming."

Khalil's glazed eyes remained on the paper, though

he did not touch it again. "I still don't understand the connection."

"Clearly," Brody explained, "we're not going to get Moses on the throne of Egypt. But, if we can manage a Jewish exodus, the very early establishment of a Jewish homeland, we might still create a long-term alliance. Jews and Arabs intermingling, even intermarrying. Maybe, just maybe, they can become allies or even an inseparable people. At worst, it would give the Arab world a reason to fight and quarrel, to remain long undeveloped, to focus on something other than modern weaponry and the destruction of those of different faiths."

Khalil pounded his fist on the table, and his tone became defensive. "The Arabs didn't do this. Just a radical fringe of lunatics."

"True," Brody assented. "Which is why we're only looking to cripple, not destroy, Egypt and why we're not targeting all of the Arab countries. That fringe was born of hatred, of raising entire generations to despise Jews, to find glory in killing them. It doesn't take much to turn *your* fanatics into *their* fanatics, to redirect those born into hate, murder, and martyrdom to targets their trainers did not anticipate. You can't ignite and fuel a bonfire of prejudice and expect to control it. When children know nothing but violence and loathing, they resort to it over the slightest perceived offense."

Jakob's heart ached. He couldn't get past what he

had seen on that newspaper. "But if the pharaoh won't release the Jews . . ."

"He will," Brody assured. "We just have to find the right incentive."

Together with Moses in the Hebrew quarter, Jakob chewed his lower lip and fought an angry tingle of guilt. His gaze played over the mud-brick houses, quiet for the night, their doors smeared with lamb's blood. Though trained assassins, not he and Khalil, had performed the terrible deed, he still dreaded the agony that would come to light with the rising sun.

For the moment, Jakob savored the clean air, the burble of the Nile, and the hum of night insects. He watched the sky turn pink, then throw radiating bands of blue and gold through the clouds. Gradually, the first edge of sun peeked over the horizon and, with it, the first screams of horror rose from the Egyptian quarters. More joined the first, then a relentless, sustained moan of anguish as they found their firstborn sons slain in their beds.

Khalil took Jakob's hand. "It's over."

Jakob nodded, knowing it was true. Even the pharaoh's own son, Moses' nephew, had not been spared; and, now, Egypt's king moved like a suffering shadow through the darkness. They watched him come, his steps measured and leaden, then stop in front of them. His dark eyes had lost all defiance, and he cast his gaze at Moses' feet. "Why . . . ?" he asked, his voice hoarse and raw with pain. "Why . . . ?"

"I'm sorry," Moses replied, his own eyes steadily trained and unwavering on the pharaoh's face. "I truly am. But *you* brought God's wrath upon yourself."

The pharaoh finally looked up, little resembling the hostile, angry giant who had weathered nine plagues and not conceded. "Take your people. Take all of them, their miserable animals, their miserable things, their miserable, terrible God, and go. Go now. I will not change my mind again." Turning, he shuffled back toward the palace.

Jakob forced himself to numbness. He dared not consider his own son, Mordecai, tucked safely in his bed. Who knew what changes their interference might have wrought on the future, who might now live and who might die, whether his own hand might have negated even his own existence. For now, he just shared the pain of a weak and weary pharaoh fighting a self-ish war he could never hope to win. The man had lost his son to keep others' sons in bondage, only to lose those slaves as well.

Jakob had not noticed the crowd of Hebrews gathering behind him until their cheers rose to the heavens. Hurriedly, they packed their meager belongings for the tenth time, harnessing their remaining beasts to crude carts, hefting their children, and began the trek toward freedom.

Walking grimly near Moses at the head of the exodus, Khalil gave Jakob a weary high five. "We did it."

"We did it," Jakob agreed, "but at what cost?" He doubted anything they did could exacerbate the situation they had learned about through Brody's newspaper, but he could not be certain. He knew better than to claim things could not get worse. The last time he had said that was during a January blizzard. He was slamming down the driveway to buy antibiotics for his sick daughter and ran over her dog.

Khalil spoke the words Jakob had avoided. "The cost cannot be any higher than the one we would have paid for failure." He joined the exodus, and Jakob walked along beside him.

Jakob cringed, despising his superstitiousness. He wanted to knock on wood, to undo the bad karma Khalil's words might have wrought. "It can *always* get worse."

Khalil stepped in front of Jakob, forcing him to stop. He seized his partner's shoulders as the Children of Israel broke ranks around them. "Listen, Koby. There's something Brody didn't tell us that you should probably know."

Jakob's heart fluttered like a captured butterfly, and he felt cold prickles of dread travel through him. "What?"

Khalil's dark eyes, usually soft and friendly, held ice. "We were taught that we can't access the future."

"Right . . ." Jakob had not expected Khalil to take off in that direction.

"Which means that, no matter how long we spend here, we'll come back to the future exactly where we left it."

"Right . . ." Jakob repeated, trying to anticipate. His eyes widened. "Are you saying the nuclear attack hap-

pened the same day we left? That we altered history so
that—"

Khalil shook his head in clear frustration. "Just listen. The date on that newspaper was April 23, 2001,
two days *after* we left."

This time, Jakob resisted the urge to guess what his
partner planned to say.

"Which means, they found a way to view the *near*
future, at least. Which means, they probably knew what
was coming when they sent us, which is probably why
they sent us, and . . ." Khalil paused, this time clearly
expecting a thoughtful interruption from Jakob.

But, shocked beyond speaking, Jakob said nothing.

Khalil's gaze never left Jakob's face. "I read enough
of that article to know retribution does occur. I think,
my friend, our true mission is to prevent *the very apoca-
lypse, the very end of the world and everyone in it.*"

Jakob could not find his tongue.

"There truly is nothing worse."

Jakob simply stared.

"Do you understand what I'm saying?"

Jakob's eyes felt as if they might explode. He forced
a dumb nod, then finally managed. "I understand."
But he didn't. Didn't understand how people could
hate with every fiber of their being, could dare to believe that God Almighty sanctioned their hatred and
their murder, that He hated right along with them.

"Now do you believe me when I say it can't get any
worse?"

"Yes," Jakob whispered. "I do understand that." He

blocked his thoughts, not wanting to move beyond the shock, beyond the denial. To do so meant considering the horrible, rending deaths of his loving wife, his parents, his children. Their mission must not fail. And he understood one thing more, why Brody had chosen them. "Do you suppose all the more experienced operatives got killed before they sent us?"

"No," Khalil said. "I think they're on other missions."

Jakob swallowed harder, recognizing the truth. If they had seen a future newspaper, it meant all of the efforts in the present had failed. It meant the lives of every person on Earth hinged on two rookies and an eighty-year-old man. He turned his attention to the tide of people flowing around them. Freeing himself from Khalil's grip, he followed the escaping slaves. "Let's go."

Khalil followed.

Jakob hummed the theme from *The Rockford Files*, examining every rock and tree, trying to focus on everything except what Khalil had told him. The more experienced operatives had probably known about the SVO's ability to look into the near future. He wondered if that information had paralyzed them or compromised their ability to assist and appreciated Khalil waiting until freedom seemed imminent to tell him. He only hoped the plan would work.

For a long time, the Children of Israel dragged themselves wearily through desert buoyed by the realization of an all but impossible freedom. Then, the sound of hoofbeats filled the air, and the ground thundered. The parade of the Hebrew exodus stopped. A great cry rose from the back and worked its way forward in a frantic wave. "Pharaoh and his men are coming!"

"Run!" Jakob shouted, charging toward the front of the column. "For God's sake, run!" *No! No! No! Not this! Anything but this!* "Run!"

In a wave, the Children of Israel obeyed, abandoning the heaviest of their carts, snapping up children. They chased after Moses in a wash of desperation and tears, laments and howls of angry frustration.

As Jakob sprinted, exhorting the people to quicken their pace, he heard a sound that came gradually to consciousness, the crash of tide on shore. Catching up to Moses, he stopped beside the leader who stood staring into the vast Red Sea.

A man beside him muttered wildly, "Nowhere to go. Trapped like rats."

"No! No!" Jakob screamed to the heavens. "No! Not this close!"

Moses alone stood stalwart, seemingly oblivious to the tumult around him. "The Lord God," he said firmly, "is with us, though we cannot see him." Raising his staff, he jabbed it at the frothing sea.

Jakob sank to his haunches, screwing his eyes shut, overwhelmed by hopelessness. *It's over.* It seemed better to die with the Hebrews than suffer the fate that the future held for him.

A hush fell over the Children of Israel, then a collective gasp rang through Jakob's hearing. He opened his eyes. At the site of Moses' staff, the waters drew back like live things. A rift grew steadily wider, surrounded by wild, white-capped pillars of water. Up, up they rose, mountains of swirling water held at bay by some force beyond even Jakob's understanding. As foolish as it seemed to wander between opposing tidal waves, he never hesitated. At Moses' side, he rushed onto the unnatural pathway left by the receding waters.

The others followed: men and women half-dragging weary animals, children racing hopefully into the spray, elders and cripples limping at the back. Khalil remained behind, watching the Egyptians close the gap between them, bravely herding the slowest stragglers into the breach. Safe on the far bank, Jakob waited and prayed for his companion, wondering what incredible device had allowed his partner to accomplish such a thing as this. The pillars of water remained, frozen in place, while the last of the Hebrews, flanked by Khalil, rushed through.

The Egyptian charioteers swiftly closed the gap, the trailing lame no match for their fleet-footed horses. The animals plunged into the spray, some whickering nervously, others balking and dancing wildly. The Egyptians whipped them onward, a few feet, then spare inches, from Khalil's back. Several raised spears.

"No!" Jakob yelled again, lunging toward his friend. Khalil's foot had nearly hit the bank when the pillars of water collapsed into thunderous cascades. Though driven to flee, nearly overwhelmed by panic, Jakob thrust his hands into the water where he had last seen Khalil. The force of the collapsing ocean hurled him to the ground. Spray bombarded his face like rocks, bruising flesh where it touched, but his hands closed around something firm. He yanked with all his strength, stumbling backward. Khalil sagged onto shore as the air filled with the savage screams of the Egyptian charioteers. The waters crashed and foamed, at first churning with bodies, then, only moments later, as clear and settled as if the parting had never occurred.

Jakob rolled over his friend. His limbs flopped like a rag doll's. Bracken clotted his dark wiry hair, and his eyes lay closed. "Khalil. Khalil, please. Wake up." Jakob shook the limp body, slapping the still cheeks. "You can't die on me, damn it. You can't. Khalil! Wake the hell up!"

A trickle of water dribbled from Khalil's lips.

Vision blurred by rising tears, Jakob sank to the ground beside him. "Khalil," he whispered, kneeling beside the body. "You're the best partner a guy could ever have. Ever. Please! Please, don't give up on me."

Jakob shook Khalil, trying to remember his CPR training through a fog of grief and abject shock. *In a moment, I'm going to wake up. This is all a bad nightmare. None of this could possibly be real.* One thought managed to wriggle through the morass, "How'd you do it, buddy? How in hell did you make *that* happen?"

A spasm of coughing racked Khalil suddenly, but he still managed to ask thinly, "Make what happen?"

Jakob laughed and let out a joyous whoop. At last,

his luck had begun to change, luck that hinged the fate of the world. "That!" He jabbed a finger toward the Red Sea, now back to its calm normalcy. "How did you make it . . . open up like that?"

Khalil sat up, still hacking. "I thought," he said between coughs. "You . . . did . . . that."

They stared at one another for several moments before Jakob helped Khalil to his feet. "You don't think . . . ?"

Khalil turned his gaze heavenward. "You never know, do you? You just never know."

In the week after his return, Jakob discovered a number of historical changes that the rest of the world would never know had once been different. After forty years of wandering, the Jews settled their homeland in Israel, where they lived for nearly two thousand years. Dispersed by pagan Romans in the first century AD, they remained scattered through the Middle East, in harmony with the religions that rose in their footsteps: Christianity and Islam. Then, in the 1940s, a villain named Hitler killed some six million who had settled in Europe. Though Jakob mourned their loss, and hated the Holocaust that took them, he realized that no one he had known before his jump had disappeared. That disgusting addition to history had served as a means to counterbalance some of what he and his partner had done, ending those bloodlines that existed only because he had prevented their deaths at the hands of taskmasters and pharaohs' decrees. The Jews officially got their country back in 1948; and, though their Arab neighbors balked then, the bickering between themselves and the lack of technology rescued the world from the devastation that might have otherwise occurred.

Jakob noticed other changes. His name had become Jacob Benjamin, his son Michael, not Mordecai, a generation anglicized by prejudice. The warring in the Middle East continued, pitting Arab against Arab and Arab against Jew. Terrorists threatened the stability of any country that did not bow to their whims. The Ten Commandments which operatives had chiseled and given to Moses found convoluted interpretations that somehow got around its remarkably simple words: Thou shalt not kill.

Yet, as Jacob sat down with his family to eat unleavened bread and foods deemed Kosher for the dwindling days of Passover 2001, he knew Khalil joined his own family in an Easter celebration. Neither holiday had existed before their jump. They had not created peace on Earth, but they had helped it dodge utter destruction. They had not driven out evil from the Middle East, but they had brought celebrations of family to Jews, Christians, and Moslems living in harmony in a myriad places.

For now, to Jacob Benjamin, that seemed enough.

TO SEE BEYOND DARKNESS

by Bill McCay

Bill McCay offers a story with a young feline hero, perhaps a holdover from his days writing young adult adventures (including those of Young Indiana Jones). He does keep trying to grow up, and his five novels continuing the story of the movie *Stargate* were well-received by adult fans (not to mention providing a crash course in ancient Egyptian lore). Bill's *Star Trek* novel (*Chains of Command*, coauthored with Eloise Flood) spent several weeks on *The New York Times* Paperback Bestseller List. "To See Beyond Darkness" is his third story about cats dealing with things which, for humans, are Unseen. The other stories appear in *A Constellation of Cats* and *Familiars*.

*O*NE *year earlier, in the hills of Judea* . . .
The ancient was toothless, her eyes blind—to the physical world. But she was full of more than just the motherwisdom passed down from generation to generation. The local cat-kindred valued her wisdom so highly, they fed her part of their kills, even chewing for her.

Crouched before her, the young one felt more like a kit facing a pair of eyes like clouded crystals. His tawny fur stood on end under the uncanny regard of those blind eyes. *You will travel far to meet your fate*, the Wise One told him. *All the way to Per-Bastet, where cats are worshiped as gods* . . .

Setting off on its strange funerary mission, Pharaoh's barge was just sliding loose of the Tanis docks when the last, unexpected, passenger leaped aboard. Like a tawny arrow, the cat launched himself from the wharf to land beside one of the oarlocks.

He teetered on the gilded wood, on the verge of tumbling into the Nile. When an oarsman reached to steady him, he got a snarl and a swipe of claws across his open hand. The movement overbalanced the cat in the other direction, leaving the animal ingloriously sprawled on the deck.

An instant later, the cat was on his feet, marching away, his arched, erect tail silently announcing, "I planned to do that."

The crewmen directed their eyes to the deck as Pharaoh strode from his canopied seat in the vessel's midsection. He looked down at the cat, eyebrows raised—or rather, the god-king raised the space where his eyebrows would have been. They were shaved in mourning, as was traditional for a household that had lost a cat. Another tradition had prompted this voyage, transporting the mummified remains of the royal pet to Per-Bastet for interment in the vast feline cemeteries surrounding the temple grounds.

Apparently unconscious of his audience, the cat curled up on the deck and began washing himself. "Valiant as . . . Miysis," Pharaoh murmured. The cat stopped, gazing up at the human standing over him. "Would you consider that an appropriate name?" Pharaoh asked. Then, shaking his head, he returned to his shaded seat.

A moment later, he had a tawny shadow following him.

The crewmen exchanged sidelong grins. Naming the cat after the lion-god had broken the pharaoh's long, worrying silence.

" 'Lord of the Slaughter' indeed," muttered the crewman who'd drawn the cat's ire, ruefully regarding the four bloody stripes across his hand.

The green delta countryside rolled slowly past as the crew rowed against the current. Arranging himself comfortably under the inlaid wood seat, the cat tasted the new name in his mind. Miysis, the tall two-leg had called him, feeding him from his own hands. Miysis was a name known to the motherwisdom of the cat-kindred. He was supposed to be the son of the cat goddess Bast, renowned for his courage. A good name for a human to choose.

Still better, Miysis had discovered this vessel was actually bound for Per-Bastet, the House of Bast. His new two-leg friend must have serious business there. Surely, he was an important human. Like a cat, he sat in the shade while the others labored.

Miysis would have found all around him satisfactory, except for the small casket on the other side of the chair—and for the cloud of sorrow surrounding the human seated above.

The wood-and-bronze box was decorated with a stylized feline face and tightly sealed. Even so, Miysis could scent natron, spices . . . and death. Cat-death.

Miysis directed a long, steady look at the chair bottom above his head. So. This human must be bringing a cat-companion to the burial fields of Per-Bastet. Miysis had heard of these during his travels. Truly, the humans in the land of Nsr treated his kind with reverence. How would it be in Per-Bastet? Miysis wondered. Was it his fate to be treated as a god?

He rose to his feet in a single flowing motion and began rubbing round the legs of the chair to mark them as his. For good measure, he also marked the human legs.

The man seated in the chair reached down to pull Miysis into his lap. Cat and human regarded one another for a moment.

Miysis reached up, one paw on the beaten-gold

necklace stretching across Pharaoh's chest, the other paw reaching for that tantalizing growth on the human's chin.

The batting blow dislodged the false beard, sending it askew—and tumbling Miysis into the human's lap. Too late, the cat recalled innumerable maternal scoldings on his overreaching nature. Instead of the expected human explosion, however, he heard laughter.

For a second, the dark eyes above him brightened, and Miysis felt pleasure. Perhaps it would only be for as long as the voyage lasted, but Miysis would do his best to clear the darkness from this man.

Not easy to do. Pharaoh shifted, and his sandaled foot touched the casket beside the chair. Sadness returned. Pharaoh was quiet as he restored the false beard to its proper place. But a practiced hand scratched the top of Miysis' head.

Slitting his eyes, Miysis pushed back against the hand. Yes. Throughout this trip, he would seek out the small brightnesses that lightened human moods, and dispel the baneful darknesses that attacked the human spirit. It always astonished Miysis that humans were unaware of these impalpable beings, but he'd seen their blindness often enough. Didn't these humans honor the cat-kindred as Those Who See Beyond Darkness?

In spite of his intention, Miysis found few shadows to hunt during the journey to Per-Bastet. Did the Banes not venture upon the water? This was Miysis' first prolonged trip by boat. He'd made his way mostly by foot at night along the edges of fields or through the desert.

Sometimes he'd had luck with caravans. Riding in a pannier on the back of an ass had not been a pleasant experience. He'd much more enjoyed traveling with the boy who'd carried him in a basket. And there had been a rich merchant's daughter in a palanquin . . .

Banes or not, Miysis did his best to divert the human through the long hours of rowing against the Nile current. Sometimes he succeeded.

When the barge arrived at the Per-Bastet docks, the crewmen put down their oars and took up spears to form the guard of honor as Pharaoh picked up the small mummy case. Miysis watched the proceedings critically. The motherwisdom spoke of much more impressive Per-Bastet processions. But times were hard in the land of Nsr. And anyway, he wouldn't be participating.

He deftly avoided the arms of the man delegated to take him up, leaping to the dock and then running for the streets. The crewman scrambled up after the escapee, even coming down the wharf before his way was blocked by townsfolk. A dangerous thing to go after a cat in Bast's city. Sometimes even fatal.

With a shrug, he returned to the jeering ranks of his comrades.

Miysis slowed his pace as he reached the marketplace. He glanced over his shoulder to make sure the crewman had given up. Then, with a flirt of his tail, he sauntered over to a town cat he'd spotted.

The other sat curled in a patch of awning shade by a

pile of fruit. *What did you look for, brother?* the town cat asked.

One who pursued me, Miysis replied, *but did not catch me.*

The other spat, back arched and fur bristling. *They dare to attempt it even by daylight!*

Attempt what? Miysis asked. *It was only a sailor from the ship I rode—*

You're newly arrived, then? the town cat said. *Beware the night, brother!*

The other had calmed, but his tail still flicked nervously. Without another word, he swung round and darted off.

Miysis didn't follow. Instead he wandered the market and the streets of the city. To tell the truth, he'd seen bigger towns farther east in the delta. Even some of the ruins which were now quarried for the stone in their buildings were more expansive—another sign of hard times for the land. That didn't matter. Miysis was busy searching out his fate. Certainly, he couldn't complain about his treatment. Passersby made way for him, and merchants fed him delicacies. It was pleasant, and yet . . .

Was this what it meant to be as a god? Miysis wondered. The tales he'd heard of Per-Bastet hadn't been clear about how cats were actually treated. There seemed to be a jarring note in all the deference he received. The humans seemed almost desperately seeking assurance as they catered to him.

As he looked around, Miysis realized he didn't see other cat-kindred.

More strangely, he spotted neither the shadows of the Banes nor the brightness of passing Benigns. As evening came on, he'd begun actively searching for them. The absence of the impalpable ones on the river might be possible. But Miysis had never encountered a place—especially a city—devoid of these beings.

Yet he found nothing—or rather, *saw* nothing.

Miysis' whiskers twitched, he stood with his mouth open, but all he detected was . . . wrongness. His senses seemed blunted, somehow.

Full darkness came as the cat ranged the city in growing disquiet. Miysis' eyes were as keen as ever against the nighttime shadows. But he found himself blind to that world the humans called the Unseen. A dullness seemed to press on his brain when he tried to pierce the veil.

Was this how the humans spent their days? His muzzle wrinkled as if he'd encountered a bad smell. Awful!

Miysis continued to cast about. The pressure seemed to ease when he went in some directions, then increased when he went in others.

He forced himself to push on to the center of the psychic blindness. It was a temple complex surrounded by a grove of trees.

The temple of Bast.

Miysis stood in the darkness beneath the trees, concentrating so hard against the psychic blindness that his normal senses didn't detect the figure coming at him.

His first warning was the bag that descended on him. Miysis got out one howl of fury, extending his claws, when the bag struck a tree trunk—not with smashing force, but enough to take the fight out of him.

Too late he remembered the town cat's warning about the darkness. But how could this be happening almost in the precincts of Bast's temple?

Reduced to the status of a furious bundle, Miysis felt the man carrying him move. And, although he could see nothing from the bag, he felt the force on his brain intensify. They weren't moving away from the temple. They were coming closer.

They stopped, and he heard a low voice. "So quick?"

"Found one in the thicket." The reply came from the man holding Miysis.

"Probably one trying to get away." The first two-leg gave a low laugh. "Didn't get far. I guess the cloud slows them up."

"They're not even supposed to know it's there," Miysis' captor said. "Or so Penmaat told us."

That was a name Miysis had heard. Penmaat was the high priest of Bast's temple!

The first human made a noncommittal noise. "Bring this one inside. If it's going to be troublesome, best to be rid of it quickly."

Miysis jounced inside the bag as his captor hurriedly moved. After a long walk, the bag—and Miysis—thumped against a stone floor. "Another one for Penmaat," he heard the human say. Then came the faint stirring of sandals on stone.

Wherever they had gone, the cloud or whatever it was pressed even more heavily on Miysis' brain. It required an effort to think. Perhaps that was what the humans meant about slowing him up.

Perhaps not him alone, but many cats. Although Miysis couldn't see, he could catch a strong scent of his kindred—as well as the stink of voided wastes. Wherever this was, it was not a good place. Extending his claws again, Miysis went to work on the rough-woven fabric that enclosed him. His jaws ached from biting into the stuff as his rear feet kicked and worried a hole. He emerged looking up to a ceiling so high, it was beyond his ability to estimate. Still looking upward, he turned round. As best he could see, he was in a large enclosed space, tall and pillared, mostly dark.

This had to be the sanctuary of the temple! None were allowed in here but the highest priests and Pharaoh himself! But the one who had snared him had walked in with no trepidation!

Then Miysis turned his attention to ground level. He seemed to be surrounded by a carpet of cats. Either they slept, or they were drugged . . . or some non-physical reason robbed them of consciousness. A very few made limp movements—not enough to help them rise.

Miysis could understand the feeling. An impalpable force seemed determined to push him to the floor as well. His movements felt slow, uncoordinated.

Chanting echoed from between the pillars. "Answer, Apep. Answer the call of Penmaat. Draw closer to this place. We offer you life and strength. Give us darkness and power."

Moving so low his belly touched the floor, Miysis crept toward the small circle of light in the center of the huge room. He saw a pair of two-legs standing beside a small brazier. One continued the chant. The other held a cat.

The chanter—Penmaat—took the cat with an almost ceremonial gesture. The priest wore a panther skin over his linen kilt, but that didn't conceal his form. While his face was still handsome, if lined, Penmaat's body was slumped and bloated. His arms and legs seemed as thin as kindling.

With the flames at his back, Penmaat seemed more like a gigantic spider than a human as he held the cat in his hands up to the darkness beyond the brazier.

Then he twisted the dazed cat's neck until Miysis heard the low but sharp *snap!* of bones breaking.

Miysis' lips writhed back from his fangs, and it took everything within him not to screech a war cry. The horror wasn't finished. As the sacrificial cat expired, a tiny spark of light seemed to escape from its head—a spark that was snuffed out by a snaky shadow-tendril that seemed a deeper darkness than the gloom beyond.

Crouched close to the floor, Miysis felt his fur stand on end. Was this to be his fate in Per-Bastet? To become a sacrifice to the foulness of the dark?

Penmaat took a new cat from his assistant, continuing his chant, and proceeded to wring the helpless beast's neck. Another escaping spark was consumed by deeper darkness.

Miysis' mind was working now. He remembered tales of humans and cat-kindred joining forces against larger baneful beings. Certain places were known as portals where these Greater Banes attained access to this world—unless blocked. The motherwisdom spoke of epic battles fought by two- and four-legged allies to vanquish bodiless, deadly creatures. Here Penmaat sought to *create* a portal, feeding the snaky tendrils the very life force of the dazed cats.

And the name Penmaat used to invoke the dark being—Apep. That was the snake-demon who eternally fought to destroy Ra and the sun-barge, to plunge the world into unending darkness.

If Penmaat gave the black being this name, it must be powerful indeed. It must be, to dull the perceptions of Those Who See Beyond Darkness, even in the place where they were most honored.

Still crouched as low as he could bring himself, Miysis slunk away.

He had to get out of this place—had to warn the people of Per-Bastet of what was happening.

But could he convince them? He remembered the desperation of the human population, the dispirited cat he'd met. Would the local cat-kindred even listen to him? A stranger denouncing the high priest of Bast, claiming that he had somehow retained his psychic senses when all others had been dimmed?

His spirits were as low as his belly as he wormed his

way back from the light—and the worse darkness beyond it.

Could he even escape? He had already been scooped as a mother captured an unruly kit. Now he was forewarned, but he was also in the center of the enemy's power.

Keep to the shadows, he told himself. The normal darkness. Shadows are your friend.

He hoped to lose sight of the blasphemous rite behind the pillars. Likewise, the priests wouldn't see him. Then to the wall—somewhere, there must be an opening to the outside.

Yet, as the brazier's light diminished behind the rows of pillars, Miysis discovered another source of illumination. It was faint, erratic. At first, he thought it might be an afterimage of the brazier's flames.

Then he realized it was not his eyes that detected this feeble flicker. What could kindle his psychic senses, dulled as they were by the presence of Apep's darkness?

Prudence dictated a quick retreat. But he was Miysis, and he would see.

He approached a larger-than-human shape, a female form wrought in bronze, kits about her feet, all seemingly caught in mid-stride. One hand held up a sistrum, a ritual basket was caught in the crook of the other elbow. The head was that of a cat with crystal eyes. Clouded crystal.

A statue of Bast.

For a moment, Miysis wondered if he had merely

been confused, seeing a reflection off stones or burnished metal.

Then he felt the tickle in his brain, softer than the barest whisper. *Little One, you do not sleep.*

Miysis froze in his tracks. But this communication did not smack of the unalloyed malevolence that rose like a stink from the snake-tendrils.

I am trapped in this image, Little One, unless you help me.

Creeping closer, Miysis stopped, fighting the urge to sneeze. There *was* a stink of evil here, but not from the statue. Tiny threads of spider silk wound round the image. They seemed to pulse with a dark energy as Miysis considered them.

These bind me in place. A note of anger crept into the mental voice. *I, who ever wandered wherever I willed.*

Having lately been imprisoned himself, Miysis understood that anger all too well. He leaped to attack the strands, spitting in disgust at their taste. As each was severed, the light within the statue grew stronger, as did the voice.

Few of my kind visit this plane, it explained. *I came—some time ago, by your reckoning. To most, I was invisible. Some saw me and feared.* An image filled Miysis' mind—a pack of dogs running. *Your kind saw me—and interacted.* Another image, this time a wild cat, eyes wide, rising up on two legs, attempting to touch . . .

Over time, the humans became aware of my presence, though they never saw me. They brought presents and pleas, fashioning images of me in this form. This faith in the unseen touched me strangely. I stayed, and helped where I could. A town grew here, and a temple. With that came priests.

A parade of human forms flickered through Miysis' mind—some good men, others less than admirable. Last was a young, slim Penmaat.

He was no worse than many, but he feared death. Feared that his heart would be found wanting in the Halls of the Dead. As he grew old, he begged for longer life, then angrily demanded. This was something I could not give. So he looked—elsewhere.

The darker ones of my kind like this world. It assuages certain—hungers. Penmaat aspired to use the trail I had forged, opening the door for one of these. While a ceremony held my attention here, tiny creatures—the web-spinners— enmeshed me. They were directed by the lesser darknesses, but they wrought cunningly. I was trapped. But no more.

Miysis had scaled the image, breaking the ensorceled web. At least now he would have an ally to convince the city's cat-kindred—

Too late merely to give warning, the glowing entity said, divining Miysis' hopes. *The Other will be established on this plane by the time resistance is roused. I can counter the nonphysical manifestations. But it will fall to you to close off the portal.*

Miysis' spirits fell. One cat against two humans and an abomination.

You will have the help of your kindred as the Other's cloud dissipates.

Still long odds. But Miysis could see the truth of Bast's words. The shadows in the temple sanctuary already seemed to curdle thicker, and the air filled with the stink of evil. Miysis made what plans he could.

Penmaat was still chanting, still feeding cats to the blackness, when a tawny bolt leaped from the floor, bounced off a pillar, and landed on his chest, claws digging into the leopard pelt as the cat surged up to savage his face.

The priest screamed, the sacrificed cat dropping to the floor as both hands went to deal with this feline intruder. Penmaat staggered back, his kilt-clad hips knocking over the brazier. Flames licked along bleached linen.

Penmaat screamed again, an entirely different tone. His hands stopped trying to dislodge Miysis. He had blundered against one of the shadowy snake-heads. The thaumaturge had instead become a victim.

His assistant had begun running with his master's first scream. Now black tendrils circled round the light to pursue him as well.

Penmaat collapsed as the dark entity fed.

Miysis knew this was a bad thing. It would only help root the darkness in this world. He left off his attack on the human. Now he must face the disembodied foe.

The very air seemed to thicken around the cat's body as he forced himself forward, seeking the point where the snake-heads issued into the world.

Baleful, raw emotion battered at Miysis' mind. Unlike the benign Bast, this one had little experience with the creatures of Earth. There was no communication, just a bludgeoning burst of negation.

Miysis staggered, drowning in darkness. Then the battering shadows receded, and the cat was surrounded in radiance. The bright spirit—Bast—had intervened!

Now Miysis could see the would-be portal—a blackness that even Bast's light could not disperse, from which the inky tendrils writhed. He knew the bulk of the creature was still on the far side. But the obscene anger of its appendages seemed dangerous enough. The snake-heads left off their feeding and their pursuit to counter this new, unexpected danger.

Body low, fangs bared, Miysis stalked forward. He was unsure what damage, if any, he could inflict on an impalpable enemy. The tendrils of shadow coalesced into a single serpent of darkness, its head alone larger than Miysis' body, arching higher than the statue of Bast, then striking at the four-legged combatant before it.

Miysis flung himself to the side. Perhaps there was little he could do to the Apep-serpent. But just a brush with that blackness was enough to unstring his limbs. A direct strike by that snake-head would snuff out his life more surely than any set of poison fangs.

Apep reared again, and the radiance surrounding Miysis seemed to dim. Was the dark spirit trying to restore its cloud of darkness? Or was Bast weakening?

Miysis wanted to run, but there was no way he could turn his back on this thing. He darted forward, dodging once more to evade the striking snake-head—

It came closer this time, leaving one of Miysis' rear

legs feeling numb. It dragged behind him as he scrabbled onward.

But in the distance, Miysis could sense stirring, hundreds of low, complaining groans.

He couldn't let that distract him. The world shrank to a snake-head so black it hurt to look at, arching back for a final strike.

And then—

The numbness vanished from Miysis' leg. But this was more than recovery. His chest seemed to swell. His fur stood on end, and a nimbus of energy filled him. He tasted hundreds of cat-minds—dazed, confused—but linking with him, offering what they could of strength, light . . .

Bast's doing.

Tail up like a battle banner, the cat leaped forward. Apep missed, and Miysis lashed out at the serpent-body. His claws passed harmlessly through the impalpable form, but his fury dissipated the darkness as dew disappeared under Ra's harsh sunlight.

Surprise, shock, pain—fear. Apep's emotions all assailed Miysis' consciousness like blaring noise. For an instant, his connection to his kindred faltered, and the world grew dim.

The dark serpent struck again as Miysis hurled himself straight up at the stabbing head. Battle fury filled him, and expanded as his brothers and sisters joined him again.

Blackness struck Miysis full on the head, driving him downward, trying to drain his very soul. But even as he fell, Miysis twisted, his rear legs pumping, claws ripping—

In his travels, he'd seen the picture many times— Bast beheading the Apep-serpent. The pictured cat usually handled a knife, but Miysis used his natural tearing weapons. The hunger sucking at him ceased, exploding in a wash of pain. Miysis kept tearing, howling a battle cry.

He had no idea how long it went on. It could have been instants, it could have been hours. But after that first decapitating stroke, the outcome of the battle was never in doubt. Connecting through Bast, Miysis and his cat-kindred extirpated Apep from the temple sanctuary—and this world.

At the end, there were lights and human voices. The tall human who had shared his barge with Miysis stood in the sanctuary, ringed with armed guards. Other armed men herded the two-leg who had assisted Penmaat, while others restrained temple servants and let cats out of bags.

I go from this place, Bast's voice filled Miysis' brain. *Perhaps I remained too long. You fought well, Little One.*

As Bast receded, so did the connection between the cats. Miysis dropped like a puppet with its strings cut, groaning with sudden exhaustion.

Then he was swept up in gentle hands. "Lord of the Slaughter, indeed," Pharaoh said, looking at the wounds on Penmaat's face. "It is quite a thing to be awakened by the cries of every cat in Per-Bast. Our first thought was attack, then we turned to the sanctuary."

His toe touched Penmaat's still form. "Where this one, it seems, was performing abominations. But it seems Bast has dealt with that transgression, through our friend here. What was it like to be the eye of a god, Miysis?"

Miysis' tail twitched as gentle hands rubbed his forehead, just where Apep had struck.

"Here—the fur has changed," Pharaoh said. "It looks like a scarab."

"Marked by the gods," one of Pharaoh's guards muttered. "Most fortunate cat."

Having found his fate, the most fortunate cat raised up his head and gently butted Pharaoh's hand. He wanted the stroking to resume, thank you very much.

Every feline fancier will tell you that cats were worshiped in ancient Egypt. They may even relate the story written by the Greek traveler Diodoros about the Roman who killed an Egyptian cat and died for it. That supposedly dates to the reign of Ptolemy Auletes (Cleopatra's father, whose rule ended in 51 BC). Herodotus, writing in the fifth century BC, mentions the custom of families shaving the eyebrows at the loss of a cat. At that point, cats and humans had been living together a good 1,500 years.

Bast or Bastet is a well-known Egyptian deity, represented as a cat or cat-headed human female. In one very old myth, she is depicted in cat-form, decapitating the Apep-serpent. Though Bast's tree-girt temple in Per-Bastet (Greek Bubastis) is ancient indeed, she became a national goddess rather late in Egyptian history, during the reign of the delta dynasties who ruled from the city of Tanis (roughly 1070–767 BC). Indiana Jones fans will recognize Tanis as the site of the archaeological dig in *Raiders of the Lost Ark*. Archaeologists have found extensive cat graveyards in Bubastis, with thousands of feline mummies. Many were unearthed during excavation of the Suez canal—and shipped off for use as fertilizer.

This story actually began when I read that some of the cat-mummies had broken necks. It's believed they date to more decadent Ptolemaic days, when priests would turn one live cat into several mummies to sell for interment to pious pilgrims.

Today, Bubastis and its temple are scattered ruins. No one goes there for the feast of Bast, where all fires in the city were doused except for one flame in the temple, which was then brought out to rekindle light everywhere. But some cat breeders have attempted to bring back the original Egyptian cat, complete with a scarab marking in the fur on the forehead. The breed is called the Egyptian Mau, after the ancient word for cat. Besides the obvious onomatopoeia, the word "mau" also means "to see."

Hmmmm . . .

A LION LET LOOSE UPON THE WORLD

by Brendan DuBois

Brendan DuBois is the award-winning author
of short stories and novels. His short fiction
has appeared in *Playboy*, *Ellery Queen's Mystery Magazine*, *Alfred Hitchcock's Mystery
Magazine*, *Mary Higgins Clark's Mystery Magazine*, and numerous anthologies. He has received the Shamus Award from the Private Eye
Writers of America for one of his short stories,
and has been nominated three times for an
Edgar Allan Poe Award by the Mystery Writers
of America. He's also the author of the Lewis
Cole mystery series: *Dead Sand*, *Black Tide*,
and *Shattered Shell*. His most recent novel,
Resurrection Day, is a suspense thriller that
looks at what might have happened had the

Cuban Missile Crisis of 1962 erupted into a nuclear war between the United States and the Soviet Union. This book received the Sidewise Award for best alternative history novel of 1999. He lives in New Hampshire with his wife Mona.

WHEN Amy Tasker went in on Sunday afternoon to visit her grandmother at St. Anne's Nursing Home in Devon, the old woman glanced up and said, "What's that hanging around your neck? Is it Egyptian?"

Amy felt her hand go up to her throat, at the thin chain and symbol that hung from it, down the front of her black sweater. A birthday gift last month from her boyfriend, Todd, a gift that really touched her for his thoughtfulness. "Yes, Grandma. It's an Egyptian ankh, and it represents the—"

Her grandmother held up a hand, still strong-looking even though the woman was now entering her ninth decade. "I don't care to know, I really don't."

Amy took a straight-backed chair across from her grandmother, who was sitting in a padded, comfortable-looking easy chair. She had a green-and-white afghan throw across her thin lap, and though her face was wrinkled and old, there was still a brightness and intelligence in her dark blue eyes. Amy visited her grandmother once a week at the nursing home, when she wasn't studying at UNH or waiting tables at the Harborside Restaurant in Porter. Some of her friends would wrinkle their noses or roll their eyes at how often she visited her grandmother, but she didn't care what her friends thought. Grandma had been one of the first women newspaper reporters in Boston, had written a couple of books about New England history, smoked unfiltered Camels until she was seventy, and even now, enjoyed a stiff sip of Irish whiskey before each meal. She was a reservoir of old stories, bawdy jokes, and funny remembrances of Amy's own father when he was young, but never had she seen her grandmother act like this before.

"What's wrong with it?" she asked, again touching the ankh jewelry.

"Wrong?" Grandma said. "It's Egyptian, right? Ancient Egyptian?"

Amy nodded. Grandma pursed her lips and said, "Then I don't like it, and that's that."

"But why? It's just a symbol, that's all, a symbol of life and—"

Grandma Tasker held her hand up. "Bah, life and all that crap. Read about the ancient Egyptians, really read about them, dear. I know they're in vogue now and there's all these specials on the television about the wonderful Egyptians and their wonderful culture, but look beyond the pyramids and pretty carvings, girl. Their culture was all about death. That's it. They worshiped death and everything associated with it."

Amy sat still, confused. Grandma Tasker's room was small—she had always been pleased to have a room to herself—and was cheerfully decorated with

framed prints of needlepoint that she had done, pho-
tographs of her relatives, and a tiny bookshelf over-
flowing with paperback romance novels. ("Since I
haven't done it in decades, I guess the only thing I
can do now is read about it," she once laughingly
told Amy.)

But now the room seemed cold, out of sorts, and
then Grandma sighed and said, "Sorry, child. I guess I
was just overreacting. You see, for a long time, I've
never liked anything to do with the pyramids and the
pharaohs and anything else about Egypt. It just brings
back bad memories."

"What kind of memories?" Amy asked.

Grandma looked out the window, to the crowded
parking lot of the rest home. "Oh, memories of my
older brother, John. Your great-uncle. He died many,
many years before you were born."

"Oh. Did he go to Egypt, is that it?"

Her grandmother shook her head. "No, not at all.
John never traveled out of the state, not once. Except
maybe to Boston a couple of times, to see the
Red Sox."

Amy said, "Grandma, I'm confused. What did the
ancient Egyptians have to do with your brother John?"

And Grandma looked at her now, with a cold look
that was nothing like Amy had ever seen from her
grandmother, and it made her shiver. Her voice was
low. "I don't like the ancient Egyptians because of
what they did to my brother, that's why."

"What did they do to him?"

"They killed him, that's what," she said.

"They did?" Amy asked, now wondering if poor Grandma was on the edges of senility. There were other residents of the nursing home who broke her heart, shrunken old men and women, alone in wheelchairs, lined up in the hallway. Grandma, though, at least she was still sharp, even if she was old. And Grandma nodded her head and said, "They killed him, they did. And do you want to know how?"

Amy could only nod. Grandma said, "All right, then. Shut the door and I'll tell you a story. I don't want somebody else hearing what I've got to say."

And that's just what Amy did, closing the door and looking out at the calm, white-clothed staff of the nursing home, strolling by on their little rounds, not knowing what kind of tale was going on in this room.

Ancient Egyptians, she thought. *Killing my great-uncle. Please.*

But still, she gently closed the door and returned to the straight-backed chair.

John was my oldest brother, Grandma started, born nine years before me. We lived on a farm up past Berlin, way up north, and my father, God rest his soul, raised dairy cattle and did some work in the woods whenever he could. There were seven of us, and when I got older, I got to see how John was different from my other brothers and sisters. Oh, he hunted and fished and trapped with our brothers, he got a job at the paper mill when he got out of high school, and did lots of things like everybody else. But he was always the quiet one, always sitting by himself at get-togethers and reunions, and he never married. Hell, I don't think John even had a girlfriend, though he was a handsome one.

We weren't that close, but we did keep in touch, and one of the last times I saw him, it was when he was in the hospital, dying. Poor fella had a problem with his liver, and this was before liver transplants were common. He was in a hospital in Nashua and I remember one day—this must have been thirty years ago—that he was resting there, eyes closed, and he was having a bad dream. His legs twitched and his breathing kicked in, and he started moaning. I couldn't stand watching that happen to him, and just before I reached over and touched his shoulder, he said in this awful, strained voice, "Conrad! Conrad! Jesus, boy, run for your life!"

So I woke him up and there was sweat on his forehead, and he looked over and managed to smile some, and said, "Jeez, Sis, thanks for waking me up. That was a bad one."

"Sure sounded that way," I said. "And who's Conrad?"

And that's when his face got really pale, and he said back to me. "What do you mean?"

"You tell me," I said. "You were huffing and puffing and saying something about Conrad, and running for your life. Who was Conrad?"

"Conrad LeClerc," he slowly said. "One of my best friends when I was younger."

"Oh. What happened to him?"

"He got himself killed," John said, turning his head on the pillow. "And it was my fault."

Well, John didn't want to tell much more than that, but I poked and prodded and got him to opening up, and maybe it was because of how sick he was, he felt like he had to unburden his soul, because unburden is what he did that warm summer day, in that hospital room. He took a drink from a plastic cup with a straw and then just sighed, like finally, he was telling his story to somebody, and not keeping it inside.

"Conrad LeClerc and Richie Boulanger," he said. "Two old buddies of mine. The woods out beyond our house, and the river, well, they belonged to us. Everything in and around Berlin belonged to us. I was the youngest, twelve, and they were a year older, but it didn't matter that much. We explored and went fishing and hunting and . . . well, we did everything together."

"I'm sorry," I said. "I don't remember those two fellas at all."

He shrugged. "No matter. They were my best friends, through thick and thin. And one summer, well, we started doing some bad things. Nothing really rotten, but going into other people's barns without them knowing it. Stealing apples and cider. Just stuff like that. And, let's see . . . it was August. We were exploring Professor Monroe's place, up on Jericho Reach. Remember that farm?"

I surely did. "Sure. But I don't remember anybody living there. It was, uh," and I laughed. "When I was your age, it was considered haunted. Nobody ever went there."

His voice was flat. "Sure. Later it was considered haunted, and for good reason . . . but when I was twelve, that summer, it belonged to Professor Monroe. I'm not sure what college he taught at—Harvard or Colby or Miskatonic or some damn place—but he had been living there for a few years, and people pretty much steered away from him. I mean, he was nutty. Retired, lived by himself. Went to the general store in a black tin lizzie, smoke billowing out, used to ask for three eggs. Not a half dozen or a dozen. Three. Just an odd fella. Old guy with a long white beard, and Mrs. Lamontagne, she once said she saw him on a rock in the far field, dancing naked."

"Naked?" I asked.

"Starkers. Hootin' and hollerin' and dancing around like he was possessed, or something. There were strange lights at night from his barn and farmhouse, and sometimes little fires, lit here and there out in the fields. Everybody else stayed away and gave him room, but we were kids, we were . . . so it didn't matter much."

He took some deep breaths, like he was gathering courage to keep on talking, and then he said, "One night, Conrad—he was the oldest of us three—said we should go see what the professor had in his barn. Richie always agreed with Conrad and me being the youngest, I just went along. So that's what we did. Even at night we knew how to get through the woods, and we went across his hayfield in the starlight, and saw that all the lights were out in his house. We crept up and got a side door open, and then . . . and then . . ."

Even though we had never been close, I couldn't bear to see him suffer like that, so I reached over and grabbed his hand, and that seemed to do something good, for he swallowed and went on. "The inside of the barn was lit up, with these candles, stuck up on the beams . . . And there were wooden crates, piled up in all parts of the barn, some with stenciling on the side that I could read. One said 'Harkin Expedition 1912' or something like that. And the smell . . . like old dust, kept buried away in stone for thousands of years. We stood there and walked around, just looking at the boxes and crates, and it was like the damn professor was waiting for us . . . you know? Like he knew we was coming . . . which is why we didn't jump much when he came out from behind one of the boxes."

I squeezed his hand and he said, "Oh, Richie jumped some, but the professor just smiled and said something like, 'Boys will be boys, eh? Curious and all that,' he said. He was wearing this long, embroidered robe and he was smiling and his beard looked so white in the light, and I knew we should have been scared, should have been embarrassed that we got caught, but it was like something was freezing us there . . . I managed to say something, though, about apologizing for trespassin', and he just held up a hand and said it was no problem. He wanted to know if we wanted to see what was in some of the boxes, and sure, we did, and he laughed and opened some of them up . . . you see, the nails had been taken off some of the tops of the crates . . ."

Another deep sigh and a wince, as if something in his gut was now paining him. "Oh, he started talkin' and showin', like the professor he was. Egypt, boys! he said. I've spent years in Egypt, hot days and cold nights and bitter sand, he said, trying to wrestle some of the secrets of the pharaohs, and he showed us old carvings and statuettes and even bits of wood and cloth he said came from toys, toys that some of the children had buried with them. He went around to each box, opening them up and showing us what was inside, and I was scared, Sis, I was so scared I wanted to leave, but I don't know. I just couldn't. He kept on talking faster and faster, talking about old Egypt and the pyramids and the pharaohs and the gods and professors and how they kept secrets from us, secrets about the past and our future . . . by then, spit was dribbling down his chin, and his eyes were wide and blue, and I thought that maybe, just maybe, we weren't getting out of that barn that night. . . ."

He looked away from me for a moment, and said, "Conrad, though, didn't look like he was being bothered at all. He looked like he was enjoying himself, enjoying what the professor was showing us, all the artifacts and stories about what went on during his trips to Egypt. Then Conrad moved around to get a closer look and bumped into a crate that had a smaller box on top. This box shook some and the professor looked right up at it, like he was making sure it didn't fall or anything. It was small, with leather and metal straps all around it, and Conrad said, 'What's that? What's in there?'"

John coughed and said, "The professor stopped and shook his head, and said, 'Oh, not tonight.' But Conrad had a way about him, wheedling and begging, and the professor said, 'Just this once, just this once . . .' And he pulled the box down and undid the clasps and fastenings, and opened it up. We all clustered around him, and I guess we all ooohed and aaahed, because there was a small statue in there, a statue nestled in dirt, if you can believe it. It was yellow and dull-looking. Conrad moved to touch it, and the professor slapped his hand away. 'No, she stays there. She stays right where she is.' And Richie piped up, asking what it was. And the professor looked dreamy and said, 'That's Sekhmet, a sun goddess.' And I said, 'It looks like a lion's head on a woman,' and the professor said, 'Yes, that's true. Sekhmet was the daughter of Nut and Geb, and wife of Ptah. She was an instrument of burning, of death, of destruction, and she was the destroyer of the enemies of Ra and Osiris.'"

I interrupted him. "You remember this, all these years later?"

He winced again. "No. I looked them up later, as I got older . . . because, well, you'll see . . . anyway, the professor went on talking about Sekhmet. The professor told us that Ra ruled the Earth for thousands of years, ruled over mankind. And the people grew tired of being ruled by Ra, and were preparing to rebel. So to stop the rebellion, Ra sent Sekhmet to Earth to kill his enemies. And this lioness roamed about the Earth, killing men and women and drinking their blood, enjoying her task. In fact, she enjoyed killing so much that Ra was fearful that all of mankind would perish, and he took pity on us and got her drunk and stole her away, the professor said. And when that happened, mankind was saved."

I just sat there, listening and wondering. You see, John had barely made it through high school. He wasn't very educated, yet for the past few minutes, he had been talking about Egypt and Egyptian mythology like he had grown up with it.

So John continued and said, "So we were sitting around the box, looking at it and looking at the statue, when Conrad again made to touch it, to pick it up. And the professor said, 'No, don't you touch that. There's a curse and I don't want that statue leaving the box.' And we were all scared, but Conrad was trying to be brave and said, 'What do you mean, a curse?' Conrad said he didn't believe in ghosts or goblins or anything like that, and the professor said, 'Boy, you better believe. I've been in places that would make you wet your shorts, would make you run away, crying for your mammy, and there's a curse on this like you wouldn't believe.' Then Richie asked him what kind of curse it was. The professor rubbed at the side of his head and said it was a dark, evil curse, that said death and destruction would come to all, if Sekhmet was removed from her native soil. Then I looked again and said, 'Then how come the statue is here, and not in Egypt?' And the professor laughed and said, 'I fooled 'em, that's how. I packed Sekhmet in the soil of Egypt and smuggled her out, and here she is, boys, safe in New Hampshire and even safer in the soil of Egypt. Come on, I've got other things to show you.'"

He licked his lips and I gave him the cup of water with a straw in it, and after drinking some of it, John said, "So with that, the professor put the lid back on the box and put it back where it was, and we went over to the other side of the barn. But Conrad, though, Conrad kept on looking up at the box with the statue in it, and I knew he was thinking about what was in there, about that statue, curse or no curse. I was going to tell him to cut it out, to leave it alone, when the professor said, 'Hey, do you boys want to see an honest-to-God mummy?'"

John managed a smile and said, "I sure as hell didn't, but Conrad and Richie did, and we stood around this large box, a real long crate, and the professor moved some candles around and said, 'You know, a few years back, it was quite common to have mummy unwrapping parties in fashionable homes. Education and entertainment, all rolled up in one. Well, I've already gone ahead and done the honors, boys,' and with that, he lifted up the lid and let it drop to the floor of the barn. Jesus."

My brother took a breath and winced, like his liver was troubling him again. He said, "You see pictures of mummies from the museums, and they're still in their coffins or whatever, painted up and looking pretty. Or maybe you see pictures of them, wrapped in their linens. But not this one, not this mummy. He had been unwrapped and he was lying there, brown and dried and dead, God, he was so dead. His hands were like claws, draped across his chest, and his neck was hardly there, and his head . . . it was like a skull, with brown skin stretched across it. Richie whimpered and I did, too, I think, but Conrad got in for a closer look, and the professor rubbed the top of his head. 'That's good,' the professor said. 'This old buzzard's been dead for years, waiting to come back to life.' And Conrad wanted to know, why did the mummy look so skinny. The professor just laughed, this cackling noise that scared me even more. He said that the royal embalmers had taken out all of the internal organs after death and had put them in jars, and he said, 'Boys, you can imagine, when the spirits reinhabit the bodies, there's going to be a lot of mending to do.'"

He paused, coughed and said, "Then Richie said, 'Who is he, what's his name?' And the professor said, 'Well, nobody else believes me, but I think this is the body of . . . well. don't laugh, boys, but his name is Aha. He has another name, too, Menes, and he was the founding king of the First Dynasty, the one to unify Upper and Lower Egypt into one empire,' and he started raving about this body, how he really believed it was the pharaoh of the First Dynasty, even though nobody else believed him . . ."

I looked at my poor brother, stubble on his face, his white hair plastered some against the pillow, and he looked away from me again and said, "That's when it happened."

"What happened?" I asked.

Another breath. "The professor was cackling, and Richie was bumping into me, like he was scared and wanted to make sure that somebody was standing next to him, and Conrad was leaning over, looking at the mummy, actually looking down toward his feet, and I was looking up at the head . . . the shrunken head and the stretched skin and . . . and . . . the eyes opened up. I swear to God and all the saints, Sis, the eyes opened up. The eyes opened up and they was looking right at me, and I'm not ashamed to say it, I screamed and I ran out of there, ran out of there and Richie was right behind me, and even by then, Conrad must have got spooked by what happened, 'cause he was with us, too. We ran and ran and ran . . . and when I got home, I got a blanket and a pillow and I got on the floor outside Mom and Dad's bedroom 'cause I was so scared . . . I shivered and laid there and didn't move, until I saw the sun coming up . . . I swear, Sis, that's what happened. The mummy's eyes opened up and looked right at me. And more than that. The eyes looked right through me."

Amy Tasker sat still, hands folded in her lap, looking at Grandma, who now gazed back at her and said, "You're thinking John was a crazy man, aren't you?"

"No, Grandma, I'm not."

"You don't believe the story."

"I don't know what to believe."

"Bah," Grandma said. "You young'uns, you grow up in your safe homes and ride your safe cars and go to your safe schools. You don't know anything about real life and what goes on out there, in the dark and beyond the shadows. You ignore death and bad things and evil, until the very end . . ."

Amy noticed her mouth was dry, and tried to swallow. "So . . . your brother, I still don't understand what you meant, about Egypt and all . . . I mean, he thought he saw the mummy open its eyes. Right?"

Grandma said firmly, "If John said the mummy got up and danced the fox-trot with the professor, I would believe him. But no, John dying and all had nothing to do with the mummy. It had to do with the second time they went back in the barn, and what happened after that."

"The second time?"

Grandma nodded. "Yep. They went in again. Poor young boys thought they were being brave." She looked out at the parking lot. "They were so young they had no idea how stupid they were."

So I tried to change the conversation around, and John would have nothing to do with it. "No, I've come this far," he said. "I've got to tell it all, Sis, tell it all before it's too late." And I knew what he meant, knew how few days were left for him in the hospital, and he went on.

"You see," he said, "after the sun came up and breakfast, and doing chores, and going for a walk, I started to think about other things. I tried to think that what I saw with that mummy was just my imagination, or a trick of the candlelight. Richie came up to me and said the same thing, that maybe we were just scared, and Conrad, he was trying to be the bravest of us all. And a few days later, after we saw the professor and what he had in his barn, that's when Conrad came up with his idea. You see, he wanted to steal the statue of Sekhmet."

I looked at my sick and scared older brother, and said, "Why?"

"Because Conrad was a fool, and thought the statue might be made of gold. And maybe he was right. He came to us one day while we were fishing off the Berlin Mills bridge and said, 'Look, my mom said that professor is crazy as a loon. Always forgets things. And you saw everything he had in his barn. You think he's gonna remember where everything is? We should go in and just take that little statue. He won't miss it.' "

John gave another wince and said, "I tried to talk him out of it. I said it was stealing, that it was wrong, and Conrad's face got dark and said, 'You tell me what's wrong. My dad got killed two years back in the woods, and who's lookin' out for us? You think I like seein' my brothers and sisters with nothin'? See my mom beg from her brothers for a sack of flour? Wear hand-me-down clothes from my cousins? Professor Monroe's a rich old coot. He don't need that statue. We do. Think of all the money we could get it for it.' I asked him where he would take it. And he said his uncle was a coin and stamp dealer, down in Concord. He said he'd get a good price from him. And then Richie said, 'Aren't you afraid of the curse?' And Conrad just laughed. 'First,' he said, 'I don't believe in curses, and second, the professor said the statue would be all right if it stayed in the box with the dirt from Egypt, right? So we just take the box and everything. Let whoever buys it from my uncle, let him worry about the curse.' "

His lips looked dry, so I gave him another sip of water. "Well. It went on like that for a few more days, talkin' and discussin', and I was still against it and Richie was so-so, but Conrad was the oldest, and well, that's how boys are when they're that age. You tend to follow the oldest one. And he said he found out that Professor Monroe had left on the train for Boston for a few days, and that it was time to go do it. And I went along, God, I shouldn't have gone but I went along. . . . It was a night with almost a full moon, so we could see just fine as we snuck through the woods, and I was thinking to myself, I know it's stealing, I know it's bad, and maybe, just maybe, the barn will be locked. And even if it wasn't locked, and Conrad managed to steal the statue, maybe I wouldn't take the money. Then it wouldn't be so bad. That's the kind of thoughts that are going through your mind when you're scared and you know you're doing wrong . . . and what happened is, right before we knew it, we were at the barn."

John gave a raspy sigh. "Oh, that stupid professor. Why didn't he lock everything up? It was like he wanted us to come back and look around, and maybe steal something from his barn. It was almost like he was scared of what he had in his barn, and didn't want to have it no more, and wanted somebody else to come along and take it. I dunno. That's just what I thought. So anyway, we got into the barn and this time, there weren't any candles, nothing at all. Just dark and dusty and cold. Even though it was warm outside, it felt real cold inside the barn. Richie . . . poor little Richie grabbed my hand and whispered, 'Maybe we shouldn't go in. Maybe we should leave.' I could feel his legs trembling, and my own legs were shakin', too. Even Conrad seemed to stand still for a moment, before he went right in . . . He said something like, 'Okay, you scaredy cats, I'll go in and do it myself . . .' And he walked right into the darkness and Richie whispered to me, 'If he doesn't come out of there real quick, I'm leavin' him behind . . .' and I said, 'Me, too . . .' Oh, it was awful, standing there at the doorway in the darkness, listening to the wind rise up and the wood of the barn creak, and hearing the rustling noises in there, hopin' it's Conrad and he's okay . . . and then he came out, laughin', carrying the box in his hands. Jesus, I felt so good right then . . . and I think I should have remembered it better, Sis, 'cause that's the last time I ever felt good about anything at all. Anything."

Well, I guess I was scared, too, right about then, sitting next to my dying brother. I really wanted to get up and say I had to go home or run an errand or some damn thing, instead of staying there, but I couldn't. He was my brother and he was unburdening his soul or whatever, and I just let him speak, let him tell me everything.

John said, "So he was there, breathin' hard, almost laughing, and then he stepped out of the barn, and the cold stayed there, right with us. You know? It was a hot August night, and it was like cold air was following us out of the barn, right when we went out to the yard. Then Richie's voice seemed to squeak, and he said, 'Guys, where's the moon? Where did it go?' And me and Conrad looked up and Richie was right. The moon was gone. There were no stars. Nothing. Just . . . it looked like these low and dark clouds were racing in above us, and they weren't high clouds. Nope. They were low clouds, just above the trees. And then I noticed something else, right away. It was quiet. Deadly quiet. You know, at night, there's always noises, the crickets, the birds, rustles in the leaves from squirrels or chipmunks. And when we were standing there, we couldn't hear a thing except our own breathing and our own voices. Richie just said, 'Gosh, I'm scared, I wanna go home,' and even Conrad seemed put off, and I said, 'C'mon, Conrad, put it back. You know it's not right. Put it back. It's all wrong.' "

Another raspy sigh. "But Conrad . . . I guess he had the gold fever or something, and who could blame him? Growin' up poor like that, knowing that you've got something in your hands, worth lots and lots of money, and he just whispered, 'No damn it, it's mine now, and I'm gonna take it.' Well, we tried moving away from the barn, but with the clouds coming over, we couldn't see so well, and the damn cold air was making me shiver, and I was thinking that something was wrong inside the box. Something was wrong . . . maybe 'cause it had to be back in the barn, with all the other Egypt stuff. I don't know. All I knew is that I was so scared it felt like my heart was tryin' to crawl up my throat, and I knew I had to do something. I was up front and I looked behind and I could see Conrad, and behind him, I could see Richie . . . and that's when I really got scared . . . because I could see 'em both, and I shouldn't have. You know? It was so dark, but yet I could see them both."

"Why was that?" I asked.

"'Cause light was coming out of the damn box, that's why," he said sharply. "Little light beams were coming through the cracks in the side of the box . . . and the place where the lid was kept shut . . . and I said to Conrad, 'That's it, that's it, you're takin' that box back in there, right now,' and Conrad said, 'The hell with you,' and that's when I went forward and started tussling with him . . ." John closed his eyes and said, "I knew I did the right thing, the only thing, but Lord, Sis . . . how many times I wish I had never done that . . . you see, we started fighting, going back and forth, me tryin' to get the box out of Conrad's hands, him tryin' to keep it there, and then the box was dropped on the ground, Sis. It felt right down and burst wide open, and the dirt flew everywhere and the little statue . . . it was glowing almost white . . . it fell out, too, right on the ground. And Richie screamed, 'The curse, the curse, we're all cursed!' I turned to run, and then there was this bright flash of light, like lightning, lit so bright I could see all around us and the trees and the clouds, and then I blinked my eyes some and Richie started screaming, 'It's got me, Jesus help me, oh, momma, it's got me . . .'"

Even then in the hospital, a nice safe place, I felt like I could be dead in any second, from the way John was talking, and he looked at me, his face white, and he said, "I'm sorry. I've gone this far, I've gotta finish it. You understand?"

And I just nodded, knowing I couldn't say a word, and John said, his voice now low and even, "I know you think I'm crazed, that I'm making all of this up, and I swear on the graves of our parents that what I say truly happened. I turned around to Richie's voice and at first, I thought shadows were playing tricks on me, making Richie look taller and bigger, and that's when I saw . . . the other thing standing there, growling . . . It had the body of a woman, dressed in this white robelike thing, but its hands were large, with long claws, and the head . . . the head was of a lion, and it was growling and blood was staining its fur . . . Richie's blood 'cause the creature had its jaws around the poor fella's waist, and was ripping him apart, like a cat with a chipmunk. . . ."

I managed to find my voice for a single word: "Sekhmet."

"Come to life . . . yes, the goddess Sekhmet, freed after thousands of years . . . and poor Richie was screaming and crying and the blood was spraying on the barn's walls, and that's when I started running. That's when I yelled at Conrad, 'Run, Conrad, Jesus, boy, run for your life!' And that's when we started running across the field, and thankfully, by then, we couldn't hear Richie anymore, and I was running and huffing and Conrad was behind me, and we didn't dare look back . . . but we could hear this low roar, this roar that sank right into our bones, and I tried running faster, trying to get to the river, the Androscoggin, and I said, 'Conrad, you there?' And he said, 'Yeah, I'm—' and then there was nothing. Just a thumping sound and a squeal, and I didn't look back, I couldn't look back. Sis, I was just running and running . . . and soon enough, I could smell the water, and then I heard something behind me, something thumping in the ground, something running right after me, and I started up with my prayers again, praying to anybody and everybody, and just then I saw the river in front of me, the river flowing nice and smooth and wide, and I've always hated to swim, always hated to get wet, but I made for that riverbank, Sis . . . made for it and just as I was getting ready to jump in, something hit me, right on the back. It didn't feel bad and didn't hurt, but something thumped me hard . . . and I got in the water . . . and the next thing I knew, it was morning . . .

and I was in the weeds downstream . . . and I was alive. That's all. I was alive."

And then I just had to get up and walk out, Amy. I couldn't take it any more. I got up and that's the last I ever spoke to my brother.

Amy Tasker thought the whole tale might have been Grandma's idea of an elaborate joke, but there was that look on the woman's face. Grandma said, "You don't believe me."

"I didn't say that."

"You didn't have to. It's plain on your face, just like that." She shifted in her seat and rearranged her afghan. "Those two friends of my brother's, Richie and Conrad, they were never seen again. Not ever. And the barn back at Professor Monroe's house, it burned to the ground that night, and the professor never came back to Berlin . . . and the house fell apart and was considered haunted when I was growing up . . . don't know what's there right now, not that it makes any difference."

Amy said, "Grandma, you mean you never saw your brother again?"

She shook her head. "I didn't say that."

"But you said—"

"No, I said I never talked to him again. But I did see him, the next day. I wanted to come in and talk to him, and give him grief about spinning such a story. I wanted to know why he said something crazy like that. I got to his room just as a couple of nurses were washing him up as he was on his side. They were talking between themselves and didn't notice me, which was fine. I got into the room and looked past the curtain, and I saw something I had never seen before. You know, we were a modest family, growing up, and John was never one for swimming or sunbathing, and that's when I found out why. For on his back, were these old scars, long lines running down his back."

"Scars?"

"Scars," Grandma said. "Like some great creature, or some great cat, had clawed at him."

Amy sat there, still, hands cold and tight in her lap, and then Grandma said, "He died a couple of days later. Poor John. I always think he lost his will to live after that night, after what happened, the guilt he carried, year after year, from all those dead people . . ."

"You mean, Conrad and Richie?"

Grandma smiled, just a bit. "No, dear child. Not just Conrad and Richie. Look, do you remember the legend of Sekhmet, what she was doing for Ra before she was captured?"

Amy recalled and said, "She was killing Ra's enemies. She was killing mankind."

"Yes," Grandma said. "She killed and killed and killed, and enjoyed it so much, killing mankind. You know your history, don't you?"

"Some."

"Here's something to think about, dear. This all happened to John and his two friends in August. In August, 1914. Do you know what happened that month?"

She could not believe she was saying the words. "The start of the First World War."

"True. The start of the First World War. Before that August, most people thought the world had finally found peace. There was the start of a global economy, global understanding, even global communications with the rise of the telegraph and telephone. Many people believed there would soon be an end to war . . . before that August, before Sekhmet returned, and the start of that war led to the bloodiest century mankind has ever seen, from the two world wars to the nations of China and the Soviet Union and Cambodia and the Congo killing millions of their own, year after bloody year, Sekhmet is still out there, Amy, Sekhmet is still enjoying her bloody work, right up to this day."

Amy could not say a word. Her grandmother was staring at her. She said, "That's what killed my brother. The guilt for what he and his friends had done, what he and his friends did to this Earth."

The door to the room opened up and a staff member of the rest home bustled in, said something about overstaying the visiting hours, and Amy stood up mechanically, bent over to kiss her grandmother on the cheek, and then found herself in the hallway, heading out, heading out to her life and her world.

And just before she went out the door, she snatched the ankh and chain from around her neck, tore it off, and tossed it in a trash can.

GAMES OF FATE

by Fiona Patton

Fiona Patton was born in Calgary Alberta in 1962 and grew up in the United States. Eventually she returned to Canada, and after several jobs which had nothing to do with each other, including carnival ride operator and electrician, moved to seventy-five acres of scrub land in rural Ontario with her partner, four cats of various sizes, and one tiny little dog. Her first book, *The Stone Prince*, was published by DAW Books in 1997. This was followed by *The Painter Knight* in 1998, *The Granite Shield* in 1999, and *The Golden Sword* in 2001, also by DAW. She is currently working on her next novel.

LAMPLIGHT flickered behind his eyelids. He smelled burning oil and unwashed bodies, felt the ground, cool and dry with a thin layer of sand, beneath him, tasted copper in his mouth and salt on his lips. Far away he heard the sounds of coughing, crying, praying, and remembered fear and pain but not much else.

Forcing his eyes open, he recognized the prison below Memphis Palace.

"Why" came to him as quickly as "where."

He closed his eyes again.

"Khet."

The sound of his name drove away the darkness, demanding his attention.

"Khet, drink."

A cup pressed against his lips and he swallowed reflexively. Warm, brackish water flowed down his throat, making him want to gag, but he finished it all, then opened his eyes again. A slight figure—creature, his awakening mind amended—crouched before him. Its face seemed to flow and merge in the lamplight, first a snake, and then a ram, a heron, then a crane, and finally the patchy features of a hyena. It grinned down at him with tiny, pointed teeth and he stared back at it in wonder.

"Who . . . ?" he managed.

It tipped Its head to one side in a curiously birdlike gesture, and the hyena face disappeared to be replaced by the sharp beak and piercing eyes of a golden hawk.

"Khepi. No, don't move," It added as Khet tried to sit up, "you've been badly beaten and your right arm may be broken."

"I can't feel it."

"The gods bestow their blessings where they will. Be grateful." The hawk face merged again to become a small, brown dog's. Khet's eyes widened.

"Are you a god?"

"A powerful one once." It sat back on Its haunches. "But merely a godling now. As Re waxes strong, so do many of us wane. We snatch what crumbs we can beneath the table of the mighty."

Khet pushed himself up to a sitting position, cradling his right arm against his chest as it began to throb. After scraping the blood from his eyelids with his good hand, he laid his head against the wall. "I feel for you," he offered.

The godling smiled mirthlessly. "I can see that you do. As I feel for you. You had a good life that might have led to great things. Born to nobility and raised right here at the palace, recruited for the Nubian campaign, where you served with distinction and honor, and chosen as one of Pharaoh's Guard. You might have eventually risen to general, perhaps even vizier, it's not unheard of. But . . ."

"But."

"But you allowed an enemy of Pharaoh to gain access to his bedchamber and he was nearly killed. Do you even know why you did it?"

Khet turned away. "I was drunk."

"A poor answer."

"But the only one I have."

"I know." The godling stood and peered down at a dead man lying nearby. "Given another chance would you have done anything differently?" It asked suddenly, turning a lean, jackal's face to regard him.

"I imagine I won't have gotten drunk," Khet snapped back. He tipped his head to one side in unconscious imitation of the godling's bird features. "Why are you here, Khepi?"

"Why, to keep you company, of course."

"But why me?"

"Why, indeed." The jackal's head disappeared to be replaced by the widespread hood of a cobra. "It's not easy to face one's final night alone," It continued. "And I thought you might like to play a game while you wait for your executioners."

Khet looked away. "I'm not really in the mood for games," he replied.

"Don't be so quick to decide. There are many kinds of games." The godling's eyes glowed red with anticipation. "There are guessing games and riddle games, games of chance and games of fate."

"Fate?"

"Ah. I thought that might strike your fancy, but I should warn you. Such games are simple on the outside but deadly on the inside and much trickier that you might at first imagine. One false answer or one wrong turn and the game is lost before you know it. A single question can hold the answer to the entire game; much like life. For example: what would you give to know your fate?"

Khet gave a harsh bark of laughter. "Nothing. I know my fate already. I'm going to die, my body will be thrown into the desert to be devoured by jackals, and my *ka* will starve and finally wither away to dust."

Khepi looked disappointed, but shook it off quickly. "True," It agreed. "And sooner than you think."

The shriek of metal hinges interrupted Its words. Khet tensed, but it was only a slave boy come to bring water for the prisoners. He let out a tight sigh of relief and, creeping forward, the godling laid one dry hand on his shoulder. "It's natural to be afraid," It assured him. "But truly unnecessary. What would you give to escape your fate, to live a long and fruitful life, to have your name honored, and your *ka* nurtured until it's drawn into the Otherworld by the Great Goddess Nut Herself?"

Khet's eyes grew pinched. "Anything, everything, but what difference does it make? I have nothing to give."

"Your have your name."

"My name? What kind of coin is that? Who am I?"

"Who, indeed?"

The prison door swung open again and two guardsmen entered. A fearful hush fell over the room as they passed a hard gaze over each prisoner, then caught one up between them. He began to beg and plead as they dragged him out by the feet. When his screams abruptly cut off, Khet turned away.

"As I was saying," Khepi continued in an even tone. "You have your name. Would you give it up to escape your fate, to escape that fate?"

The guardsmen returned. One looked Khet's way and his eyes narrowed in recognition.

"Decide quickly," Khepi hissed. "Your death is written in that one's gaze."

The guardsmen marched forward and Khet shrank against the wall. "Yes."

"Yes, what?"

"Yes, I give you my name. Turn them away."

"Done."

The guardsmen swerved suddenly and caught up a different prisoner. Khet turned.

"Was that it?"

"Was that what?"

"My fate escaped?"

The room seemed to grow suddenly cold as Khepi turned a frightful scorpion's gaze upon him. "Merely averted. Now you need to chose."

"Chose?

"Whose fate you will make the exchange for. That's how the game is played. The fate of each and every person is already known to the gods. Someone has to live them or the world falls out of balance."

"So I choose to live and someone else dies?"

"Precisely."

"Why would I do that?"

Khepi shrugged, but Its eyes gleamed slightly. "Do you want to live or don't you?" It asked in an indifferent tone. "This is the only bargain the gods are offering today."

"So, who should I chose? Someone who deserves to die?"

"You should choose whoever will best advance the game and keep the interest of the gods." Khepi waved one hand to take in the entire prison. "Choose whoever you wish from those you see about you."

Khet glanced around with an incredulous expression. "From in here? Everyone's a prisoner. So I gain an extra day or two in prison. What good will that do?"

The godling's face twisted into the sharp visage of a crocodile. "There are more than just prisoners in this room," It snapped back impatiently. "Open your eyes. There are your fellow guardsmen, for example."

Khet's expression hardened. "I was one of the pharaoh's Elite Bodyguard," he replied haughtily. "These are the dregs of the pharaoh's army, worthy only to guard the doomed far from Re's regard."

"As inferior as you may think them, at least they can move freely beyond these prison walls," Khepi sniffed back. "If you wish to do the same, I suggest you lower your standards."

A line of Palace Guard entered the prison and the godling's face shorted and became the sharp, pointed features of the hyena again. "Your death approaches, *He Who Guards*. Choose now!"

Khet glanced around in panic, then his eyes lit upon a tall, cold-eyed guardsman watching the others march forward with an amused sneer on his face. "All right. That one."

"Done."

"Wha . . ."

There was a sudden jerk and everything went dark for an instant, then he was reeling against the wall as the Palace Guards brushed by him. They caught a man up and, with a start, Khet saw his own features, made almost unrecognizable by a mask of blood. He flinched as they jerked him up by his broken arm, and nearly fainted as they dragged him through the door. Gripping the smooth half of his spear until it creaked, he stared at the godling, his black eyes wide until the man's—until his own—screams cut off. Slowly, as if loath to draw too near, he approached It.

"So quickly," he whispered.

It shrugged. "It's usually that way. Thank the gods the guards don't linger over their work."

Khet fell back against the wall, his head spinning. "I'm dead."

"No. Khet is dead. You are Rekhm now."

"I don't feel like Rekhm."

"How do you know?" The godling waved one hand dismissively before he could answer. "Then be Khet if you want to, but remember to answer as Rekhm or people will think you're fevered."

His face pale, Khet swiped at his mouth, expecting blood and finding only sweat. "He didn't know. Rekhm, when the exchange was made, he didn't realize."

"He didn't need to."

"But I do?"

"You can hardly play the game if you can't remember the rules."

"I took his life."

The godling rose. "You did. The choice was made—and just in time, too—I might add. You'd do well to choose more swiftly in the future."

"The future?"

Khepi turned Its cold, cobra eyes on him, Its tongue darting out to dance at the air. "The game is ongoing, *Rekhm*," It hissed, weaving slowly back and forth in the flickering lamplight, "until you're satisfied with your choices or the gods are."

Mesmerized by the movement, Khet stared back at it. "How will I know if the gods are satisfied?" he asked, unsure of whether he really wanted to know the answer.

"You will die."

"Die."

"If the gods allow you to take a lethal wound or if you're so foolish—or so unlucky—as to choose a fate which is almost at an end through disease or misstep, then you will die, and the game will be over." It stood. "No game, like no life, lasts forever, Khet."

"So what happens now?"

"Now? Now you stand your watch as Rekhm—no one will know the difference, just as no one will observe us conversing—then you will take me from this place and find me a warm bed to sleep in. After that,

only the gods can say. No doubt they're wagering on
your choices right now."

Khet couldn't help but glance about fearfully. "I
hope I make the right ones," he observed.

Khepi looked suddenly very weary. "So do I," It
replied in a dark tone.

The godling was as light as a child, it wrapped Its
soft, fine-boned fingers about Khet's neck as he carried
It to Rekhm's bed in the nearby barracks room, and
covered It with a coarse linen sheet. The godling fell
asleep immediately, but Khet sat for a long time, watching Its features shift and merge. The lamplight flickered
across the wall, causing the shadows to jump and
dance, enacting a story he almost remembered. As his
eyes slowly closed of their own volition, he dreamed.

"What will you give to escape your fate?"

*The godling's breath was hot on the back of his neck and,
with a snort of disgust, he thrust It aside.*

*"Nothing. Ask rather what I would give to be the means
to bring about the pharaoh's fate."*

"That's not the game we play."

"No? It would be a lot more entertaining." He gave a
*dark laugh deep in his throat. "Let's see if we might make it
so, regardless."*

The next morning, the godling nibbled delicately at
a piece of shat-cake as Khet tried to shake off the disturbing images of his dream.

"So," It began, catching him up in Its now familiar birdlike stare. "Are you ready to continue the game? Unless you'd rather live out the remainder of your life down here with the murderers and the disgraced guardsmen, of course?"

"No, I don't."

"Then reach for the life you want and choose again."

"I want the life I had."

The godling grinned at him with the sharp, white teeth of the hyena face. "Oh, I know you do," It agreed.

Khet frowned. "All right." He glanced around. "The life of another prison guard will not advance me at all," he noted.

"Nor will it advance the game," Khepi agreed.

"So, who do I choose? There are only guardsmen and prisoners on this level."

The godling gave an explosive sigh. "Once again, I fear that your limited sight will be the end of you."

Khet looked mystified and It snapped Its teeth together in frustration. "I think this last incarnation has addled your wits; you used to be much better at this."

"At what?"

"Nothing. Think, who else might come down here during the course of their duties?"

"Um . . . priests."

"Did you really want to take a priest?" Khepi's fine, black whiskers bristled, and Khet could almost feel Its anticipation of a wrong move.

"No," he said hastily, "but who else could there be?"

"There's another in this very room who would do nicely; must I show you every turn of the game?"

Khet stared about him in confusion. "Where?"

"By the bread table."

"I don't see anyone."

"Are you blind?" Finally the godling snorted and, catching Khet by the ears, drew his head around. "Do you think that tray is hovering in midair?"

Finally Khet's gaze focused on the boy who carried the tray. His eyes widened.

"You want me to trade fates with a slave?"

"That slave travels through every hall and room above in a day," the godling answered slowly as if to a child. "He can go outside to the palace gardens and into the fields beyond, even down to the very Nile itself. In many ways he has much more freedom than Rekhm has."

"But he's a slave," Khet protested.

"So take his fate and give him the life of a guardsman. It's a decent enough move for him."

"But not for me. A slave's life would hardly keep the interest of the gods."

"Your inability to grasp the nuances of the game is what will lose the interest the gods," Khepi snapped back. "Do you know nothing of strategy? This boy has access to unlimited areas of the palace. *Unlimited.* He is invisible to everyone. It took *you* an hour to notice him. How long will it take the pharaoh's Elite Bodyguard?"

Grinding his teeth, Khet nodded sharply. "Very

well. I choose him, whatever his name is, assuming he
even has a name."

The smell of cooking oil hit him like a blow as he entered the kitchens. The actual blow caught him across
the left ear and sent him flying into a pile of rush baskets. Struggling to stand, he looked up into the angry
face of the chief cook.

"When I say be quick, Enna, you're quick, or by
Ptah, I'll beat the speed into you," the man snarled, his
fist raised once again.

Khet surged to his feet, fury turning the boy's face a
dangerous crimson and the godling caught him before
he could launch himself at the older man.

"What will you do?" It hissed "He's three times your
present size and a mile above you in rank and status.
Do you want to end the game dead on the kitchen
floor?"

Khet turned, his eyes blazing. "He struck me," he
grated.

"And how will you enact vengeance upon him?
Think. Play the game."

"How do you feel?"

Khet flexed in the unfamiliar body. "Old. And fat."

"Only old compared to Enna and fat compared to
Rekhm."

"And both compared to Khet."

"You are Khet no longer. You are Senmut now, chief
cook at Memphis Palace."

"But I'm still a servant who carries no weapons."

"I'd say his fists are weapons enough." The godling flashed him a predatory grin. "But if you're unsatisfied with the life of a chief cook, move on. Choose another."

Khet's eyes flashed. "In a moment. I still have some unfinished business with *him*."

He took a step forward, but the sight of the cowering boy, blood smeared across his temple, gave him pause.

"He doesn't remember, does he?"

"No. He is Enna and always has been. If you strike him, it will only be for the second time this morning, nothing more."

Khet turned away. "Your game leaves a sour taste in the mouth, Khepi."

"So end it here."

"And spend the rest of my life as a fat, old cook? No thank you. I was one of Great Pharaoh's Elite. And I will be again." He made for the door.

The godling watched him go, an odd little smile playing across the hawk's head visage. "Yes," It agreed, "you will be and other things besides."

"So who *will* be cook?" It asked, after catching up to him as he strode down the hall. The sunlight pooling through the row of high, narrow apertures, bounced across the pale stone walls, making seeing difficult. Khet shrugged. "I don't know yet. But I don't think I want to take much more advice from you. You said Enna was invisible."

Khepi shrugged. "If I'd said mostly invisible, you'd still be debating the ins and outs of a slave boy's life."

"Hardly," Khet replied. "I probably would have headed up the stairs and taken my chances as Rekhm."

A breath of perfume cut off their debate and Khet stared as one of the Great Queen's handmaidens slipped by him, her arms laden with lotus flowers. The godling shook Its head. "You would make lovely Neri a fat, old cook?"

"What? No, I . . . wasn't thinking about that."

The godling glanced down at Khet's loincloth. "I can see you that weren't. But if you want her you'd best exchange your fate with someone with the right to her."

"Like who?"

"Oh, I don't know, her husband perhaps?"

"What is he?"

"A junior scribe."

Khet's heavy face twisted in disdain "No."

"Picky. Then carry on."

They continued down the hall, pausing before a long flight of stone steps.

"That leads to the main level," Khepi offered.

"I know."

"Glittering hallways, lush gardens, beautiful women . . ."

"I know."

"And people, many different people living many different lives."

Smiling, it followed as Khet took the stairs at a run.

He had to jump immediately into the life of an upper guardsman as Senmut was stopped at the head of the stairs. The cook returned to the kitchen level with a confused look on his face while Khet stared out at the sunlit world with a hungry expression. Servants, artisans, scribes, and traders bustled past him, and, as he breathed in the spicy scents of flowers and blooming trees wafting in from pharaoh's gardens, he swallowed painfully.

"I almost lost it all forever," he whispered.

"Yes," Khepi agreed with a soft, sibilant hiss. "And here you are once more basking in Re's regard. It only took you four moves. Not bad."

Unable to answer, Khet could only nod.

"You risk a fatal blow," the godling snarled. *"And the anger of the gods."*

Khet dreamed. He stood in an ornate bedchamber with friezes on the walls and mosaics on the floor, all depicting the life and deeds of the pharaoh. As he crept forward, he felt a sudden desire to kill the figure slumbering in the bed before him, although he couldn't understand why. He turned to glance at his ever-present companion.

"You might want to choose a different head to wear next

*time you threaten me, Khepi." He observed, gently moving
the fine bedcurtain aside with the tip of his dagger. "A pi-
geon's face is not particularly frightening, only foolish." He
raised the dagger above the sleeping figure and suddenly a
body hurled itself upon him. There was a flash of metal and
the godling cursed, but the blow missed and, with a word,
he was suddenly Ahkm, Chief of Guards, pinning the poten-
tial murderer of the Living God to the floor as more of the
Pharaoh's Elite poured into the room.*

Khet started awake, listening to the beating of his
heart pounding overloud in the quiet barracks room.
The moon cast a bright strip of light across Khepi's
jackal face, and with a shudder, Khet lay back down
again and tried to will himself to sleep without
dreaming.

It was high summer in Memphis and the palace was
filled with exotic visitors: Nubian warriors rubbed
shoulders with Mesopotamian scientists and Greek
philosophers; the elite of both Upper and Lower Egypt
sat beneath the brightly painted archways and debated trade, politics, and war while servants hovered
close at hand with jugs of wine and plates heaped
high with round, tiny cakes.

Khet had spent the better part of a month standing
guard in the palace's huge entrance hall, drinking it all
in, his pleasure marred only by the dreams that grew
increasingly clear and violent each night. Khepi would
not discuss them with him, merely crouched on the

floor nearby each day, Its multifaced visage betraying none of Its thoughts, content also to watch the world flow by. Today, however, It smiled as a host of dancers swept past, the tiny silver bells on their wrists and ankles filling the air with music and the most beautiful among them turned a smile full of promise on Khet.

"So, will you end the game here?" It asked, wearing a strangely eager dog's face. "This fellow . . ."

"Mehti."

"Mehti, he is both young and beautiful. Will you choose this life full of promise and pleasure?"

Khet frowned. "I don't know. I should. He—I—am well fed and well liked. I could have my choice of duties and half a dozen palace women would willingly be my wife."

"True, you would have love, family, honor, children to give you comfort and build your tomb all a man could wish for. Simply say the word and it will be so."

"Yes, but . . ."

"But what."

"I don't know, I feel like there's something else, some other life I'm meant to live. These dreams . . ."

"Hush!"

Khepi caught his arm just as the sound of horns blared through the hall. "Pharaoh approaches."

Khet started, the blood draining from his face. "Pharaoh," he repeated.

"The Great Qa'a himself. God among us and ruler over a strong and prosperous Egypt."

"I . . ."

"What?"

"Nothing."

"I ask again, Khet, will you keep the life of Mehti, loyal guardsman of Pharaoh's Palace at Memphis?"

Khet moved forward as if in a dream. "No."

The godling sighed, the dog's head merging to become the hyena once again. "I didn't think so," It grumbled.

He heard the music give way to chanting and singing as if from far away, smelled the strong scent of incense and felt a sudden twist of fearful excitement in his bowels as the great, mahogany-and-beaten-gold doors to the private areas of the palace were flung open. First a line of Bodyguards marched forward, their ceremonial armor flashing in the sun. A line of white-garbed priests came next and then finally the pharaoh. Khet stared, unable to tear his eyes away.

Qa'a, Ruler of Upper and Lower Egypt, terror of Nubia and Syria, husband to the Great Queen Nebet, son of Anedjib and brother of Semerkhet, pharaohs both before him, was a tall, well-muscled man in his early thirties. Wigged and bejeweled, he wore the formal false beard and cobra's hood headpiece of his exalted rank and walked with a warrior's powerful stride. As he and his entourage passed Khet's position, the guardsman forced himself to look away. He locked eyes with Khepi and fell suddenly into the snake-head's fathomless gaze.

*   *   *

The corridor was still and quiet, even the wind which had sent thousands of tiny grains of sand flying through the air that evening, had died down. Khet stood his watch, weaving slightly back and forth, remembering the sweet scent of Nofret's hair and the feel of her fingers, warm and soft, clasping his. He would see her again. Tomorrow likely, in the company of her mother and sisters, but at least he would see her.

His bladder twinged and, as he turned to relieve himself through the narrow window, he saw a dark figure slither over the wall and make, as silent as a snake, toward the pharaoh's bedchamber. As he watched, it struck down the guards on duty before the God-King's door, and slipped inside.

He opened his mouth to shout the alarm, but no words came out. He tried to move, to run to the pharaoh's aid, but his feet were frozen to the floor. The guardsman beside him made an inquiring noise in his throat and Khet turned, knowing it would mean the pharaoh's death, and shrugged. Deep inside him something, someone, chuckled in triumph.

When Khet came back to himself, Qa'a had passed through the doors to the main temple, leaving only the heavy scent of sandalwood behind.

It took him two days to get noticed by Kenamun, the Chief of Guards. Throughout, Khepi pestered him to make a choice. Khet ignored It, finally asking It bluntly about his dreams. The godling backed off, muttering, but the day Khet was assigned to the pharaoh's hunting procession, It followed him reluctantly, the brown dog's head whining quietly.

The morning breeze was warm and sweet as the procession wound its stately way down to the marshes along the west bank of the Nile. Having put aside his formal attire, Qa'a walked easily, his long, black sheep's wool wig sweeping across his back at every stride. He wore a simple but finely made loincloth and carried his own spear across one shoulder. Bending down, he whispered a joke into the hair of his tiny daughter, the six-year-old Princess Meryet, and she laughed with the pleasure of just being at his side. Behind her, the older Princess Henet and their mother, the queen, smiled indulgently.

Khet gripped his spear, his palms suddenly slick, and tried to concentrate on the path.

Arriving at the marshes, Qa'a immediately waded into the shallow, reed-filled water while his family gathered on the bank to watch. The Chief of Guards stood beside him, his sharp, black eyes sweeping the water for fish, while his guardsmen formed a ring about them both, watching intently for signs of crocodiles or hippos. Khet stood just to one side of the pharaoh, a series of conflicting emotions chasing themselves around and around within his heart. When Khepi spoke to him from the reeds, he started guiltily.

Twisting the long, graceful neck of a crested heron to regard him, It fixed him with one large eye.

"It's a warm day," it observed mildly.

Khet frowned without taking his gaze away from Qa'a.

"What?"

"A warm day. The enemy is sunning themselves on the east bank."

Glancing quickly across the river, Khet noted the line of dozing crocodiles before returning his gaze to the pharaoh.

"Yes," he answered absently.

"Keep your eyes open. You never know when one might sneak past your guard."

"Yes, all right."

The pharaoh moved a step closer and Khet gripped his spear as tightly as he had that first night as Rekhm. His head began to spin.

"The game has progressed nicely," Khepi continued. "You've chosen well and the gods are pleased. So I will ask you again; will you now take Mehti's life and fate as your own?"

Something in the urgency of Its voice cut through his daze and Khet glanced down at him as the heron face melted away. For an instant, it seemed to become the blunt visage of a great scarab beetle, then the heron face returned as if it had never left.

"What?"

"Mehti?"

Khet shook his head in distracted annoyance. "Not now, Khepi."

"If not now, then when?"

"Later. Tonight, when we return."

The godling laid Its hand on his arm, staring up at him with the pleading eyes of the brown dog. "We are nearing the end of the game, Khet," It said quietly. "Won't you choose now?"

He met Its gaze. "I can't."

"You can. Put anger and betrayal aside and make the right move at last."

The pharaoh turned his back to him. Khet's hand twitched.

"Khet."

"What?"

"Choose now. Mehti's is a good fate. Trust me."

The sun beat down upon the sparkling sand as Khet looked across at Memphis Palace standing large and formidable on the spit of land bank between Upper and Lower Egypt. He thought of his life, of Mehti's life, and of all the things he might have and do, and suddenly it seemed as if he'd wasted his entire life—a life much longer than Mehti's or even Khet's, on an obsession even he couldn't understand anymore.

He stared at Khepi for a long time, then slowly nodded. "Yes," he said at last. "I choose Mehti."

With a relieved smile, the godling nodded.

"Done."

Khet opened his mouth to speak, but suddenly a crocodile launched from the water between two of his fellow guardsmen. On the bank, Meryet screamed and, as Khet spun around, he could almost feel the gods holding their breath, then he was plunging through the water, knocking the pharaoh aside in his haste to throw himself between him and the deadly creature. His spear caught it in the mouth, drove through and out, but it kept coming, rising up to catch him around the waist. It snapped its teeth together and he felt a terrible, slashing pain, then nothing. The pharaoh's Elite rushed forward, thrusting and stabbing, and finally the creature released him and fled back to deeper water, trailing a line of blood behind it. Khet fell.

Somehow, he found himself on the bank, lying with his head cradled in Kenamun's lap. Khepi sat beside him, Its cobra's face inscrutable.

He tried to speak, coughed blood across his face, and the godling reached down to gently wipe it away.

"That's the end of the game, child," It said kindly. "You chose well in both Mehti and Khet."

Khet blinked, trying to keep It in focus, then just closed his eyes. "I can't . . . feel my legs," he breathed.

"The gods bestow their blessing where they will. Be grateful." It sat back on Its haunches. "One final question remains, my very first question: What would you give to know your fate?"

Khet struggled to open his eyes. Khepi's face flowed and changed, becoming in quick succession every form It had taken while asking Its question. He shook his head weakly.

"Khepi . . . you know I have . . . nothing left to give," he whispered.

"You have your name."

"I gave you . . . my name."

"You gave Khet's name. A Palace Guardsman, valuable yes, but do you really think that he alone could command the gods to give him a second chance to rewrite the deeds of his life. Think, feel, and remember, *He Who Guards*, remember your name."

The cobra's eyes stared into his, and suddenly he knew. "Hello, old friend," he whispered.

"What would you give?"

He smiled faintly. "I don't know. How about my gratitude?"

"That will do fine, Semerkhet."

The word echoed through the marshes, making the hair on the back of his arms and legs stand on end, and suddenly he was in another place and another time. There were guards at his door, a doom on his head, and a great rage in his heart. Khepi stood before him, the tiny pointed teeth of Its hyena face flashing white in the moonlight.

"What would you give to escape your fate?"

He shrugged in disdain. "Very little. What do you want?"

"Your name."

"No."

"That's all you have to offer."

"Then depart empty-handed and I will make the journey to the Otherworld without your help."

"You'll only make it with my help," It hissed. "You

*enraged the gods when you took the throne of Egypt and the
mantle of Godhead through bloodshed.*"

"*It was my right.*"

"*Perhaps some day, but you murdered your own father to
achieve it!*"

"*He planned to pass the throne to Qa'a on his death. He
plotted it with his vizier. I was older and stronger. It should
have gone to me.*"

"*He was pharaoh.*"

"*And now I am pharaoh.*"

"*Technically, Qa'a is now pharaoh.*"

"*Not until my death.*"

"*Which is imminent.*"

Semerkhet fell silent. "What do I do?"

"*Play the game and choose. Who here would you exchange your fate with?*"

"*How about my executioner?*"

"*A good choice. Here he comes now.*"

The marshes slowly returned. He blinked.

"I . . . murdered Anedjib?"

"And tried to murder Qa'a. That first night you took
the fate of Derj, Pharaoh's Chief Executioner—and the
earthly representative of Anubis, too, I might add—
which did not endear you to that particular god at all.
You went immediately to the pharaoh's bedchamber
and tried to gut him. You failed, of course. Nekhebt
spread her great wings above his body and you were
taken by the guard; the first of many times."

"Many? How many lives have I chosen?"

"A few more than might have been necessary if you'd used your head."

He frowned. "Why didn't I remember all this as Khet?"

The Godling cocked Its crested head to one side. "Because Khet was a truly loyal member of the pharaoh's Bodyguard for all you tried to corrupt him. Fortunately, however, he succeeded in corrupting you, as we hoped he would."

"We?"

"Your fellow gods." It stood. "Now, Great Pharaoh, are you ready to cross over to the Realms of Bliss?"

Suddenly unbearably tired, Semerkhet nodded. "I am."

It reached out Its hand. "Then come. The Goddess Nut is waiting for you in Her sycamore tree, and I have business with yet another of your kind this night."

It pulled him to his feet. Together, Semerkhet, sixth Pharaoh of a united Egypt and Khepi, Scarab God of the Dead, turned their backs on the world, while the Bodyguard of the pharaoh carried one of their own back to the palace at Memphis to honor his sacrifice.

THE SPIN WIZARD

by Laura Resnick

Laura Resnick, a cum laude graduate of Georgetown University, won the 1993 John W. Campbell Award for best new science fiction/fantasy writer. Since then she has never looked back, having written the best-selling novels *In Legend Born* and *In Fire Forged*, with more on the way. She has also written award—winning nonfiction, an account of her journey across Africa, entitled *A Blonde in Africa*. She has written several short travel pieces as well as numerous articles about the publishing business. She also writes a monthly opinion column for *Nink*, the newsletter of Novelists, Inc. You can find her on the Web at *www.sff.net./people/laresnick*.

R AMSES the Mediocre was having a bad day.

"Have you *seen* today's scrolls?" he demanded of his favorite wife, Nefertari.

"Well, I've *seen* them," she said, "but since I can't read—"

"Then let me read them *to* you!"

"It's a little inconvenient right now, dear. I was just about to go have my body shaved."

"That can wait," he snapped. "Just listen to this piece of venomous drivel in the *Theban Times!*"

"And after my shave, I was thinking of having a pedicure. Or maybe a manicure? Hmmm . . . Pedicure, manicure? Manicure, pedicure?"

Happily for the sake of posterity, a palace scribe was nearby, busily writing down every precious word which tumbled from the dewy lips of the divine king's consort. Without such attentions, history might never learn how well-groomed pharaoh's wives were, in which case subsequent generations might let their appearances decline to the standards of your average Hyksos kitchen wench.

" 'Ramses the Ineffectual!' " Ramses quoted, pacing up and down the polished palace floor as he read from the *Times*. " 'His father Seti successfully fought Palestine, Syria, and those darned Libyans, and then built the temple at Abydos in his downtime. But what has Ramses done so far? Gotten huge numbers of Egyptian soldiers slaughtered, that's what! The battle of Kadesh would be farcical if it weren't so costly and tragic, not to mention embarrassing.'" Ramses snarled with impotent rage as he tore the scroll to pieces.

"Well, they never really have liked you in Thebes, darling," said Nefertari soothingly while browsing among her eight hundred pairs of sandals. "Shall I wear the beige pair today? Or the tan? Hmmm . . . Beige or tan? Tan or beige?"

"If it were only those pesky Thebans, I'd shrug it off," Ramses replied furiously, "but the *Elephantine Express* is even worse!" He waved the *Express* at Nefertari before unrolling it and reading, " 'According to our ace scribe on the scene in Kadesh, the Hittites claim *they* won the battle that the pharaoh claims *he* won. Ramses owes the people of Egypt an explanation! And the people are going to get it! Whether they want it or not! Exclusive sources have informed our award–winning scribes that the priests of Ma'at are already petitioning their goddess to weigh Pharaoh's heart against her ostrich feather to determine if he should come under investigation for the travesty which was Kadesh."

"Ostrich feathers!" Nefertari turned to her dressers and said, "What do you think?"

"No," they all three said in unison.

One of them added, "Not with that outfit."

"Hmm . . ." Her exquisite brow puckered with concentrated thought. "Perhaps I should change."

"Or perhaps," Ramses continued, "you'd prefer a selection from the *Memphis Messenger*? One of their scribes got an exclusive interview with Muwatallis, and that rat bastard has told them—"

"Who, dear?"

"Muwatallis! The damn king of the damn Hittites!"

"Foreigners." Nefertari rolled her kohl-rimmed eyes. "Where *do* they get those silly names?"

"Muwatallis says that I retreated in haste and lost a big chunk of the territory that my father Seti held!"

"Good gracious," Nefertari exclaimed while letting Nubians daub scent behind her ears and knees, "why ever would he say a thing like that?"

"Possibly," said a newcomer, "because it's true."

Ramses whirled around and confronted the intruder. "These are our private rooms! How did you get in here? Guar—"

"No, no, don't call the guards," said the stranger. "They can't see me."

"That's absurd!" Ramses shouted.

"Who are you talking to?" Nefertari asked.

"To this short, fat fellow, of course!"

"Fat?" the stranger repeated. "*Fat?* I haven't eaten in centuries, I'll have you know!"

"*What* short fat fellow?" Nefertari asked.

Ramses stared at her. "You can't see him?"

The short, fat fellow said, "Told you so."

"It's a spirit!" Ramses cried. "An afreet! A demon!"

"Oh, pull yourself together, would you?" the afreet snapped.

"Or possibly," Ramses added uncertainly, "it's that palm wine I had last night."

"I *told* you I thought it had gone bad," Nefertari reminded him.

"I am neither a demon nor a palm wine illusion!" the intruder said with offended dignity. "*I* am Imhotep."

"Imhotep?" Ramses frowned dubiously. "Not *the* Imhotep?"

"The very same," was the smug reply. "Architect, physician, scribe, and the great Zoser's vizier."

"Who's Imhotep?" Nefertari asked Ramses, looking around in confusion.

"He's the one," Ramses told her, "who came up with the idea for the Step Pyramid at Sakkara."

"*Don't* let him remodel the palace, dear," Nefertari said quickly.

"Don't worry," Ramses advised her while Imhotep sputtered in indignation, "he's dead. Been dead for more than a thousand years."

"So . . ." Nefertari pondered the ramifications of this. "That means he won't be staying for dinner?"

"Oh," Imhotep sighed longingly, "if only I could."

Ramses eyed him uncertainly. "Well, if you'd really like to dine with us—"

"There's nothing I'd like better, dear boy, but it's impossible. Ever since the embalmers removed and mummified my digestive tract . . . Well, suffice it to say that eating's just not what it used to be." Imhotep sighed again. "Can you imagine? A thousand years without a meal? Trust me, immortality isn't all it's cracked up to be. Nor is divinity."

"Divinity . . ." Ramses sucked in his breath on a horrible gasp. "That's right! You're a patron god of . . . *scribes*."

"Ah . . ." Imhotep smiled. "Perhaps you're not quite the slow-witted ignoramus they all said you were."

"*Scribes!*" Ramses repeated with furious loathing. "You fiend! You unholy swine! You . . . um, *who* said I'm a slow-witted ignoramus?"

"I shouldn't have brought it up," Imhotep apologized.

" 'They?' They who? Who are '*they?* ' "

Nefertari looked nervous. "They, dear? Are you saying there are more demons here now?"

Imhotep scowled. "Please inform the chief royal wife that I'm not a demon, I'm a *god*. Primarily a god of medicine, of course, but one does try to keep one's hand in—"

"Ah-hah!" Ramses waved some of the daily scrolls in Imhotep's pudgy face. "This is all *your* doing, you villain!"

"No, Ramses," the god said tersely, "frankly, it's *your* doing. What in the name of Isis were you *thinking* of at Kadesh? I've seen pubescent priestesses at remote desert shrines who could've run a better battle than you, the king of Egypt, ran against the Hittites!"

"Hindsight," Ramses said through gritted teeth, "is of no use to me. Where were you when I needed you?"

"We never realized—"

"We?"

"You know: the gods of Egypt. *Us*. We never realized that you'd need help." Imhotep gazed innocently at the high ceiling. "Seti, after all, never needed any help."

"Could we just leave the old man out of this discussion?" Ramses snapped. "Is that too much to ask?"

"I can see it's a sore subject," Imhotep said gravely. "So I'm guessing that it's a *very* sore subject that even Hatshepsut was a better military leader than you."

"Hatshepsut!" Ramses sputtered. "How can you even compare me to that—that—female in a beard?"

"You're right." Imhotep nodded. "It's not fair to Hatshepsut. When *she* was pharaoh, after all, she waged triumphant military campaigns, launched successful trading expeditions, and constructed exceptional monuments. So, as you say, what comparison could there possibly be between her and the likes of y—"

"I don't believe anyone invited you here," Ramses said stiffly.

"Oh, dear," Imhotep murmured, "I've offended you, haven't I?"

"Ramses, dear," said Nefertari, "you're turning purple and talking nonsense. What has Hatshepsut, surely the worst-dressed woman in royal history, got to do with anything?"

"The great royal wife," Imhotep noted, "has a one-rut mind, doesn't she?"

"Leave my wives out of this!" Ramses warned.

"Wives? I only see the one," Imhotep said.

"The rest are all in the harem," Ramses explained. "I keep Nefertari close by in case I need a second opinion."

"She being such an intellectual?" Imhotep asked.

"Compared to my other wives," Ramses replied.

"Sad. I *never* thought all this inbreeding was a good idea," Imhotep confided.

"You'd think even less of it if you were me and had to marry some of *my* female relatives," Ramses said morosely.

"Not to mention the Hittite princess you're going to have to marry," Imhotep added.

Ramses fell back with a gasp of horror. *"Marry a Hittite?"*

"Naturally," Imhotep replied.

Nefertari repeated, *"Marry a Hittite?"*

"I can't!" Ramses cried. "Have you ever *seen* a Hittite princess? At least Hatshepsut's beard was fake! But *Hittite* girls—"

"Nonetheless—" Imhotep began.

"No, no!" Ramses pleaded.

"Do try to show some spine," Imhotep urged the Lord of the Two Lands. "After the way Muddy Wallace trounced you—"

"Muwatallis," Ramses corrected. "And he didn't *trounce*—"

"After the way he slaughtered your army and sent you running home with your tail between your skinny legs—"

"They're not skinny!"

Nefertari repeated, *"Marry a Hittite?"*

"—you're going to have to make a royal alliance to keep Egypt secure, which means—face up to it, old boy—marrying a Hittite."

"Hittite girls have hair on their bodies in places where even *I* don't have hair!" Ramses protested.

"How do you know that?" Imhotep asked curiously.

"How do you know that?" Nefertari demanded.

Ramses blushed furiously. "Um, I, er . . . hear rumors, dear."

"Very convincing," Imhotep said dryly.

Nefertari's sloe-eyed glare was penetrating. "If you bring a Hittite into our home," she warned Ramses, "I will fling myself into the Nile."

"Good gods!" Imhotep frowned. "She's taking this rather hard, isn't she?"

"Not really," Ramses confided. "She's an excellent swimmer. Never ever drowns when she flings herself into the Nile."

Nefertari scowled, made an imperious gesture to her thirteen body servants, and said icily to pharaoh, "I can see you're busy talking to thin air—"

"To a *god*," Imhotep interjected.

"—so I will leave you in peace!" She stalked majestically out of the room. Many sandals scuffled noisily in her wake as her servants trailed behind her.

"Well, thank you very much," Ramses said sourly to Imhotep. "Do you do this sort of thing for everyone's domestic life, or just mine?"

"Oh, don't fret so much. You can probably stall the Hittites on this marital alliance for years. So her gracious majesty, the Lady of Charm, will have plenty of time to get used to the idea."

"No, she'll just have years in which to plan how

she'll make me suffer if I bring home a Hittite," Ramses said despondently.

"I'm beginning to see why you managed Kadesh so badly."

Ramses flung himself into a gold-encrusted chair. "Did you come here just to goad me, or does this unexpected visit have some more specific purpose?"

Imhotep gestured to the daily scrolls. "They're calling you Ramses the Forgettable. Ramses the Incompetent. Ramses the Mediocre."

"Yes, yes, I know, you needn't repeat everything you read."

"Ramses the Destined to Obscurity—which is quite a mouthful, and also hard to work casually into a sentence."

Ramses watched him warily. "Are you going to demand I quit the job?"

"No, no," Imhotep assured him. "Divine right of kings and all that. Oh, admittedly, you were chosen for the job late one night after we'd all had way too much to drink; but we don't go back on divine mandate. So you've got the job for life."

Ramses drew his knees up to his chest in sudden alarm. "For life? Er, does that mean . . ."

"Hmm? Oh!" Imhotep chuckled merrily. "No. Anubis would be here instead of me if we wanted to whack you. No, dear boy, what I'm trying to tell you is that this is our mess, too, and we're going to help clean it up. After all, the future of Egypt matters a great deal to us. We don't want to have to apply for work as Assyrian or Babylonian deities."

"No, I suppose not." Ramses asked hopefully, "Does that mean you're going to kill a lot of scribes? particularly the one who interviewed that rat bastard Muwatallis?"

"Oh, have you got that interview here?" Imhotep asked with interest. "I'd love to read it! Hathor says it's insightful, audacious, and all correctly spelled."

Ramses handed him the *Memphis Messenger*. "Please, take it with you when you leave. The door's right over there."

Ignoring the hint, Imhotep continued, "We've all talked it over together, and we've decided that what you need—"

"Is a terrible public death and a guarantee of no afterlife whatsoever for any scribe who writes such malicious tripe about me," Ramses said with conviction.

"No."

The pharaoh tried not to let his lower lip tremble. "No?"

"No." Imhotep shook his head. "You don't need them dead, what you need—"

"Yes, I do! Dead would be good!"

"What you need," Imhotep continued doggedly, "is to get all of the scribes praising you and extolling your virtues."

Ramses frowned. "How do I do that?"

"Well, it would have helped if you'd given them something to work with," Imhotep admitted, "such as even a soupçon of military skill or intelligent leadersh—"

"Under the circumstances," Ramses said through gritted teeth, "how do I do it?"

"Why, you do what every other incompetent ruler with a shred of self-preservation does, my dear boy." Imhotep waved his chubby hand and produced a little cartouche out of thin air. "You hire an expert."

Ramses accepted the little stone tablet from him and read the hieroglyphs there. " 'Miriam of Mahoza . . .' " He frowned in puzzlement as he concluded, " 'Spin Wizard to the Gods'?"

"Exactly!" Imhotep beamed at him.

"But what's a—"

Suddenly an unfamiliar nasal voice echoed through the serene halls of the palace. "Hull-o-o-o! Anybody home?"

The pharaoh's chief personal steward appeared an instant later. "Your gracious majesty," he began, "Lord of the Two Lands, He Who Rules—"

"Yes, yes, what is it?" Ramses rose from his chair.

"There is . . ." The steward's expression struggled with profound distaste for a moment. "A *person* here to see your divine magnificence."

"A person?"

"In all honesty, gracious king of all that is civilized, I could not possibly describe her as a *lady*."

"Ah! It's Miriam," said Imhotep cheerfully. "Impeccable timing, as always."

A tall, beautiful, big-boned, and immensely vulgar

woman strode into the palatial room wherein Ramses and Imhotep awaited her. "Imhotep? Boychik!" she cried with noisy glee.

Ramses asked, "You can see him?"

"She's a wizard," Imhotep explained as Miriam of Mahoza enveloped him in a sturdy embrace.

"And *you* can see him," Miriam said, turning to Ramses with robust energy, "because you're descended from the gods. Or so the theory goes." She seized his hands and squeezed them—hard enough to hurt. "How ya doin', your divine majesty? It's a pleasure to meet you!"

Ramses protested, "A commoner such as yourself should never touch Pharaoh's divine person without—"

"This is such a thrill for me," Miriam burbled. "Let me tell you, I was such a fan of your father's."

"Really?" Ramses tried to pull his hands out of her agonizing grip.

"Such a king!" she beamed. "If he had ever hired *me* . . . Well! Imhotep! Imagine if Seti had hired me!"

"It boggles the mind," Imhotep assured her.

"He would be even bigger than Hatshepsut."

Ramses finally succeeded in freeing his hands. He staggered back a few steps and snapped, "Hatshepsut?"

"Only one of the greatest pharaohs in history!" Miriam assured him. "Only destined to be remembered through the ages as a ruler eons ahead of her time. As a woman who showed men what a woman can really do! As a great military—"

"Did you work for her?" Ramses demanded suspiciously.

"If only!" Miriam waved her hands. "No, no. Before my time, I'm afraid."

"Well," Ramses said, attempting to gain control of the conversation, "if we could just leave Seti and Hatshepsut out of this and—"

"Of course, of course!" Miriam agreed. "We have *sooooo* much work to do."

"Work?"

"Oy! I wish, your gracious majesty, that you hadn't waited so long to summon me. You needed someone of my expertise on the scene in Kadesh, or at least there in time to spin the story the moment the battle was over. But now, what with having waited until—"

"Are you a military wizard?" Ramses asked in disbelief.

Miriam of Mahoza laughed—or, at least, a rhythmic snorting sound came out of her nose. "No, sire. Anyhow, it's definitely too late for that, isn't it? I mean, you lost, what, one fourth of the army at Kadesh? No, if you wanted a military wiz—"

"Then what *do* you do, woman?"

Her eyes widened in surprise. "But I thought . . ."

"No, Miriam," Imhotep intervened. "It wasn't Pharaoh who summoned you, it was us." He frowned. "We? Us?"

She said, "You and the other gods?"

"Yes."

"*Ohhhh*. So this is, like, a referral, right?"

"Exactly," Imhotep said.

Ramses was perplexed. "Referral?"

"I did some work for the gods of Egypt," Miriam explained. "It was a big contract. Completely turned things around for the whole pantheon."

"She's not exaggerating," Imhotep assured him.

Ramses stared at Imhotep. "You and the other gods employed this woman?"

"Frankly," Imhotep admitted, "she saved our, er, posteriors."

"*This* woman," Ramses said, "saved the gods of Egypt?"

"I certainly did," Miriam confirmed. "So if anyone can save your *tuchas* after Kadesh, Lord of Much Less Than All Seti Used to Survey, it's me."

"I *said* you're to leave the old man out of this!"

"Oops! Sore spot?" Miriam asked Imhotep.

"Very," the chubby god confirmed.

"I don't understand," Ramses said to Imhotep. "How did this pestilent woman help you and the other gods?"

"Pestilent?" Miriam repeated. "I would take that personally if I didn't have the hide of a Nile hippo."

"And the figure of one, too," Ramses said malevolently.

"Now, now, mortals," chided Imhotep. "Let's be nice."

"If this woman is a wizard, then I'm—"

"A great military leader?" Imhotep asked gently.

Ramses flung himself into another gold-encrusted chair and said sulkily, "All right. I'm listening."

"Ramses, my boy," Imhotep began, "you have no idea what things were like when Akhenaten died."

"The heretic?"

"*Now* he's a heretic." Miriam gave a satisfied nod. "*That's* spin."

"Huh?" said Ramses.

"Now he's a heretic," Imhotep repeated, "but at the end of his reign, huge portions of the population had converted to that hippie cult of his. Don't ask me why. I mean, honestly—*one sole* god? Good grief! Even now it boggles my mind that mortals can be that gullible." Imhotep sighed. "But I digress."

"You certainly do," Ramses agreed.

"When Tutankhaten was crowned—"

"Who?" Ramses asked.

"Tutankhamon," Imhotep replied. "He changed it after he became king."

"Oh."

"Such a pity," Miriam said, "dying so young like that. And the funeral! So shabby."

"Not to mention that tomb," Imhotep shook his head.

"Pathetic," Miriam agreed. "No way of putting a good spin on *that* tomb."

"You'd think the king's dog had died instead of the king himself," Imhotep added.

"And what were they *thinking,* putting the tomb where they did?" Miriam demanded. "I'll bet you a pair of gold sandals that tomb robbers find it before the end of the year."

"No bet," said Imhotep sadly.

"Could we leave Tutankhaten—Tutankhamon— *whoever*—out of this?" Ramses said wearily.

"Not really," Imhotep said. "You see, my boy, thanks to Akhenaten, when Tutankhamon was crowned, the temples and shrines of the traditional gods, all the way from Elephantine to the delta, had become overgrown, dusty, depressing ruins."

"Not really?" Ramses said.

"Well, I may be exaggerating slightly, but things were bad."

"And *why* did Aten worship take over Egypt like a bad rash?" Miriam interjected.

"Because," Ramses said with dignity. "Pharaoh decreed it should be so."

More of those noises came out of her nose. "That's cute. I like it. Keep that."

"Keep what?"

"That whole 'I am Pharaoh' vibe you've got going."

"But I *am* Pharaoh."

"Now don't overdo it," Miriam cautioned. "A little is good, but too much is worse than none at all."

"Pearls from the master," Imhotep told Ramses.

"Where was I?" Miriam said. "Oh, yes! The gods lost so much ground so fast because no one was handling their image. They were just floating around being deities, like that was all you had to do!"

"It's not?" Ramses asked doubtfully.

"*Bubeleh*." Miriam pinched his royal cheek. "You are so sweet. A little pathetic, but sweet."

"You know the jeweled statues of all the gods that Tutankhamon set up, the rites and sacrifices he performed on such a colossal scale, all of it designed to get people back to our side of the street?" Imhotep prodded.

"Um . . ." said Ramses. "No."

"But you do know who Isis is?" Miriam said.

"Well, of course!"

Imhotep added, "As well as Osiris, Anubis, Bast, Thoth, Hathor, Horus—"

"Naturally!" Ramses assured them both.

Miriam continued, "Qebehsenuef—"

"*Who?*"

"Ah-hah!" Miriam looked at Imhotep. "Was I right, or was I right?"

Imhotep spread his hands. "You were right, as always, Miriam. I tried to talk sense into him, but it was useless. He was a schmuck."

Miriam explained to Ramses, "Qebehsenuef is a god wh—"

"Surely not."

"Would I lie to you?" Miriam raised her hands as if declaiming all responsibility for Qebehsenuef. "I told him, and I *told* him. 'Qebbie,' I said, 'if you want to make a comeback, you have *got* to be a patron of something more alluring than the intestines of the dead. You need to take a snappy, glamorous cause under your protection, like seeing-eye cats or homeless dancing girls.' But did he listen? *Noooo*."

"The result being," Imhotep said, "that hardly anyone even knows who he is. While those of us who *did* follow Miriam's advice currently find our polls running at an all-time high."

"Plus there was that whole *look* of his." Miriam shook her head. "Head of a falcon on a mummified human body. I mean, really! What was I supposed to do with *that*? But, no, you couldn't tell Mr. Protector-of-Dead-Intestines a thing. *He* knew best, *he* knew what the people wanted after all that Aten worship: dead intestines and a molting bird's head on a moldy mummy. I ask you!"

"We felt your pain," Imhotep assured her.

"I sometimes wonder if it's all that inbreeding," she mused. "I *never* thought that was a good idea."

"So if I understand you correctly," Ramses said, his head already spinning, "you're here to create a favorable image for me in the eyes of the Egyptian people?"

"Boychik, let's think bigger than that! In the eyes of the world! In the eyes of *history*. Posterity! I'm here to guarantee that you become known as 'Ramses the Great,' not only to your subjects, but to everyone, everywhere, for generations to come!"

"Well. That sounds pretty good," Ramses conceded.

"I'm afraid it's a very tall order, Miriam."

"You know I love a challenge," she replied, pulling Ramses to his feet and circling him with an assessing gaze. "Is there anything we can do about those skinny legs?"

"They're not skinny!" Ramses protested.

"The rest isn't too bad," Miriam continued. "The schnozz is a little big, but we can work that to our advantage."

"How dare—"

"How?" Imhotep asked Miriam.

"Oh, easy. We spread the word that a big schnozz means a man has a big—"

"Well, now that you mention it . . ." Ramses began.

"People will believe any lie," Miriam explained, "as long as you tell it with conviction."

Ramses frowned. "It happens to be tr—"

"Ah! Yes, now I remember," said Imhotep. "You did something similar for Sobek and that huge crocodile snout of his."

"And believe me, that was a lot harder to work with than Ramses' beak."

"*Excuse* me, it is not—"

"So the real problem," Miriam continued, "is not the unimpressive physical material—"

"Unimpressive? I will have you know that Nefertari says—"

"—but rather the disastrous military background combined with the utterly mediocre domestic record. Hmmm . . ."

"Mediocre," Ramses muttered bitterly.

"Tell me more about Kadesh," Miriam said.

"I don't want to talk about Kadesh anymore," Ramses insisted.

Imhotep began, "Ramses heard that Mut the Wallis—"

"*Muwatallis.*"

"—had gathered thirty-five thousand men and several thousand chariots. The Hittite king claimed he'd done it solely to keep Hyksos barbarians off the streets at night—"

"But I just *knew*," Ramses said, "that rat bastard meant to attack Egyptian territory."

"So Ramses departed posthaste for Kadesh, taking four infantry divisions with him." Imhotep paused before continuing, "Then some Hittite deserters got caught and brought before Pharaoh. They explained that their king and all his troops had fled in terror before our advancing army and were already far to the north." After another pause, he added, "Ramses believed them."

Miriam put her head in her hands. "Dear gods."

"They *said* they were deserters!" Ramses protested.

"In reality," Imhotep said, "they were, of course—"

"Decoys sent by Muwatallis," Miriam guessed.

"Bingo," said Imhotep.

"They *looked* like deserters," Ramses muttered.

"So Ramses took only one of his four divisions," Imhotep continued, "and dashed ahead to Kadesh, eager—for reasons which he has never coherently explained—to catch up with the retreating Hittites."

"And Muwatallis," said Miriam, "struck him."

"Naturally. Ramses had run—not walked, but *run*—straight into a trap. Our boys were hopelessly outnumbered, and the rest of our army was strung out way behind them."

"This is terrible," Miriam said.

"Ramses survived—just barely—to counterattack the next day, but the Hittites were too strong and he had to retreat back to Egypt. The Hittites are now in control of Kadesh and the rest of the territory they've taken from us."

"Who could spin *this?*" Miriam said despairingly. "Let me make sure I've got this right. The king of Egypt was easily duped by a couple of Hittite peasants, he nearly got our army destroyed, and he lost Egyptian territory."

"In a nutshell," Imhotep confirmed.

"I feel ill," Miriam moaned.

"It's discouraging, I admit," Imhotep said. "But surely a wizard of your—"

"Maybe we could claim some sort of psychotic incident?" Miriam mused aloud.

"Possibly," Imhotep said as he considered this. "Because when Ramses found himself outwitted, trapped, and outnumbered, he fought the Hittites while our boys, quite sensibly, ran for their lives. For all the good it did them."

"I *thought* they were right at my side." Ramses shook his head. "When I turned to give orders and discovered they were gone, I had a bad moment, believe you me."

Miriam looked at him sharply, her black brows knitting in fierce concentration. "So you . . . attacked the Hittites in the face of certain death?"

"Not exactly. The only possible means of escape, by

then, involved cutting through a seething hoard of Hittites."

"And you were all alone?" Miriam persisted.

"No," Ramses said testily, "there were thirty-five thousand Hittites there. Aren't you listening, woman?"

"I mean, there were no other Egyptians?"

"There were a *few*," Ramses said defensively. "*Some* of them are loyal to me, you know. Not every single one of them bolted."

"How many stayed to fight with you?" Miriam asked.

"Um, well, uh . . . Three." Ramses shrugged awkwardly. "Four, if you count the guy driving my chariot."

"But this is wonderful!" cried Miriam.

"It is?" Imhotep asked.

"Ramses, you beautiful hunk of man!"

"You shouldn't touch the pharaoh's divine—"

"Yes, yes, never mind that right now." She turned to Imhotep. "This is our angle! This is how we're going to make this boy the biggest thing since irrigation!"

"I knew we'd hired the right wizard for the job!" Imhotep paused, then asked, "Er, how?"

"Well, I admit," said Miriam, "there's not much we can do about the way he fell for that pathetic 'we're helpless deserters who just happen to be spewing exactly the improbable story you want to hear' ploy. I think flat-out denial is really our only reasonable strategy there."

"Agreed," said Imhotep.

"They *looked* like deserters," Ramses muttered.

"As for the rest, we claim that Ramses single-handedly won the battle."

"But, er . . ." Imhotep frowned. "The Hittites won it."

"So *they* say," Miriam said. "But who are you going to believe, huh? Pharaoh himself, Lord of All That the Sun Encircles, King of Upper and Lower Egypt, Lord of the Two Lands, blah blah blah? Or some smelly Hittite upstart who can't even scratch his own name in legible hieroglyphics?"

"Miriam!" Imhotep cried. "Brilliant!"

Ramses looked at them both doubtfully. "We simply . . . say that I won at Kadesh?"

"Yes!"

"Even though I didn't? Even though those damn Hittites now hold it?"

"Yes!"

"But how can we get away with that?"

"Because," Miriam reminded him, "people will believe any lie, as long as you tell it with conviction."

"We'll add verisimilitude with plausible details," Imhotep said.

"Huh?"

"Exactly," said Miriam. "Trapped by Hittite treachery and abandoned by his weak-kneed army—"

"Aw, come on," Ramses protested, "your knees would have been weak, too, if you'd seen those Hittites come down like the wolf on the fold, their cohorts all gleaming in—"

"—the brave and noble pharaoh, Ramses the *Great*, single-handedly attacked the Hittite army—"

"I told you, I didn't *intentionally* attack thirty-five thousand men," Ramses insisted. "I'm not *that* stupid. I was just trying to esc—"

"Fighting against overwhelming odds," Imhotep chimed in, "Ramses battled alone against the entire enemy army—"

"Hey, there were three other guys with me," Ramses reminded them. "Four, if you count the guy who drove my—"

"The pharaoh's fierce resistance and courage in the face of overwhelming odds terrified the enemy, who screamed like schoolgirls as they fled—"

"They didn't flee," Ramses pointed out, "they just—"

"Then Ramses rallied his troops, who came storming back to his aid, so deeply moved were they by the king's unconquerable bravery."

"Actually, I caught up with them, and we realized we'd forgotten—"

"Your magnificent victory at Kadesh," Miriam told Ramses, "must be recorded on all your temples, obelisks, and monuments for all of Egypt and all of posterity!"

"I, um, don't have any temples, obelisks, or monuments," Ramses pointed out.

"Well, obviously, we're going to write all about your heroic deeds on other pharaohs' temples and monuments, as well as scratch out their names and replace them with yours. But we're also going to start a massive building program. That's the beauty of my plan," Miriam explained. "We'll obliterate your military debacle and do something about your utterly mediocre domestic policy at the very same time."

"But how are monuments covered with lies going to improve my domestic policy?"

"Oh, that's good! Keep that in!" Miriam urged, snorting.

"Huh?"

"Dear boy," Imhotep said, "you don't need to improve your domestic policy, or even *have* one. You just need to make it *look* as if you have one."

"By building a lot of stuff?" Ramses frowned. "How will that—"

"Trust me," Miriam said. "It always works. Spend the entire treasury immortalizing yourself, and you will come out history's winner, boychik."

"Well . . ." Ramses considered the plan. "I like it. Don't get me wrong, I like it a lot. It just seems a little . . . uncertain. Don't you think we need a . . . I don't know— a fall guy? Just in case anything else goes wrong."

"Hmmm." Imhotep stroked his chins as he pondered this suggestion. "You mean someone we can handily blame for any future problems the nation may have?"

"Someone who *isn't* Muwatallis," Miriam said, thinking it over, "since it wouldn't be smart to risk another Kadesh, even with me on the payroll."

"Actually, Ramses, it's not a bad idea."

"Back-up plans are always good." Miriam agreed.

"Hmmm. A fall guy . . ." She snapped her fingers. "I may have someone!"

"Didn't I tell you she's the best?" Imhotep said.

"There's a foreign god—"

"Foreign god?" Imhotep said warily.

"Don't worry," Miriam said, "Egypt's not on his agenda. He's making a push to take over the Land of Canaan."

"That backwater? You can't be serious."

"Foreign gods." Miriam shrugged dismissively. "Go figure."

"What's his angle?" Imhotep asked.

"And how can it help me?" Ramses added.

"Well, he's got his eye on this plucky local kid called Moses . . ."

"Our fall guy?" Ramses asked.

"Will it spin well?" Imhotep asked.

Miriam smiled at them both. "Leave everything to me."

THAT GOD WON'T HUNT

by Susan Sizemore

Susan Sizemore lives in the midwest and spends most of her time writing. She works in many genres, from contemporary romance to epic fantasy and horror. She's the winner of the Romance Writers of America's Golden Heart Award, and a nominee for the RWA Rita Award. Her available books include historical romance novels, and a dark fantasy series, *The Laws of the Blood.*

"REJOICE, Princess Ipuit, for my son is of an age to marry, and who better than you to be chosen as one of his queens?"

Ipuit bowed low before the chair of the Queen Mother, her forehead touching the flank of a hippopotamus that was part of a hunting scene painted on the reception room floor. "I am blessed by this honor, Queen Ankhnes-Mery-Re."

Ipuit did not feel quite as blessed as perhaps she should, for she had been happy far away from the royal city of Menfi. The mud brick palace crowded with people disconcerted her after years spent studying in a quiet, isolated temple. But duty and family obligation called her from her quiet retreat, and she could not feel sorry for herself, either. Being a great wife to the Lord of the Two Lands was hardly a fate to cry herself to sleep over. She and Pepi had been friends when they were children, she had missed him when she went away, and enjoyed their occasional exchange of letters and presents. Still, it had been nearly a year since she'd heard from him, which was one of the reasons the Queen Mother's summons had taken Ipuit so much by surprise.

"Come, girl, and sit beside me," the Queen Mother ordered. "For I am your great-aunt as well as your husband's mother, if you recall."

A servant moved swiftly to place a low stool beside the queen's carved ebony chair, and Ipuit moved with some trepidation to take this seat of honor. Though she was a princess of the royal blood, daughter to the young pharaoh's predecessor and half-brother, Nemtyemzaf, Ipuit did not think the mother of the present Lord of the Two Lands bestowed such a mark of favor on her out of deep family feeling.

When Ipuit was seated, Ankhnes-Mery-Re dismissed her attendants. When they were alone, the Queen Mother took Ipuit's hand in hers and said, "You have been away from Menfi for a long time, child. Look at me, and tell me of your life in the temple of Meresger."

Initiated into the mysteries of a goddess who was known as the Lover of Silence, Ipuit had been trained to listen. She heard the importance her answer held in the Queen Mother's sociable words. Her aunt was deeply troubled, and looking for reassurance. As a woman, or as the Queen Mother? Ipuit wondered. From a princess, or from a priestess? Was her concern for her son, or for the kingdom? But of course all these different parts of personality were mingled together, were they not, like the *ba* and *ka* that made up the totality of the living soul? Pepi was god and ruler, as well as the beloved child of Ankhnes-Mery-Re. And Ipuit reminded herself that she was priestess and princess, and capable of being useful as both.

"I have learned to love justice from serving in the temple of the Lady of Heaven," she answered Ankhnes-Mery-Re.

"You are a great scholar, I hear," Ankhnes-Mery-Re said, squeezing Ipuit's hand. "A student of the great mysteries and magics."

The Queen Mother sounded eager to know about Ipuit's knowledge of magic, but the reception room door opened before Ipuit could answer.

The dogs entered first, half a dozen rollicking young hounds with prick ears and sleek red coats. Ipuit could not help but smile at the sight of such lively creatures, for she had always dearly loved dogs. She rose to her feet as the largest of the hounds came right up to her and began to eagerly sniff her all over. She laughed, and pushed the familiar creature's head away, then almost forgot about the animal as a dozen men followed the dogs into Ankhnes-Mery-Re's reception hall.

"Oh, my dear," the Queen Mother complained to the young man who entered at the head of this entourage, "must you bring those beasts with you everywhere? They raise an awful stench."

"These beautiful hunters are my brothers and sisters. I would not be happy unless they were always with me. Besides, they're as washed and perfumed as I am," the king replied airily. "Though they don't like taking baths any better than I do."

Only the friendly hound's bumping her hand with its very cold nose distracted Ipuit enough not to gasp with shock at Pepi's claim to dislike bathing, for being ritually cleansed in the water of the Nile was one of the pharaoh's daily duties.

Pepi came forward and kissed his mother on the cheek. At the same time he gestured that there was no need for Ipuit to bow. He kissed her on the cheek a moment later, leaving her skin rather damp. The informality surprised her, but it also pleased Ipuit to see that her future husband was affectionate in private despite being the pharaoh.

Her favorable impression was dimmed a moment later when Pepi stepped back and announced petulantly, "Djau said I had to come see you before I could go hunting." He looked Ipuit over critically, then his gaze shifted to contemplate the shafts of sunlight coming in the windows set high in the thick wall.

Ipuit looked toward the king's entourage, and saw several familiar faces. One was Queen Ankhnes-Mery-Re's brother, the vizier Djau who had served as co-regent with the Queen Mother during Pepi's childhood. From the bold, and very nearly disdainful, way the vizier returned her regard, Ipuit surmised that he was very confident in the influence he held over the king, though Pepi was now a man. Ipuit was careful to bow slightly to the vizier, as a niece to an honored great-uncle.

As if Djau's attitude was not disturbing enough, Ipuit saw that a priest of Set stood at the vizier's side. She firmly believed that Set was a god of darkness and mischief, though his priests defended his role as a god of love. Dark magic came where Set was. Seeing Set's priest so close to the vizier gave Ipuit at least one answer to the meaning behind Ankhnes-Mery-Re's questions. Perhaps Ankhnes-Mery-Re hoped Ipuit would influence Pepi to favor the goddess of justice over the god of chaos. When the Set priest looked at her and smiled a thin, contemptuous smile, Ipuit knew he was aware the Queen Mother might think this as well, and he did not believe Ipuit had any hope of succeeding.

Ipuit saw the man's scorn as a challenge, but gave him no indication she accepted it. She stayed as quiet and unobtrusive as she could, willing herself to seem no more than a meek shadow at the Queen Mother's side, but for the enthusiastic young hound that continued to lean against her and nudge at her hand for a petting.

"You are a persistent thing," she murmured to the dog, and the king heard her.

"That's Nebshedd. He's a house hound, that one." The pharaoh sounded disappointed in this lean red hound. He looked at the vizier. "I have seen my mother and my new queen. Can I go hunting now, Djau?"

"But, my dear, there are ambassadors. And the marriage, and—" The appalled Queen Mother began.

"Pharaoh is no longer a child for you to rebuke, Sister," Djau interrupted. "He will do as he pleases, and we will loyally wait for him to turn his attention to us—when it pleases him." He bowed, then gestured toward the door. "If it pleases you to go hunting, my lord, then we rejoice in what pleases you."

The pharaoh yelped with joy at this encouragement to ignore his duties, and he rushed from the reception hall without a further word or glance for his mother or wife-to-be. The dogs bounded out on his heels, with Djau and the rest moving almost as quickly to follow the king.

The Queen Mother and Ipuit looked at each other in shock and amazement, but neither voiced any complaints about Pharaoh's behavior. A god could do as he pleased, and it was traitorous to say anything about it. "If my lady allows," Ipuit said instead, "I should take my leave as well. The journey to Menfi has been tiring, and I have much to do to settle into my new household."

And much to think on, she added to herself, as she made a formal bow to Ankhnes-Mery-Re.

What do I know so far? Ipuit asked herself now that she was alone in her large new bedroom. *How much more do I need to know? And what will I do about it when I have all the knowledge I need?* This last question was more of a prayer to her wise goddess than a question to herself, but Ipuit knew she must be the one to act upon the insight Meresger granted her.

She had changed from the carefully pleated court dress into a straight linen shift, the carefully applied makeup had been washed off, and her heavy wig now sat on a stand in the nearby dressing room. Her rooms surrounded a private courtyard that held a fragrant garden and a delightful blue-tiled fish pool planted with reeds and lotus. Her personal quarters opened onto a shaded verandah, and a pleasant breeze wafted in to cool the room.

Now that she had sent her women away, Ipuit stepped out to the veranda, took a seat on a bench by the wall and combed out her shoulder-length hair while she thought over what she knew after less than a day back at the palace. She had heard rumors from people she'd talked to on the river journey from her quiet temple. Rumors that the young king was more frivolous now that he'd reached his majority than he had ever been while under the tutelage of his co-regent mother and uncle. She remembered Pepi as a dutiful boy. He loved to hunt, she'd been told. He hated being confined in the palace of Menfi. More than anything else he loved to be out for days on end, living for the exhilaration of the chase. This endless holiday had been going on for nearly a year.

What she thought she knew from her observations was that the vizier Djau was encouraging Pharaoh's immature behavior because he did not want to give up the power he wielded during Pepi's childhood. The Queen Mother was trying to counter Djau's influence by insisting Pepi take wives and other trappings of adulthood. Djau kept a priest of Set by his side. The priests of Set were adepts at dark magic. The Queen Mother—

"Rrrrawfff, rawff, rrraff!"

The loud barking not a foot away from her startled Ipuit out of her reverie and brought her to her feet. "By Lioness' wrath!" she swore, then looked down and said, "Oh, it's you."

The long-legged red hound dropped to his haunches in front of her, tilted his head and looked at her with what she would have sworn was laughter in his large brown eyes. Nebshedd, she remembered the hound was called. He wore a gold collar inset with carnelian and lapis. "Quite the court beauty, aren't you?" she asked. She stepped into the hot afternoon sunlight of the garden long enough to see if any human had come into her quarters with the dog, but decided after a few moments that Nebshedd had found his way to her on his own. She was rather pleased by the animal's interest, actually. It was nice to have one friend she could utterly trust in the palace.

When she turned and went back into her bedroom, the dog followed her inside. Nebshedd showed no respect for her person or property as a Queen of the Two Lands as he immediately jumped onto her bed and made himself comfortable.

Ipuit crossed her arms and looked at the beast with tolerant amusement. "Why aren't you out hunting with the king? That's right, I recall he said you preferred staying in the palace. Is that any way to earn your keep? Are you hiding from the master of the hounds, you lazy creature?" Nebshedd yawned in response to her questions. "Stay if you like," she told him. "I have some work to do."

There were several small chests in a corner of the room that she had not allowed the servants to unpack. She went to them now. First she knelt and said the appropriate prayers before the inlaid chest that held a statue and ritual objects of her goddess. Then Ipuit reverently opened the chest and set up a small altar on a low table with the contents of the chest. After she had lit incense and two alabaster lamps, she picked up one of the other boxes and brought it back to the bed, where she took a seat and opened the box. The dog looked at her curiously when she brought out a papyrus roll.

"What's this, you're wondering?" she said to the dog. "Not something for you to chew on, my pretty one. This," this told Nebshedd, "is a book of wisdom.

Magic of the deepest kind. For if I am called upon to battle a priest of Set, I will need to study and pray and prepare myself."

The dog looked at her as if he actually understood, and as if to guard her privacy, Nebshedd got up off the bed and went to sit alertly at the door. He watched vigilantly while Ipuit read until the sun set and her servants insisted she eat and bathe and be prepared for bed.

The servants wanted to send for the master of hounds to take the dog away, for they were wary of the large hunting hound despite his lazy ways and friendly manner. They wanted to bring her a cat, if she must have a pet. Ipuit was nearly as fond of cats as she was of dogs, but cats did not make particularly good guardians. At least she'd never heard of a cat that barked at the sound of intruders in the night. Besides, she felt that it was meant that the hunting hound had come to her. She did not let them take the dog away, or send for a cat, but she did feed Nebshedd a good part of her dinner. She was glad to have him with her when the dark drew down.

She sent up a silent prayer to Meresger for having at least one true friend as she settled into her bed on her first night back at Menfi. She did not trust the vizier, or his priest of Set, or any servants but the two maids she'd brought with her. She thought that the Queen Mother had sent for her out of good motives, but Ipuit knew that the favor of royalty was a chancy thing. If she did not bring about the results Ankhnes-Mery-Re desired, then the Queen Mother would discard her in favor of a new tool to do her bidding. Ipuit did not resent Ankhnes-Mery-Re in any way. She was the daughter of a pharaoh herself; she knew how royal games were played. She also believed Ankhnes-Mery-Re believed the good of the two lands and her son's best interests were at stake in this game with the vizier. Ipuit would do what she could to help.

But what was she to do? She fell asleep pondering that question.

She did not think it was much later when the dog's wet nose pressed against her cheek woke her. She blinked a few times, then turned her head to look at the dog. The small lamps of her shrine gave enough light for Ipuit to see that Nebshedd had something in his mouth.

"What have you got?" she asked as she sat up.

When he dropped the dead asp in her lap, she wished she hadn't asked.

"Ah."

She sighed, and examined the corpse of the deadly creature carefully, holding it up with one hand while she rubbed Nebshedd's ears and head with the other. She wondered which of the servants had left the snake in her room. The one who had protested the most about the dog, she supposed. What to do? To make a fuss about an assassination attempt would make her seem weak in her enemies' eyes, while to act as if nothing had occurred might make her seem enigmatic and mysterious. That she was shaking like an acacia in a windstorm right now was something no one but she and the dog need ever know.

She calmed down when Nebshedd whined a little and licked her hand. "Good dog," she said. You saved my life, she thought, and wondered what sort of reward she could give a creature who already wore a gold collar and was the pampered pet of Pharaoh. Because he was a dog, she did what dogs love best, she patted him and praised him and scratched his belly for a while.

When she was done petting Nebshedd, Ipuit took the dead snake outside and tossed the body into a patch of flowers. Then she looked up at the moon, shining round and full tonight, the finest jewel in the garb of the goddess of the night. She closed her eyes and lost herself for a few moments in prayers of thanks to the Lover of Silence and the goddess with a thousand souls. She was still caught in the rapture of worship when she stepped back into her bedroom. At first all she heard was a fluttering in the darkness, like the sound of a bat or a bird trapped up near the ceiling. The sound drew her rather than sparking any fear of another attack. The dog was not barking. In fact, but for the fluttering of small wings, there was a deep, intense silence about the room. Ipuit stepped from the veranda into total darkness. No moonlight entered through the door or windows. There was no tiny flicker of flames from the lamps in the shrine. Darkness, deep, thick, and swirling with the manifestation of deep mystery. Magic had entered this room where a short time before death had been unloosed to strike at her.

Ipuit stood very still, set her body aside, and looked upon the room with eyes trained to see beyond the physical world. Once she drew upon her own magical senses, the chamber became as clear to her as if it was midday in the desert. Nebshedd stood quivering in the center of the room, his keen hound's eyes fixed upon the thing that fluttered a few feet above his sharply pointed ears. She became aware of the dog's yearning, and a hunger beyond the physical. There was loneliness, confusion, and even hope emanating from the animal as well. Ipuit's magical self did not doubt that the animal experienced such complex emotions, for she saw them, flowing around the creature like multicolored mists.

When she turned her gaze up to where the dog was staring, she immediately recognized what the dog was staring at. It was not a bird, or a bat. The delicate creature with the head of a human and the body of a bright-colored bird was a *ba*, one part of a human soul, though who it belonged to and what it was doing here she could not at first fathom. The *ka* was the strongest part of the soul, the essence of all a person was, it resided in the body and in the spirit world. The *ba* was the *ka*'s messenger and servant. The two blended spirits made up the essence of a complete soul. The *ba* could not survive without the *ka*, but it was known that *ba* spirits could become lost and be led astray.

Poor little spirit, she thought. What was it doing here? And what did it have to do with one of the pharaoh's hunting dogs? Poor Nebshedd, she thought, to be haunted by a *ba* when you should be chasing hares or sleeping on the end of the bed.

Then she suddenly understood exactly what it all

meant. Ipuit did not know if the knowledge that came to her in a flash of clarity was a gift of the goddess, or if it was simply the only possible explanation. To do such a thing to any soul was a heinous crime—but to do it to the pharaoh—it went beyond crime to the deepest type of sin. It was blasphemy and heresy and wickedness so vile only the priest of Set, the god of chaos, could possibly have contemplated it. Even to think of what had been done made Ipuit feel unclean and tainted.

But what was to be done? What needed to be done? Justice needed to be done, of course. And she was the priestess of Meresger, the savage lioness who pursued evildoers until they were brought to justice. Ipuit felt as much compassion for Nebshedd as she did for Pepi. She would do what she could for both of them.

The *ba* still fluttered above Nebshedd's head. Ipuit debated whether she should try to capture the tiny piece of fractured soul, then decided on a different course, for capturing the fragile *ba* might destroy rather than save it. Instead, she grabbed Nebshedd by the collar and forced the reluctant hound away from the little soul bird. She took the dog with her to the shrine, and made him sit while she knelt before the small gold statue of her goddess.

With her eyes closed, one hand on the dog and the other held out in supplication to Meresger, Ipuit said a prayer for protection, then opened herself further to danger. She sent her own *ba* and *ka*, twined together as they should be in a living soul, out of her body and into the world beside the world where spells were given form and sent to bring mischief or healing to the living world. With her she took the spirit image of Nebshedd, the lean red hound, and for a dog she'd been told did not like to hunt, he was quick to find the dark trail she looked for.

All magic leaves a path back to its source. With Nebshedd leading the way, this one was easy to follow. She was not surprised to find the priest of Set as the source of the evil. He was surprised to find her in the place of his abomination, and this surprise gave her an advantage in the battle they waged for the soul of the pharaoh. She had another advantage as well. For though darkness mixed with blinding light disoriented her, and pain and confusion tore at her mind, Ipuit was certain she caught the occasional glimpse of Nebshedd darting in to bite Set's priest whenever and wherever he could.

You're a good dog, she thought, but it was the last thought she had before she gathered all her strength to drive one last blast of magic at her enemy's defenses. Once that spell was cast, Ipuit became aware of nothing else, not even the darkness.

"Are you awake, my princess?"

The voice was familiar, but Ipuit could not place it just yet. Was she awake? "I am not sure." The words issued from such a dry throat that Ipuit was not sure the voice was hers. She was not sure where she was, and that was most disconcerting. "Have I been ill?"

"Very. But all is well with all three of us now."

The voice was male, young, and confident. It didn't belong to any priest she knew. Where had she heard—?

"Pepi!"

She sat up, even before her eyes were open, trying to find a way to bow in bed. Hands gently grasped her shoulders and kept her from falling to the floor.

"Easy," he said. "You've been asleep for days, and you're weak. Don't fuss. Let me help you. I've had to chase out my mother, and every servant and priestess in the palace to claim the privilege of taking care of you."

"You came back from hunting!" Excited as she was, the words came out as a faint whisper.

He laughed. "Of course. My place is here, ruling the Two Lands. Here I will stay. And in bed is where you will stay until you are well enough for the wedding feast. Then we will stay in bed together, but we will talk about that when you are better."

Ipuit smiled at his words, and was glad of his aid in helping her to lie down again. Once he had helped settle her back on the bed, Ipuit stared wide-eyed at the pharaoh. He smiled at her regard, young and handsome, and quite self-possessed. They were alone in her bedchamber, and Pepi was seated near her on the bed. There was something very familiar about the look in his eyes, but she was used to seeing that enthusiastic intelligence shining out of the hunting hound's farseeing eyes. Now, she thought, Pepi's *ka* was back where it belonged.

"Yes," he said after she had studied him for a while. He pointed to himself. "I am all here." Then he pointed to the dog. "And Nebshedd is here," he added, patting the dog that sat close to him, leaning against Pepi's thigh. "We were both very confused for a while."

Ipuit was very curious. She was also very weak, yet she felt a bone-deep satisfaction. She knew that the goddess had worked through her to break the curse. "How did it happen?" she whispered. "How did Set's priest—?"

"How did his evil magic trap a god in the body of a dog?" Pepi shook his head in disgust. "I do not know, but I will learn. Perhaps my excuse is that I am a young god, and my uncle did not allow me to learn all that I should have during his regency. With your help, royal wife, I will learn the magic a pharaoh needs to know. But that is for the future. What I remember before the curse struck me was that my uncle presented me with the gift of a litter of the finest red hunting hounds. Even as a pup Nebshedd was the most beautiful. I remember picking him up and making a fuss over him. Then I grew dizzy and the world became dark. The next thing I knew I was in a kennel with the rest of the pups, and I knew that somehow this was all wrong."

"You knew you were Pepi?"

He gestured. "Sometimes. Mostly I was aware of scents and sounds, and all the things dogs are aware of. I remember being sad when I heard my mother cry. I remember whimpering and whining and scratching at her door once, but the kennel master wouldn't let me get to her. I was part of the pack, but not part of it. When Nebshedd wore my body, he was as confused as

I was, but the vizier and his priest of Set kept him under control. They let him hunt with the pack, which was true to his dog self, while I roamed the palace knowing that was where I belonged. Sometimes I would hear my *ba* trying to reach me, but my dog self did not understand it was trying to draw me home." He shook his head. "It was all very confusing until you came back." He took her hands in his. "I knew you." He bent to sniff her palm, and licked it. "You smelled and tasted right. I knew you would help me." He lifted his head and looked her into her eyes. "And you did."

"How—how?" She wished she could concentrate more, and that her dry throat did not make it so hard to speak. "When the spell was broken—how did it— how did you feel— What did you do?"

"I woke from a dream I knew had been real. One moment I was contentedly asleep under the desert stars surrounded by my hunting pack. The next I was on my feet and shouting for my guards and my chariot, and for my traitorous uncle and the priest to be brought before me. The priest I had executed, and my uncle will live out his life exiled on one of his estates. Then I rushed back to Menfi to take up my life and duties." He brushed fingers across her forehead. "Mostly I rushed home to be with you. My *ka* remembered being with you, and what you had done to save me. I feared you might have died when you broke the spell."

She was gratified at his concern, but shocked at what she had heard. "The vizier was only exiled? For such a crime?" She was too tired to properly show her outrage.

"Officially, he has retired from public life for the sake of his health." Pepi looked very stern when he added, "It would not be wise for any word of what was done to Pharaoh to be known." He kissed her hands again. "You, I know, will never tell. Neither will I." He glanced at the dog, who looked up at him worshipfully. "And I think our secret will remain safe with Nebshedd as well."

The dog responded to this attention by jumping up on the bed. It was not that large a bed, and Nebshedd took up quite a bit of space. Pepi laughed, and pushed him back down on the floor. "Oh, no, my spoiled brother, " he said, and looked at Ipuit with a wicked gleam in his eyes. "The only one of us who will be sleeping in Ipuit's bed from now on will be me."

BASTED

by Alan Dean Foster

Alan Dean Foster was born in New York City and raised in Los Angeles. He has a bachelor's degree in political science and a master of fine arts in cinema from UCLA. He has traveled extensively around the world, from Australia to Papua, New Guinea. He has also written fiction in just about every genre, and is known for his excellent movie novelizations. Currently, he lives in Prescott, Arizona, with his wife, assorted dogs, cats, fish, javelina, and other animals, and where he is working on several new novels and media projects.

IT was Harima who drove Ali out of his home and into the desert that night. Harima was his wife.

There had been a time in the not-so-distant past when Ali had thought Harima a great beauty, as had a number of his friends. When, exactly, had that time been? he tried to remember. How long ago? He could not recall.

Now his wife was rather larger than he remembered from their dates of courtship. In fact, the joke around the village was that she was as big as the pyramids at Giza—and her voice shrill and loud enough to wake everyone in the City of the Dead. Whatever she had become, she was no longer the sweet and alluring woman he had married. Her voice, old Mustapha Kalem was fond of saying over strong coffee in the village café, was harsh enough to drown out the morning call to prayer.

Ali was sick of that voice, just as he was sick of what his life had become.

Once, long ago, he was a bright and promising student who had done well in school. Well enough to be considered for attending the university, in Cairo. But his hard-working family, Allah's blessings be upon them, had been dirt poor—which in soil-poor Egypt is a description to be taken literally. Even with Ali being an only child, there had been barely enough money for food, let alone higher schooling. As for the university, it was made clear to Ali that such a notion was out of the question.

Forced to look for a job to help support himself and his increasingly feeble parents, the ever resourceful Ali had seen how rich tourists paid incredible amounts of money to visit and view the fabled wonders of his country. The guides who escorted such people through temples and tombs not only received honest salaries from the tour companies, they were also the recipients of frequent tips, sometimes in hard currency, from the grateful visitors. Espying an opportunity where there seemed to be none (something Ali had always been good at), he proceeded to apprentice himself to one of the best-known and most successful local guide groups.

Alas, many years had passed, and he was still carrying heavy luggage, and fetching cold drinks, and doing only the most menial of tasks for the guide service. They guarded their privileges jealously, did the guides. Many times, Ali had seen less qualified apprentices promoted over him, only because they had connections: this one was somebody's cousin, or that one wealthy Aunt Aamal's son. A poor boy like himself was kept down.

This sorry state of affairs continued despite his excellent and ever improving command of English, as well as his knowledge of many things ancient that he had acquired from listening to the other guides, reading guidebooks, and humbly asking questions of the more knowledgeable tourists themselves. In truth, it had to be said that the visitors from overseas encouraged him in his efforts more than did his own countrymen.

Especially Harima. He was not good enough for her, she was fond of telling anyone who would listen. He was too short, too dark, he didn't make enough money, he was a lousy lover—ah, Harima, he mused! Wild-haired, lovely, full-lipped Harima—who once was the love of his life and he, he'd thought, of hers. No longer. Black visions of drooling jackals and squawking buzzards helping themselves to hearty hunks of the hefty Harima filled his head. Unworthy thoughts, he knew. But he could not help them.

To get away from her, he had taken Suhar, his favorite camel (truth be told, his only camel) for a nocturnal jaunt into the desert, in the direction of the canal. A piece of the desert, the real desert, was very near to Ali's village. It was not hard to get away from contemporary civilization and back to that of the great pharaohs and kings of ancient Egypt. It was their temples that brought the tourists to his town, and kept them coming back. Neither Ali nor the guides for whom he worked were ashamed to admit that the best thing about the temples was the money they continued to bring in, thousands of years after their builders had vanished.

The moon that floated high in the star-flecked sky was nearly full. Ali enjoyed the ride, as did Suhar. The farther from the village they rode, the more a calming peace settled on both man and camel, and the farther the lights of the city of Zagazig faded into the distance. He took a different track than usual. As his mount's wide, splayed feet shushed over the sands away from the roads and trails that led to the main tourist sites, the steady yammering of televisions and boom boxes and yes, of Harima, faded from memory as well as from earshot.

It was just past midnight when Suhar suddenly stopped. Ali frowned. Nothing lay in front of them but flat desert and the still distant canal. Giving her a firm nudge in the ribs, he yelled "Hut, hut!" Still, she refused to move.

What ailed the beast? he wondered. Dismounting, he strode out in front of her. If he failed to return before sunrise, Harima would lay into him even more than usual. She would accuse him of spending their money, her money, on illegal liquor, or women, or khat. He winced as he envisioned the knowing smiles that would appear on the faces of his neighbors, and the disapproving expressions he would encounter the next time he went into town for coffee.

Taking the reins, he began tugging. Gently at first, then more sharply. But neither sharp gesture nor angry words could persuade the camel to budge.

"Spawn of the devil! Giver of sour milk! Why do I waste good money on food for you? If not for the tourists who like to have their picture taken with you, I would sell you for steaks and chops!" Unimpressed, in the manner of camels, Suhar stood and chewed and said nothing.

"Come *on*," he snapped. Leaning back, he put his full weight into the reins. As he took a step, Suhar emitted an outraged bawl. This was overridden by the sound of a loud *crack* beneath Ali's feet. With a yelp and a shout, he felt himself plunge downward and out of sight.

Above, Suhar stood quietly masticating her cud. She did not move forward toward the yawning cavity that had appeared in the desert.

Spitting out dust and grit, a groaning Ali rolled over and climbed slowly to his feet. Though his backside throbbed where he had landed, the fall had wounded his dignity more than his body. Feeling himself, he decided that nothing was broken. Looking up, he saw that the hole through which he had fallen was no more than a meter wide. Sand continued to spill from the edges of the opening, the trickling grains illuminated by the moon that was still high in the night sky.

What had he tumbled into? An old well, perhaps. But a well would have been deeper. Turning as he continued to dust himself off, he let his eyes adjust to the subdued moonlight.

And sucked in his breath.

Surrounding him were beautifully painted walls. Fourth or Fifth Dynasty, he decided, drawing upon his years of accumulated knowledge about his ancestors' works. The elaborate murals were intact and completely undamaged. At the four corners of the chamber stood four massive diorite statues of Bastet, the cat goddess of the ancient Egyptians. Except for them, the tomb, for such it had to be with a stone sarcophagus in its center, was empty. His heart, which had leaped so high the instant he had recognized his surroundings, now fell. No golden chariots blinded his gaze, no metal chests of precious stones stood waiting to be opened. The tomb was in excellent condition, but it had either been looted or else was the resting place of some poor man.

And yet—the quality of the murals was exceptional. That did not square with the apparent emptiness of the chamber. And then there was the single sarcophagus, resting in isolated majesty in the exact center of the chamber. It was not large, indicating that this was perhaps the final resting place of a child. Or an intended resting place, given the bareness of the chamber.

He consoled himself with the knowledge that, while there might not be any great riches present, the four massive and well-made statues of Bastet would surely be worth something. Even mummies themselves could be sold. He hesitated. Provided there was a mummy here, of course, and that the sarcophagus was not empty.

It took him nearly an hour to shift the heavy stone lid far enough to one side to let him get at the inner sarcophagus. For a second time, his heart jumped, this time at the flash of gold within, Sadly, the inner container was only of gilded wood. It opened far more easily than had the upper cover. Another person might have been frightened, working there alone beneath the desert in a previously undiscovered tomb, opening ancient sarcophagi. Not Ali. The desert, the nearby ancient city of Bubastis, were his home. He had spent all his life among such relics of the distant past. The only

danger in doing what he was doing, he knew, came
from inhaling too much dust and mold, or being discovered by the authorities.

The inner cover was pushed aside, allowing him to
see within. His brows furrowed uncertainly. The inner
sarcophagus contained a mummy, all right—but a
mummy unlike any he had ever seen. It was too big to
be a child, and the wrong shape for a man or woman.
What could it be? From local excavations in and around
Tell-Basta, Ali knew that the rulers of Bubastis had
sometimes selected holy cats to be interred beside
them along with human members of their household.
The statues of Bastet pointed the way to the answer,
helping him to finally recognize the shape.

It was indeed a mummified feline, not unlike those
from the famous graveyard of mummified holy cats—
but this was no house cat. This was big, much bigger.
Was it unusual or unique enough to be particularly
valuable? There was no way of telling without calling
on expert help. It didn't look particularly heavy—
certainly no heavier than the stone lid of the main sarcophagus had been. He knew a man who, for a reasonable price, could identify such things and who would
ask no awkward questions.

Ali was very strong in the arms and shoulders from
years of carrying tourists' overstuffed luggage. Suhar
could manage the dual burden of man and mummy
easily. Reaching in to the inner container, he carefully
slipped both hands under the wrappings that had lain

undisturbed for thousands of years, preparatory to lifting it out.

Something moved against his fingers. And coughed.

"Inshallah!" he exclaimed involuntarily as he dropped the weight and stumbled backward. Eyes wide, back pressed against the far wall, he gaped at the sarcophagus.

The mummy was getting up.

It rose slowly on all four feet, a lean and lithe bundle of unimaginably ancient linen and encrusted preservatives. Trembling, Ali scuttled to his right. But there was no stairway that led to freedom, no ladder with which to climb out of the chamber. Come to think of it, how had he intended to get the mummy out of the tomb, much less himself? Excited by his accidental discovery, he hadn't thought that far ahead. Now he looked at the circle of moonlight overhead as if it represented the route to heaven. He would have screamed, but there was no one to hear him.

An odor reached his nostrils; the smell of something incredibly ancient, but rapidly reviving. Suhar caught a whiff of it, too. He heard her snort once, in fear, before the clomp-clomp of her big, oversized, suddenly lovable feet began to recede rapidly into the distance.

Now he was well and truly alone. Alone with—something.

Oh God, he thought. *It's looking at me.*

Indeed, the bandage-swathed head had turned toward him. Behind the disintegrating wrappings, a pair of intense yellow eyes were gazing directly back into his own. They seemed to burn into his soul, to still his very heart. And yet, and yet—there was no murder in them, but something else. Curiosity, perhaps. Curiosity, and—intelligence.

That was impossible, he knew. But then, to have a millennia-old mummy suddenly stand up and stare back at you was not exactly possible, either, and that was happening before his eyes.

The animal shape coughed again. Louder, this time. Then it seemed to stretch, to expand, as if taking a deep breath. It shook violently. Before his terrified eyes, desiccated, ancient linens snapped and crumbled. Chewing hard on the knuckles of his left hand, Ali could only stare, and pray.

In the full flush of vibrant, new life, the cheetah concluded its yawning stretch. When it turned toward him again, there was no mistaking what it was. When it started toward him, he closed his eyes. Mummy or magic, anything this old with teeth like that was bound to be hungry.

Shivering, Ali felt a powerful paw reach out to touch his thigh. He could smell the creature clearly now, much as Suhar had smelled it—and fled. He waited for the sharp caress of claw against his throat. It would all be over in a minute, he knew. His friends in the village would never know what had happened to him. Maybe some day some one would find his gnawed, whitened bones. At least, he reflected, he would no longer have to listen to Harima's shrill, shrewish insults. There were some small good things to be said even for death.

"Open your eyes, man. I'm not going to kill you."

Somehow, the idea of a talking cheetah struck him as even more absurd than that of a revivified mummy. But since there was no one else in the tomb with him, the words had to be coming from the cat. Opening his eyes, still shaking with fear, Ali found himself looking down at the creature. A truly magnificent specimen it was, too, he thought.

"Thank you," the cheetah responded politely, which was when Ali realized that they were not speaking aloud, but speaking athink, as it were. Whether he was reading the cat's mind, or it his, he did not know. Nor did it seem to matter much.

"It doesn't," the cat thought at him. Slowly, deliberately, it looked around the chamber before its eyes settled on him once more. Some of his trembling having ceased, Ali could not keep from thinking half-sensible thoughts.

"Who are you, peace be unto him?"

"I do not know who 'him' may be, but I am Unarhotep, Pharaoh of Egypt, son of Arenatem IV, grandson of Arenatem III, Lord of the Upper and Lower Kingdoms, Ruler of the Nile. Who are *you?*"

"Just Ali. Ali Kedal. That's all. I'm a guide. I show to visitors the wonders of this part of my country." He took a chance. He'd always been a bit of a gambler. "Our country."

"I see. Then you are not a servant of Osiris, and this is not the Underworld." The cheetah paced thoughtfully for a moment before looking up again. "What year is this, Ali Kedal?"

Ali considered. The modern calendar would mean nothing to someone from so ancient a time. Unarhotep would have no reference for it. "As near as I can tell, it has been some four thousand eight hundred years since your entombment, my lord."

"So long! The mere thinking of it makes me tired. If this is the truth, then I cannot be your lord. You may call me Unar. My mother did. The kingdom of Egypt still exists, then?"

"As it ever has been, Egypt remains a wonder of the world. Its history and its monuments are still revered by all mankind." He hesitated briefly. "Might I ask, oh lor—Unar, how you came to be in this—form?"

The pharaonic feline began to pace restlessly; back and forth, back and forth. "I was Pharaoh only for a very short time. I contracted a wasting illness with which my court physicians were, sadly, unfamiliar. There was at that time working in Thebes a certain mystic. A sorcerer named, if I remember correctly, Horexx. A venerable man. Nubian, I believe. He claimed to be able to oversee the transfer of a soul from one body to another. But not to that of another human person. To do that would require chasing the soul from that other person's body. This feat was beyond Horexx's powers.

"But he felt certain that, if given the opportunity, he could shift a person's soul into any other kind of body. As it rapidly became clear that the disease that was consuming my person would leave me with nothing in which to dwell in the otherworld, it was left to me to choose the vessel for my soul's life after death. Following much discussion among my most learned advisers, it was decided to put me in this body, of my beloved pet Musat, and consecrate the result to the cat-goddess Bastet." Raising up on hind legs (a thing Ali had never before seen or heard of), the cheetah pawed gently at the air in the direction of the open sarcophagus.

"Though the procedure was both torturous and painful, in the end Musat's body welcomed me. It is a powerful form; handsome, swift and elegant. A fitting container for the soul of a pharaoh. Unfortunately, so shocking was the transfer that it resulted in the death of Musat's body as well as mine." The big cat dropped back down onto all fours. "It was declared by Horexx that the first person who should touch my preserved form would have the ability to think 'with' me, and that that person alone should be my guide through the Underworld for all eternity." A paw gestured, taking in the modest chamber.

"I determined to be interred here, in this simple place, so that my person would not be disturbed by those lowborn ones who live by pillaging the tombs of better men who went before them."

"I am sorry, Unar." Ali was genuinely apologetic. "I have disturbed your sleep of thousands of years only to have to welcome you yet again to the real world, and not that of Osiris and Horus, of Bastet and Anubis." Privately, he knew that such imaginary beings did not exist, nor did the Underworld they were supposed to rule. But he could hardly venture that opinion to one who believed in them as deeply and personally as did Unarhotep. One man's superstitious nonsense is another man's true religion.

But the revived pharaoh surprised him.

"Perhaps it is just as well. I was never so certain of the existence of Osiris' realm myself. To the unending frustration of my scholars, I was always a free-thinking sort of man. Such beliefs could be discussed freely only on rare, private occasions." The cat's head came up proudly. "A pharaoh must be strong for his people.

"If I am to live again, perhaps this real world is not such a bad place, or time, in which to do so. Is Egypt still the ruler of the known world?"

Emboldened by both his knowledge and the continued friendliness of the most ancient one, Ali stepped a little bit away from the beautifully painted wall.

"The world has changed in ways you cannot imagine, Unar. There are many more countries and lands than when you reigned. Science has changed the way the world runs. There are great things about it that even I do not understand. Computers, atomic energy, the Internet . . ."

The cat raised a paw to forestall him. "Do men still lie with women, and thus make children?"

"Yes." Ali could not keep from smiling. "That, at least, has not changed."

"And what of riches, of the material wealth of men? Do they still value such things as gold and silver, and precious stones?" Once again, Ali nodded. "Then it may be," the cheetah thought clearly, "that it is only the superficial things that have changed as much as you say, and that at heart and at base, men are still much the same. Do they still choose others to rule over them?"

"It is indeed so. If I may say so, Unar, you are handling this very well."

"Though I did not rule long, I ruled well. To do so, one must learn to adapt to new things very quickly, be they an unexpected war, foreign alliances, or something as small as a new way of raising cut stones. Even for a pharaoh, for a living god, life is a constant battle: to learn, and to retain mastery over others." He looked down at himself. "Yet I confess that for all my experience and knowledge, I cannot see how I can make myself again even a little bit of what once I was: a lord over men, wealthy and admired, with a host of concubines at my side and great men trembling and waiting at my every move. Because for as long as I may live again, I will have to live in this form."

It was then that Ali had the idea. He was, after all, sophisticated from long contact with foreign tourists. And while his village was poor, it was not isolated. There were things about the world that Ali had learned, and remembered. Things that anyone who lives in the real world learns very quickly.

"I think, my lo—Unar—that I may be able to help you, to regain some of what you once had. Some of your stature, some of the effect you had on other people. Maybe even the company of beautiful concubines."

"This is a true thing? You do not lie?" The cheetah grinned, which unfortunately had the opposite effect on Ali than what was intended. "If you can do such a thing, Ali, then you will truly be my friend for the remainder of my life in this world, as well as in the next."

"We can but try," Ali confessed. Turning, he looked up at the circle of moonlight overhead. "Hopefully, someone will come along and find us before the desert overtakes us." He gestured helplessly. "I found this place by accident, by falling, and have no way out."

"Is that all?" Unarlotep asked. And with a single bound, he leaped upward and through the opening.

It does not matter how Unarlotep helped Ali to get out of the tomb. It only matters that he did. Nor need it be dwelled upon how the two got themselves out of Egypt. Only that they did.

So it was one day that camel guide and cat found themselves in another country far, far from the desiccated delights of Thebes and that haranguing harridan Harima. A tall man was standing next to Ali, who wore a very fine shirt and pants indeed, together with sunglasses that themselves would have cost him six months earnings as a guide's assistant. The tall man was nervous, and made no effort to hide it.

"You're sure about your animal, now, Ali? We can't take any chances here. I'm not using a double for Tiffany. She really wants to do this shot herself, and I want her to do it. But if anything goes wrong, the studio, the insurance company, and the ASPCA will have my ass for it."

Ali waved off the concerns. "I assure you, Carl, that my cat will do exactly as I instruct it. You have nothing to worry about. Nothing whatsoever."

The director still looked uncertain. "Yeah, well, you'd better be right. I mean, when the time came to do the animal casting for this picture, your name was at the top of the list. I'm told you're the best big cat trainer in the business, even if you only work with the one animal."

"I only need one," Ali replied loftily. "Do your shot, Carl. I'll be right here, watching in case I am needed."

But he wouldn't be needed, he knew as he watched the final touches being put on the elaborate setup for the next sequence. He wouldn't be needed because Unar, the wonder cheetah, the best trained and by far the most famous big cat in Hollywood, who was now known and admired all over the world, had demonstrated again and again an astonishing ability to carry out the most complex series of owner commands, in response to hand and eye gestures even the most experienced animal trainers were unable to perceive.

So it was that Ali was able to relax and watch the action unfold as the director called for action, the cameras rolled, and the snarling cheetah, Guardian of the mysterious lost Temple of Unak-Pathon, approached the two nearly naked heroines. It proceeded to paw and lick them threateningly and thoroughly, but yet with the most astonishing self-control. . . .